Early

Also by Whitney Dineen

Romantic Comedies

Relatively Normal

Relativey Sane

She Sins at Midnight

The Reinvention of Mimi Finnegan

Mimi Plus Two

Kindred Spirits

Going Up?

Thrillers

See No More

Non-Fiction Humor

Motherhood, Martyrdom & Costco Runs

Middle Reader

Wilhelmina and the Willamette Wig Factory

Who the Heck is Harvey Stingle?

Children's Books

The Friendship Bench

Relatively Happy

Whitney Dineen

Relatively Happy
By Whitney Dineen

https://whitneydineen.com/newsletter/
33 Partners Publishing

Made in the United States of America

September 2019

Print Edition
ISBN-13: 978-16-873035-0-9

This book is dedicated to all of you lovelies
riding the rollercoaster of life with me.

Prologue

I've dreamed about the county fair for as long as I can remember. I've been to every single one since the year I was born. I started out in my mom's arms, then moved to a stroller, before graduating to my dad's shoulders—affording me a view like none other. When I was old enough to go with my friends, it was just one great big cotton-candy-eating, tilt-a-whirl-riding, tractor-pulling adventure.

Walking behind two little blonde girls, my heart is full of love for them as they busily whisper secrets to one another. They're wearing typical kid clothes: shorts, tank tops, and flip flops. The one on the right has a sort of wild excitement emanating from her. Her hair, which looks like it hasn't been brushed in a couple of days, adds to the feeling that she marches to the beat of a different drummer. She leans in and tells her friend, "When we grow up, I'm gonna come here every single day the fair is open, and I'm gonna eat nothing but corn dogs and elephant ears!"

The other little girl laughs and says, "I've got five whole dollars in my pocket, and I'm going to spend every last penny on the ring toss, so I can finally win that giant stuffed octopus."

I walk behind these two cuties for quite a while, enjoying

their youthful energy and anticipation. Once they hit the arcade, we go our separate ways. They're going to stay there until they win seven goldfish between them, and an assortment of junky plastic toys, one pair of giant clown-like sunglasses, and a foot-long super-soaker squirt gun. No stuffed animals, but neither is going to care.

The one with the nicely braided hair is going to grow up and move to New York City and run a successful party planning business. Then, she's going to come home for Thanksgiving one year and fall for her high school boyfriend all over again. She'll move back to our hometown as much for herself as for him.

The more rumpled girl is going to stay in Gelson and take over her family farm. She's going to keep the same fashion-sense—shorts, tank tops, and flip-flops. Although she'll grow into those gangly legs, and she'll eventually brush her hair every day, her devil-may-care attitude will only get bigger with age.

How do I know this? I'm the little girl with the messy hair and the corn dog fetish. I revisit the fair all the time in my dreams. Though not exactly lucid dreaming, I have come to understand that when I see my spirit guide, Terraz, she's planning to use my memories in dreams to bring me messages. I'm never sure what age I'll be when I get here, but between her guidance and the sounds of happy people, the smell of fried delicacies, and the blur of activity, I feel the thrill just as much as I did when I came here as a kid.

I see Terraz waiting for me next to my favorite ride, and I join her. "Hey, T! What do you have for me tonight?"

"Let's get on, and I'll tell you."

Terraz comes in all kinds of forms. Sometimes she's a bright light. Sometimes she's an animal. She's even been a seashell before. Tonight, she's a dolphin. You'd think she'd be totally out of place at the Illinois Ford County Fair hopping around on a dolphin tail, but no one seems to notice. That's the beauty of dreams—anything goes.

Once we get on the carousel, she points to an animal on the ride and says, "Go sit on the black bear's back and we'll talk."

I follow her instructions. But, as I near the bear, I realize it's real, not plastic or wood or even a stuffed animal. It looks down at me and briefly bares its teeth before turning away. I look at Terraz to make sure I'm really supposed to sit on him, but she just motions with her flipper for me to do as I'm told.

Terraz says, "I know you love the merry-go-round."

"I do!" I tell her enthusiastically. "I love the brightly painted animals, and the sparkling lights, and the happy music. I love everything about it."

"But Sarah, you're thirty-two years old. It's time you graduated to a ride with a height requirement."

"Why?" I demand. "I don't think you need to change rides until you're tired of the one you're on."

"You've outgrown this ride, Sarah. Come with me."

When the ride comes to a stop, I follow her across the fairgrounds to the roller coaster. Only a handful of people are waiting as we walk right up to the height chart. At five feet seven inches, I tower over the thick black line of the "acceptable height requirement" measurement sign. "I don't know, Terraz. I'm not one for crazy highs and lows. I'm pretty happy going around in circles."

She lifts a fin and indicates the back of a man in line, who, if

I do say so myself, looks pretty spectacular from behind. He's easily over six feet with dark brown hair, and he's built like he bench-presses cows in his free time. "It's time to share your life, Sarah. Staying on the same path isn't going to find you that person. Ask the universe. It's time. Go on."

I obediently follow her instructions. I walk over to stand behind the man in line and my dream ends as I roll over in bed and say:

Dear Universe,

What do you say we blow things open? I know you've got some great things in store for me. Let's start with a boyfriend, shall we?

I drift back to sleep with the knowledge that my world is about to change.

Chapter One
Because I'm Happy

Before I know it, I'm standing in the dandelion field waiting for the first sign of morning. I reflect on my feelings like I do every day before my sun salutations. The one undeniable truth about me is that I, Sarah Ellen Hastings, am happy. Every molecule of my person wears a smiley face emoji and flashes a big thumbs up.

I let the warmth of this thought flow through me before trying to remember everything that happened in my sleep last night. I want to grab the memory before it slips away. With my eyes closed, I see it. Cat and I are at the county fair. We were nine, and it was the first year we were allowed to go off by ourselves. I ate three corn dogs and remember feeling nauseated the whole next day. But it was so worth it!

Terraz was there with a message. Something about a man. I've been too busy to acknowledge the dating deficit in my life, but I realize a relationship would be nice. Oh, yep, there it is, she had me ask the universe. Excellent! I know, once that happens, it's only a matter of time.

The first time Terraz came to me, I was twelve years old. She was in human form that time, probably so as not to scare me away. At any rate, I didn't believe her when she told me she was my spirit guide. "Prove it," I said.

She'd asked, "What would it take for you to believe me?"

I thought long and hard about what I wanted and was about to tell her she needed to turn a pumpkin into a stagecoach, but then I thought I should have her do something useful, so I said, "I want to win the lottery."

She shrugged her shoulders. "Fine, but just this once. You have to ask the universe, as well."

"How do I do that?" I asked.

"Just say, 'Dear Universe, I'd like to win the lottery.' You might also want to add that this is the only time you'll take advantage of this privilege for something as trivial as personal gain, when you clearly don't need it."

When I woke up, I was filled with a sensation that Terraz was not only real, but that she was going to come through with a win. I had told my folks I was going to win the lottery that day, and they laughed at my over-confidence. My dad had said, "Sar-bear, hardly anyone ever wins the lottery, and when they do, they sure as heck don't expect it."

"Then why do they play?" I had demanded.

"For the fantasy!"

"That's silly. Why would you waste a dollar on something you didn't expect to have happen? I'm not playing for some dream. I'm playing for victory!" Plus, I knew if I really won, my whole life would change for the better. I figured a spirit guide was just another name for a fairy godmother.

Standing in line at the gas station, Dad had asked, "How many tickets do you want me to buy for you?"

"Just one."

He'd laughed again. "Clearly, this is a lesson you're going to have to learn the hard way. Although it won't be *that* hard being that you're only investing a dollar."

I remember rolling my eyes in a neat 360—a maneuver that only a preteen can manage without doing permanent bodily damage and saying, "You don't have to believe me, Dad. Because I know I'm going to win."

And I did. Not the twenty-four million I was expecting, but, back in the late nineties, eight thousand wasn't anything to sneeze at. Heck, I'd take eight thousand any day of the week. I had put most of the money in the bank, but kept a thousand out to blow on things like a new rabbit hutch; a swing for my chickens; and a gorgeous cowbell for Adelaide, my favorite cow. Oh, and I went to Claire's boutique and got my eyebrow pierced. Watch out, this farm girl has an edge.

Obviously, the biggest thing to come out of that experience was confidence in Terraz. Every time she's come to me after that, I've believed her implicitly.

She also said something else last night about my world changing. Something about getting off the merry-go-round and being ready for the roller coaster. I'm not sure what that was all about. I just know that if she came to tell me, then it was real. I also know she's going to deliver on a boyfriend and I'm super excited about that.

Chapter Two
The Snowbirds are Coming

I see the sun beginning to peek above the horizon as Scottie Schweer runs my way, calling, "Wait for me!" He's hopping and skipping and jumping the whole way as bits of sharp grass and ground poke at him. I keep telling him he doesn't have to take his shoes off until he gets out here, but he leaves his yurt barefoot every morning. The direct contact with the earth is essential for ridding the body of pain as well as energizing it. Although it's less painful if you wear your shoes until you're in a soft place.

Scottie arrives at the exact moment the first whisper of pink appears on the horizon, bidding the darkness adieu. My body erupts in chills of gratitude and anticipation.

"Is it just me or is morning arriving earlier and earlier?" he demands while getting into position and releasing a giant yawn.

I ignore him as I try to concentrate on my sun salutation and not the fact that I've got to pee. I overslept by thirty-two minutes because I was having the most delicious dream about a man I saw in the roller coaster line. It was so good I didn't want to wake up. As a result, I didn't have time to use the facilities before running out to the east field and getting into my current position. Missing the first glimpse of a new day simply isn't an option.

I inhale deeply, move my hands from prayer position to high above my head, and arch my back slightly. Tingles of electricity radiate from my scalp straight to the tips of my toes. Pure radiance rushes through me as my chakras gain full alignment. Perfect physical and spiritual balance are achieved—if only it didn't feel like the Clydesdales were performing Riverdance on my bladder.

On the exhale, I bend forward, resting my forehead on my knees and placing my hands on either side of my feet, releasing any negativity that might have crept in during the night.

"Did you smell that skunk last night? Woweeeeee, that was a powerful stink!"

I've recently discovered that Scottie is super chatty in the morning. "Stop talking, Scottie, I'm becoming one with the universe," I shush him.

I lunge into plank position and stick my pose. This is followed by an Upward Dog—one of my all-time favorite poses. With my body flush to the ground, I feel the strength of the earth fortifying my core. Pushing up on my elbows causes the most sublime stretch down my spine. Then I lift my bum up to the sun, sliding straight into Downward Dog. One more backwards lunge, followed by hands straight up, and I'm back into Mountain Pose. With the completion of my sun salutation, I know the world is my oyster. Another pearl of a day is upon me.

"I wonder why skunks have to smell so bad. You'd think there was another way to protect themselves. Take porcupines. Nothing says back off like a bunch of poisonous quills shooting at you."

I tell him, "They're not poisonous, they have barbs that make them super hard to get out."

He releases a full body shiver. "Either God has a wicked sense of humor or he's out to get us."

Ignoring his train of thought, I ask, "What do you have on your agenda today?"

"Nothin' much. I have to," he makes air quotes and says, "apply for some jobs I might be right for so I can collect my unemployment check," and then he returns to his normal self, "but other than that, I'm gonna chill."

The advertising company Scottie worked for just went belly up. He's decided to take a break from city life, sublet his apartment, and come back home for the summer. He's staying with me so I can help him regain emotional balance.

"How 'bout you? Saving the planet one mortal at a time, or do you have something less daunting on your agenda?"

"I'd like to spend another twenty minutes out here and go through a few more poses, but I really need to pee. So, first I'll take care of that, and then I've got deliveries to make," I say. "See you at dinner?"

"I'll be there," he assures me enthusiastically. Scottie's only been here for a week, but it's been nice to have the regular company. We've known each other since we were kids, so it's almost like having a little brother stay with me.

I run through the backdoor of my farmhouse and immediately hear a macaw chirp. Mom's calling.

"Hello?" I grab the phone on the way to the powder room.

"Sweetheart, it's Mom. How are you this morning?"

"I'm wonderful. Why are you calling so early?" My parents

spend most of the year in Florida, preferring the sun and fresh citrus fruit to the biting cold of a central Illinois winter ... and spring ... and often fall, come to think of it.

My dad, who's eighty-three, has rheumatoid arthritis and claims the heat is the best thing for his pain. He's an old-school farm boy who doesn't much go in for naturopathy. He's of the generation that happily takes a multitude of pills for whatever ails him, but is very skeptical when I suggest a completely natural plant-based cure.

"It's six forty-eight here, dear. I've been up for an hour."

"But you never call before noon," I reply as I sit on the toilet and experience sweet relief.

"I wanted to give you as much notice as possible." Pause. "Dad and I are coming back early."

My parents never leave Florida before the Fourth of the July, and since it's only May this revelation causes me a bit of concern. "When will you be here?"

"Two weeks from today. I'll email you the details so you can pick us up at the airport."

"Why are you coming home so soon?"

"We miss you and want to spend more time with you." She adds, "I hope this won't cause any trouble with business."

I've taken over the family farm and am here alone nine months out of the year while my parents snowbird in Florida. I supply organic fruits and vegetables to twenty restaurants between our place in central Illinois and Chicago. I also have a farm stand, gift shop, and several yurts—one currently inhabited by Scottie—on the property that I rent out to people looking to get back to nature, many of whom experience health issues who come to me to detoxify the pollutants from their bodies. Needless to say, I stay pretty busy.

"You won't cause any trouble. In fact, you'll be here for the opening of *Eat Me!*." That's with an exclamation point, 'cause you know, I really mean it.

I've turned one of the yurts on the property into a vegan cafe we're going to serve breakfast and lunch to my guests and any locals brave enough to eat an animal-free meal. I'm not sure how busy it'll be since most people in our neck of the woods expect meat served every time they open their mouths. I take it as a challenge to help them expand their boundaries, and plan on doing so with tasty dishes like garbanzo bean cutlets, cashew sour cream, and cocoa nib brownies. Yum!

Though I have a terrible weakness for certain meats myself—which started with my love of corn dogs—I manage to maintain about a ninety-six-and-a-half percent vegetarian diet. Of course, I don't let anyone else know that or I'd lose my street cred. A girl should practice what she preaches, right?

"I don't mean to cut you short, dear," Mom says, "but I really need to take a shower before my hair and nail appointment. Then I'm going to Publix to pick up some ground beef. I promised your dad a taco casserole for dinner tonight."

My stomach involuntarily rumbles in response. Taco casserole was my favorite Tuesday night mainstay from childhood. Apparently, it's still going strong.

"Love you, Mom. Can't wait to see you," I say, but she's already hung up the phone.

My parents were older when they had me. Dad was fifty-one and my mom was thirty-nine. As a later-in-life match, they weren't expecting to have a family. My surprise entrance into the world kept them from the boring existence they would have had to endure without me (see previous note about taco Tuesday). I remind them of their good fortune regularly.

Dad had a whole other family before Mom and me. He was married for twenty years to a lady name Jeannie, and they had two daughters together, Naomi and Caroline. My sisters were twelve and fourteen when they died in a car crash with their mom. They would have been fifty-four and fifty-six if they were still alive today. Strangely, I've never thought of myself as an only child, even though I grew up without siblings in physical form.

My mind travels back to my parents' early arrival. Being they're such creatures of habit, it makes zero sense that they're coming home early just because they miss me. Worry niggles in my brain; I wonder if something bigger is afoot.

It's not even six, so I decide to go back out to the pasture and spend a few minutes in Bird of Paradise pose. Not only will it massage my internal organs, facilitating proper digestion, it'll also help focus my mind. My record is three minutes, but my goal is to be able to hold it for five. Today could be my lucky day!

As I point my toe toward the sky and wrap my arms around my thigh to support it, I breathe in the early summer air. The sun has begun to warm the plants, releasing their unique fragrances; its beams reach into my heart and fill me with contentment. Life is so darn good. I can't imagine anything upsetting this tranquility.

Chapter Three
Land Opportunities & Faith

It's ten thirty and I'm in the herb greenhouse when I hear, "Sarah!" I hear Ethan before I see him. "SARAH!"

My childhood bff's ex-fiancé screeches to a halt mere inches from me. He's panting like he just ran a three-minute mile and is more excited than I've ever seen him.

I continue to cut and wrap Thai basil for today's restaurant deliveries. "What in the world has gotten into you?" I ask because Ethan is a very staid individual, not one prone to great bursts of excitement.

"My mom called. My apartment in New York City sold. I'm officially homeless. Isn't that great?"

Ethan's been living here for several months so I can help him explore his recent diagnosis of Autism Spectrum Disorder. He's super high functioning and extremely intelligent, as many ASD people are, yet his diagnosis forced him to confront his differences and make some decisions about how he wants to live his life. He decided to get out of the hustle and bustle of the Big Apple to try something calmer.

"Congratulations. Does that mean you've decided to stay in Gelson?"

He shifts uncomfortably from foot to foot, adding a little toe tap as he goes. "I don't know. I mean, I'd like to. I feel comfortable here, but I need to talk to Catriona first. I don't want her to feel like I'm intruding on her new life."

Cat and Ethan were a couple for two years in New York City before they drifted apart. Part of the divide was due to Ethan's rigidity, the other was a result of Cat never fully getting over her first love, our old classmate Sam Hawking. When Cat brought Ethan home last Thanksgiving to meet her family, it all exploded. She returned home shortly after.

"I think she'll be delighted. She truly wants the best for you."

He shrugs his shoulders and tilts his head. "She's a good friend. I just don't want it to be uncomfortable for her."

Cat and Ethan are one of those rare couples who made the transition from life partners to friends with little drama. While it's strange to think of them both leaving the Big Apple to live in our tiny hole-in-the-wall town in central Illinois, if anyone can pull it off, they can.

"Let me know how it goes. I'd be more than happy to help you look for a place in town."

Ethan's reached the point where he's ready for his own space. I've gone as far as I can with him. He's been living a clean lifestyle for the better part of five months. With a steady schedule of guided meditations, sweat lodging, and yoga, he's about as deprogrammed as he'll ever be.

Ethan hands me a large priority-mail envelope. "This was delivered for you. I signed for it. I hope that's okay."

Setting my clippers on the greenhouse table, I wonder who the heck sent me something that requires a signature. I hope I'm not getting sued or anything.

Ethan watches closely as I rip open the back tab on the envelope and pull out a sheet of paper on a legal letterhead.

To Sarah Hastings,
The Greers' two-hundred-twenty-acre property next door
to yours has been vacant for six years since the passing of
Herman Greer. The family has decided to proceed with
its sale and offers you the first opportunity at ownership.

Blah, blah, blah, yada, yada, yada … It's more money than I could possibly hope to swing, so I crumple up the letter without finishing it. Ethan raises his eyebrows in question. "The neighboring farm is for sale and their family trust is giving me first crack at buying it."

"Wouldn't that be a great opportunity for you?" he asks.

"Yes, but the cost is prohibitive. Plus, I'm as busy as I can handle. Now isn't the right time to consider expanding my operation." *Especially if I'm trying to free up time to have a social life.*

"I see." Shoving his hands deep into his jean's pockets, he adds, "I'm going to drive over to Catriona's then and see if she's available to talk. Do you need me to pick up anything in town while I'm out?"

Ethan and I didn't start out on great footing, but he's turned into a real doll. While he definitely marches to his own tune, he's proven to be very hardworking and thoughtful—two essential qualities in my book.

"Would you mind stopping at the pharmacy to see if my new

book has arrived?" I recently joined a book club along with Cat's grandmother, Nan; Dorcas Abernathy, the retired Presbyterian minister's wife; and Emily Rickle, the gal who runs the cafeteria at the hospital and soon to be caterer for Cat's event business she's running out of her family barn. It's a very cool party venue.

"Sure. What's the name of it?"

"I think it's called *The Laird's Unsoiled Lover* or something like that. Ask Mrs. Fleming, she's holding a copy for me." Our sole reading material subject is erotic historical Scottish romances. You'd think we'd run out of books, but apparently this genre is chock-a-block full of authors, with new ones publishing daily. While it wouldn't be my genre of choice, I find the steamy romance angle makes up for the rather alarming deficiency in my own social life. However, I like to imagine they had toothbrushes back then, making sure all those heated encounters were minty fresh.

Ethan doesn't blink when I tell him the name of the book. He's aware of Nan's penchant for trashy novels. "Anything from the IGA? I thought I'd stop and see if they got in the vegan ice cream I asked them to order."

"No, thanks. I'm driving to Chicago to deliver produce. If your ice cream doesn't come in, let me know. I can make a stop in the city."

Ethan nods before turning around and marching off like a fully-wound toy soldier. I hurry to finish loading my pickup with today's deliveries. I want to be back on the road to Gelson by three to avoid as much rush hour traffic as possible.

Once I settle into the cab, sipping my stinging nettle tea, I turn on my favorite Pandora station. Stevie Wonder and Ariana

Grande blast out "Faith," and I bop along with my usual undeterred optimism—certain the day ahead will be full of gorgeous men and romantic opportunities.

Chapter Four
Bad Roads and Burgers

Nine hours later, standing in front of the open fridge, I'm no longer feeling the love. Nearly every road or freeway I've driven on was undergoing some kind of repair. Midwestern winters destroy the pavement, and once the spring rains end, it's back-to-back construction until it starts all over again. There's a reason I live in the middle of nowhere. The concrete jungle wreaks havoc on my chakras.

I grab a bottle of beer and slam half of it back instead of waiting for a cup of hops tea to work its calming magic. I take the rest outside with me to the medicinal garden. I need to transplant my German thyme seedlings, which is hands down the best expectorant during cold and flu season.

I'm happiest when I'm tending my plants and have my hands in the soil. I feel connected to life on a spiritual level. After transplanting the herbs and singing to the lemon balm—it's grown four inches since I started serenading it with Blind Melon—I start to unwind a bit.

I love supplying quality food to restaurants in the Chicago area, but that drive is going to turn me bitter. I decide I need to go unwind in the dandelion field.

Most people consider dandelions a weed that needs killing. How these beautiful yellow flowers got such a bad rap is beyond me. I grow an entire acre of them. They're part of the daisy family, and people are supposed to love daisies. Not only are they stunning, but one hundred percent of the plant is edible and highly nutritious. I'm serving dandelion fritters and dandelion wine on my cafe menu and using the blossoms as a cheery garnish in salads and on dessert plates. Take that, you negative Nellies who murder these beautiful blooms that dare to grow in your lawn.

I love standing in the dandelion field at the end of summer and picking the flowers that have gone to seed. I bet I've made millions of wishes blowing tiny tufts of possibility into the cool late-summer breeze. The plants mostly reseed themselves, but what kid doesn't like to help spread dandelion seeds?

Before I can get to the dandelion field, I see a 1974 Dodge Monaco sedan plowing up my driveway like it's on a mission from God. *Holy crap, I totally forgot I'm hosting book club tonight!* I run toward the car and try to signal Mrs. Abernathy away from the hydrangea bushes she seems bent on driving over.

When the car eventually comes to a halt, causing a dust storm of gravel to fill the air, Dorcas and Nan emerge from the interior. Both ladies are eighty and graduated from the same high school class right here in Gelson. They're an imposing duo. Dorcas has to be at least five foot ten with an impressively large set of knockers, and Nan, who is barely five foot five, has the attitude of an entire football team and half the Navy. Seriously, don't cross her.

Nan fans the dusty cloud of air out of her face with one hand and raises the other high in the air. She's holding a bag from a fast food stand in town. "I brought meat!"

"Of course, you did," I laugh before leading the older ladies up to the porch. "Why don't you both sit down. I'll grab us some iced tea and put together a vegetarian option."

Mrs. Abernathy offers, "Can I help, dear?"

"No need, Mrs. A. Just keep Nan company. I won't be a minute."

"I don't want iced tea," Nan calls out. "The doctors still won't let me drive, so I say we have a pitcher of margaritas."

Nan had a brain aneurysm which burst right before Christmas. It could have easily killed her, and the doctors are being very careful about letting her back behind the wheel. It's my secret hope they never give her the go-ahead. She's not a great driver under the best of circumstances. According to Cat, she's taken out five of their mailboxes in the last three years alone.

In the kitchen, I rustle up some guacamole and chips to go with the margaritas and put together a quick fruit salad. By the time I get back to the porch, Nan is surrounded by an assortment of food wrappers. She smiles up at me. "I finished the nuggets, but I've still got a quarter pound patty if you want some."

I shake my head. "No thanks, Nan," *but, good lord that smells amazing.* I have a top-secret day every year where I allow myself to eat meat, and that day is only a couple of weeks away. The closer I get to it, the weaker I become.

"More for me," she declares as she unwraps another bundle of delicious smelling grease.

I see Scottie heading up the driveway flailing his arms about with a certain degree of flamboyance. He looks like he's trying to swat away flies, but then I see his headset. He's on the phone. As he nears us, we hear him say, "I'm more than just gay, you know. Tad, I'm not coming back until I'm good and ready … I want to be home long enough to figure some stuff out … uh huh, whatever."

He hangs up as he nears the porch and declares, "Nan, Mrs. A. You joining us for supper tonight?"

Nan throws her arms out as though she's expecting a hug. "Come here, Schweer, and give me some sugar."

He eyes her hamburger. "Naughty, Nan. You brought meat. Can I have a bite?" Scottie's childhood's best friend is Nan's grandson, so she knows him well. Pretty much everyone who's been in this town for over ten years is entwined in some way.

"Course you can. You poor thing, living out here with no real sustenance. Why, you're just going to waste away!"

I intervene, "I forgot about book club tonight, Scottie. So, we're having guacamole and margaritas for dinner. You good with that?"

He takes a bite of Nan's burger and decides, "Sounds perfect."

Dorcas announces, "I saw Emily in town earlier today and she said to tell you she'll be a few minutes late. She had a doctor's appointment at the end of the day."

Emily was a year behind me and Cat at school. As such, we didn't know her very well back then. She took over running the hospital cafeteria a few years back and has done a bang-up job. So much so that Cat asked her to cater the parties she's started to book at her new barn venue.

Nan says, "We can wait to discuss the book until she gets here. In the meantime, where are the margaritas? I'm ready to get this party started."

Chapter Five
Emotional Support Pigs

Scottie tells us, "Tad is convinced I've come back to Gelson to try to win my mother's love, but I assured him that I'm going nowhere near the woman and that I don't care whether she accepts me or not."

Dorcas says, "Good for you, honey. You're just the way the good lord made you, and if your mother can't understand that, then it's her problem, not yours."

Nan demands, "What's going on between you and that hipster TV producer anyway? Trouble in paradise?"

Scottie shakes his head. "No, he's just away shooting with the Renovation Brothers all the time. I'll go back to the city on the weekends he's there." He continues, "I'm glad Sarah invited me out here. It'll give me time to think."

"You know what I like to think about?" Nan asks.

We all turn and face her as if we're all on pins and needles waiting for her to share her deepest, darkest thoughts. "I like to think about that Jamie Fraser, from *Outlander*. He can fry my bacon any time he wants! The griddle might take longer to warm up, but I'm sure I could keep him busy while it does."

"Right?" Scottie declares. "That man was built to fry bacon. What about you, Sarah? You want some of that bacon?" He gives me a secret smile. He might have caught me about to eat a piece of microwave bacon yesterday, but I'll have you know I stayed strong and didn't succumb to its call. You know, because I got caught and all.

I ignore his innuendo and say, "I believe I do." I've mentioned the deficit in my social calendar, right? The much awaited-and wanted-guy will have to show up on my doorstep and offer to woo me while I mixed organic fertilizer for me to fit him into my schedule. *Get on with it, Universe!*

Dorcas offers, "Sarah, I've been thinking I could introduce you to my grandson, Johnny."

Nan's eyes open wide. "The pig farmer?"

Dorcas nods. "Unless he's raising those pigs as emotional support animals, I'm pretty sure our Sarah won't approve."

Emotional support pigs—I briefly wonder if there's a market for such a thing. Then I answer, "I can't see myself in a relationship with a pig farmer, Mrs. A. Sorry about that."

Dorcas's face turns red with what I assume is embarrassment or offense before she says, "I thought with you both being farmers and all ..."

I offer a conciliatory smile. "It's a very nice idea and I thank you. It's just that being I'm a vegetarian it might cause some troubles." Those troubles being that I wouldn't be able to pass as vegetarian for very long if I was dating a bacon farmer. Which is really what he is, right?

Before I can figure out a way to make things right, Emily's car pulls up the drive.

When she steps out, I notice her normally icy-blue aura is dim. Her posture is lagging and she's dragging her feet like she's wading through knee-deep molasses.

I call out, "Welcome, stranger. Glad you could make it."

Nan rubs her hands together in anticipation and declares, "Time to talk trash."

Once Emily arrives on the porch, it's clear she's in shock. Nan demands, "Girl, what happened? You need me to take my cane to someone's backside for you?"

Emily shakes her head slowly before accepting the margarita Nan passes her. She drinks the whole thing down in one shot before answering, "I just found out I don't have breast cancer."

"What?" I ask. "Is that why you were at the doctor today?"

"I found a lump last month. They scheduled a mammogram for last week and the doctor called me in to talk about the results. I thought for sure he was going to tell me that I was dying or something, but he said it was benign."

"Praise the Lord!" Dorcas exclaims. "Come here and let me hug you."

"I would have made you a voodoo doll!" Nan exclaims.

I offer, "I have a supplement protocol that kills cancer with incredible accuracy. I would have given you that."

"I'm out of my element here," Scottie says, "but I would have said some rosaries for you or maybe some Buddhist chants or something."

As much as we all want to talk trashy novels, our conversation detours into how we would have healed Emily had we needed to. Apparently, prayer, black magic, and herbs were our arsenal—the trifecta of health.

"Cancer can kiss my Aunt Fanny," Nan declares. "Not only did it take my Hugh from me too soon, but it's getting its claws into too many people I hold dear. Viola Petersen down at the senior center found out her skin cancer is back. All those years of greasing up with Crisco and tanning with a reflective board have taken their toll on that girl." *Girl* is not the word for Viola. She isn't a day younger than Nan, but that's how Nan remembers her. It must be nice to get old and be surrounded by people you've known for your whole life.

Dorcas shakes her fist in the air like she's leading a protest march. "It can kiss my butt, too."

A brilliant idea pops into my head. "What are you all doing tomorrow?"

"It's my day off," Emily answers. "I was going to work on a tasting menu with Cat for the first wedding she's hosting in the new barn, but I think I need to sleep and recover from the drama of the last month."

"Why don't you all come over here? I'm giving a class to some of the ladies from the senior center about how to prevent breast cancer. You all can join us."

Scottie teasingly asks, "Can men get breast cancer?"

"Yep," I tell him, "although it's rare. But you should come anyway. Healing is always more effective the more people you have participating in it." The grin melts off his face.

Having seen the results of my work with Ethan and others, they agree to come, and then we dive into the highlights of our trashy novel—not quite as satisfying as the real deal, but still pretty good. After more margaritas and a discussion about the benefits of our book club visiting Scotland together, I see Dorcas and Nan to their car. Dorcas only had one drink and doesn't appear any the worse for wear, so I don't have any problem with her driving. Nan, on the other hand, needs an arm to lean on so she doesn't fall over. Also, she kind of smells like a frat party.

I love Cat's grandmother like she is my own. She makes no apologies for who she is. She lives an alarmingly honest life, as in, don't ask for her opinion if you don't really want it. She's not going to shine you on out of politeness. I admire that quality and wish more people would say it like it is.

Once the older half of our book club leaves, I pour Emily and Scottie another drink. I say to Emily, "Why don't you to stay here tonight? That way you don't have to worry about driving."

She takes a big gulp and holds out the glass for me to top it off. "Sounds like a plan."

Chapter Six
Naked Yoga

Emily is already sitting at the table when I walk into the kitchen, ready to greet the day. "Hey, Em, how'd you sleep?" Clearly not well, as she looks about as perky as fresh roadkill, but you gotta pull out the niceties in life. I'm a firm believer in that.

"I might still be drunk."

"I'm glad you're up. You can join me in the east field and learn how to greet the day properly. I promise after five sun salutations you'll feel like a new woman."

She eyes me dubiously, but I know of what I speak. Pointing down at the T-shirt I gave her to sleep in, she asks, "Is this enough or do I need to put my clothes on?"

Spokesmodeling my own oversized T-shirt, I answer, "The less constricted you are when you do yoga, the better. Ideally, nothing should hinder the energy flow while performing poses."

"You mean naked yoga?"

"Yup. But just to warn you, if we go out there naked, Scottie's robably going to get naked too, and that might get a little weird. 1 good with it, but I'll leave that up to you."

Emily releases a rusty-sounding laugh. "OMG, Sarah, I was

kidding! I promise I won't be comfortable doing naked yoga by myself."

How disappointing. It's a pretty delicious sensation to feel the elements directly on your person with no barriers.

I reach my hand out to my new friend and say, "Let's bounce. The sun waits for no woman." Emily's hand feels like ice in mine. She's got to sweat the alcohol out and spend the day rehydrating her body.

"Do you know how to do a sun salutation?"

She tells me, "I took that free class at the high school last summer. It was pretty cool. I regularly do shoulder stands after a long day on my feet and baby pose is one of my favorite ways to relax."

I inhale deeply as we step outside. The air is still coolish even though the forecast promises an unseasonably warm day. "Fantastic. I won't talk while we do it then. If you get lost, watch me, and it should come back to you."

When we get to the field, we find Ethan and Scottie already there. Ethan usually does his sun salutations in his room, claiming he doesn't like the feel of morning dew on his bare feet, but I guess he's had a change of heart. Thank goodness we've stayed dressed. I don't think Ethan could have handled the shock.

"Morning, boys," I greet.

Ethan nods his head once, "Sarah." Then he turns his attentions toward Emily. "Emily, good morning."

She smiles pleasantly and rather coyly drawls, "Ethan." I swear there's an eye bat and side-smile that indicates something akin to romantic interest. I briefly wonder if the universe got my plea wrong and is sending Emily love. Not that I mind, but I mean really, I'm the one who asked.

We all face the sun and, like synchronized swimmers, begin to greet the day as one.

Ethan has taken to yoga like a fifth grader to YouTube. After his first session he declared it life altering. Months later, he's a regular Gumby. He lets out small grunts as he goes which he tells me are completely involuntary. Negative energy releases differently in everyone. I assume this is his body's way of clearing its channels.

Scottie performs his salutation with a bit of bounce like he's dancing along to music only he can hear.

I watch Emily's first poses to make sure she's on track before losing myself in my own postures. This morning's exercise feels like rockets going off. The energy exchange between us, the earth, and the sky is positively transcendental. I wish there was some way I could bottle this feeling and hand it out to the world, free of charge.

I lose track of how many salutations we do, as we are *that* lost in the moment. When we hit the last prayer pose, and no one seems to be moved to carry on, I ask, "Ethan, would you like to join us for breakfast?"

"I would," he says, smiling at Emily. "But I'm going to meditate this morning before I go into town to apartment hunt." I'm happy Ethan is planning a proper meditation. A mind can't explore the ethos for answers if the body isn't in total repose. And a body can't relax when it's busy digesting food.

"I take it that means Cat's okay with you staying in Gelson?"

"She's an amazing woman. She and Sam even offered to help me find a place."

I can't, for the life of me, imagine my friend being with Ethan for two whole years. They're such different people. But I can definitely see the love between them and am happy they've opted to stay friends. It says a lot about how evolved they are.

Ethan says, "I'll see you all at dinner tonight. Will you still be here, Emily?"

She smiles in return. "That's the plan."

Oh cupid, you wily little cherub, I see you're hard at work. Don't forget about me. As we walk into the house, Emily says, "I'm super excited to sit in on your class today. How is it that you know so much about cancer, since you've never had it?"

"Who says I haven't?" I answer.

Chapter Seven
Undulating for the Cure

"You've had cancer?" Emily's shock rings in her voice.

"I was diagnosed with Hodgkin's disease when I was a sophomore in college."

"I didn't know."

"It's not something I talk about a lot. But I promise it changed my life for the better."

Shaking her head, she demands, "How in the world did it do that?"

"It made me profoundly grateful for every day. It made me stop thinking about the future and forced me to live in the moment. It also gave me the courage to believe in my own ability to heal."

Emily sat silent for several moments before deciding, "Wow, I guess you do know what you're talking about."

I deliver gorgeous plates of food to Emily and Scottie, who just joined us. "Eat and enjoy every single bite, appreciate every flavor. The objective isn't to finish breakfast, it's to experience it."

While Emily eats, I squeeze fresh orange and grapefruit juice and place the pitcher on the table. "It's important to reduce processed sugar from your diet. Fruit is very useful in satisfying a sweet tooth."

Scottie leans in and whispers loudly to Emily, "Just nod your head like you're going to do what she tells you. I have chocolate in my yurt." I love Scottie. He's here because he knows this is a great place to figure his stuff out. It's no skin off my nose how he goes about it. And let's face it, eating chocolate *can* be a pretty mystical experience.

We hear the roar of an old car coming up the driveway. "Nan and Dorcas must be here."

Emily jumps up. "I better run upstairs and change."

I wave off her suggestion. "Nope. What we're going to be doing today doesn't require clothes."

Scottie says, "Just my luck, we're flying commando and I'm stuck in a group of women."

"You're not talking naked yoga again, are you?" Emily asks in alarm.

"You keep your T-shirt on, if you want." Then I look at Scottie and add, "And you, keep your pants on."

Even though Emily looks uncertain, I feel like her trust in me has grown exponentially now that she understands I have experience with what I teach.

Nan walks into the kitchen first, carrying a box of donuts. "Apple fritters fresh out of the fryer," she announces.

"We're cutting back on sugar," I tell her.

"Why?" she demands as though I've suggested we stop breathing air. "Sugar heals the heart!"

Emily replies, "But Sarah says it feeds cancer."

"You don't have that, girl," Nan protests.

"I'm learning how to avoid getting it."

Nan looks unconvinced. "More for me, then." Scottie leans over and grabs one out of the box while it's still within his reach.

Dorcas walks in next, looking like she's going to church. She's wearing a summer dress full on with high heels and a pretty summer hat. She puts a vase of flowers on the table and announces, "I didn't know what time we should come so I figured the earlier the better."

"We're happy you're here. But Mrs. A., Nan, you're going to need to change clothes."

"What's wrong with what we've got on?" Nan demands.

"Our whole objective today is to ground ourselves in nature so that we can ask Mother Earth to help facilitate health in our bodies," I explain.

"Girl, are you high?" Nan asks.

"You know I'm not into drugs, Nan." I laugh because until rather recently, Cat's grandmother enjoyed smoking marijuana with her grandson. She claimed it helped keep her from being too mean to people. Cat made her stop. Turns out her lack of mean wasn't related to pot-smoking, but a whole attitude change. Nan felt like she was disappearing right in front of people's eyes as she aged, she figured she needed to be outrageous to be seen. Don't get me wrong, she's still outrageous, she's just nice about it now.

"How in the world are you planning to have us get in touch with *Mother Earth*?" Dorcas asks. She said "Mother Earth" like she'd say Mork from Ork. This thinking is clearly outside her comfort zone.

"First off, we're going to take our bras off to let our breasts undulate as nature intended."

Scottie announces, "I'm out of here. I mean, I'm happy to lend support and all, but only when it doesn't involve a boob fest." He grabs another apple fritter on his way out the door.

Dorcas looks faint. Nan looks intrigued. Emily appears concerned. "Take our bras off?" the latter asks. "Why in the world do we have to take our bras off?"

Instead of answering, I ask, "How many of you wear an underwire?" All three women raise their hands.

"I like to keep the girls looking alert," Nan says. "I consider it a public service."

"My bosoms would be down around my waist without one," Dorcas declares.

"All the cute bras come with an underwire," Emily adds.

"Underwires restrict the proper drainage of the lymphatic system," I explain. "If you don't release the toxins, they can build up and cause problems." My audience goes mute. "Come with me, ladies. I have extra T-shirts upstairs. You can change in my room."

I hear some grumbling behind me, but I have no doubt everyone will do as they're told.

As soon as the bras come off, I hear Nan declare, "Good lord, Dorcas, you're gonna need to be careful or you're gonna trip over those things!"

Chapter Eight
Hemp and Hunks

Once we're outside in our white hemp T-shirts, sans all mammary support, I lead everyone out to the dandelion field. The rest of the class is already assembled and waiting. Abigail Smothers, Elsie Farnsworth, Dottie Jacobs, and Reba Lindstrom attend religiously and haven't missed a session yet. This is the third in this particular series. I just wish I had some younger women in the group. I'm going to post a notice at the library to see about broadening my demographic.

The ladies all greet each other, and I can't help but feel incredible joy at our assemblage. It does a heart good to share healthy knowledge and have a community interested in hearing it. I announce, "First, we need to sit in a circle and face each other."

Poor Dorcas looks about as comfortable as a plump cow in a wagon train full of starving pioneers.

"If I get down on that ground, I'm gonna need some help getting back up," Nan grumbles.

"No worries, Nan, I'm here for you."

Elsie says, "We all need help, honey. Getting down on the

ground and back up takes half the class."

Dottie agrees, "But we have nowhere else to be, so we might as well."

Once we're all situated, I announce, "I want us all to take turns and thank our breasts for their service."

The funny thing with older people in general, and Nan and Dorcas in particular, is that they talk loudly—even when they think they're whispering— they have no idea they're being overheard. It's hard to keep a straight face when these two get going.

Nan grumbles, "Mark my words, next week she's going to have us all sitting on the ground with mirrors looking at our hoo-ha's!"

"I don't have any of those, so I don't think I'll be able to participate in that class," Dorcas says.

"Good lord, woman, you've got the same lady business as the rest of us."

"What lady-business? I thought you were talking about hoo-ha's," the minister's wife exclaims.

"For the love of god, Dorcas, what do you think a hoo-ha is?" Nan's exasperation is positively oozing out of her.

"Aren't they those cute new running shoes the kids are wearing today?"

Nan nearly chokes on her laughter. "No honey, your hoo-ha is your lady bits—or what those new shows on the Netflix call your va-jay-jay."

Dorcas's eyes double in size and she yells, "Why in the world would we want to see that in a mirror?"

"So's you know where everything is. I think it's so you know what parts bring you pleasure or something."

I'm pretty progressive, and I'm all *for someone* teaching this class. Just not me. I've got enough on my plate without branching out into lessons on achieving the geriatric orgasm.

Shaking her head vigorously, Dorcas declares, "No, ma'am. It's one thing to take my bra off, but my knickers stay on. That right there is a deal breaker for me ever coming back to these classes."

I try to regain control of the class and reiterate, "Time to thank our *breasts*."

"Out loud?" Emily gasps.

"Totally, out loud. We're here in a healing sisterhood. There shouldn't be anything we're afraid to say in front of each other. Why don't I start?" I take a deep breath before stating, "I want to thank my breasts for being strong and healthy and pretty darn cute, if I do say so myself."

Nan pipes in. "Girls, I want to thank you for hiding my belly from me. It's nice of you to block that little pooch from my view."

The other gals add their two cents, before Emily says, "Um, thanks for helping me look better in swimming suits?"

Nothing from Dorcas. I nudge, "Your turn, Mrs. A. How have your breasts served you?"

"Well, I guess they fed my babies. So, thanks for that." Then she adds, "I'm guessing you don't want me to thank them for the infected milk ducts, all the backaches, and the years of leering men."

I ignore the unexpected sarcasm and ask, "Anyone else?"

There are no takers, so I jump up and announce, "It's time

to encourage our lymph nodes to open up and drain!"

"How are we gonna do that?" Nan demands.

"Follow me." I keep my promise and help Nan to her feet before lending a hand to the minister's wife. Sarah takes care of helping the other ladies. When we're all ready, I start to skip around the field in zigzagging lines. I feel the warm sun on my face and the soft dandelions underfoot, then I start to wave my arms around like I'm an exotic bird about to take flight. It's a deliriously freeing sensation.

When I look behind me to see if the others are following my lead, I find my regulars are doing their part, but Nan's laughing her head off, and Dorcas and Emily look borderline appalled.

"Girl, if Dorcas does that, she's gonna have black eyes for a month," Nan declares before doubling over with renewed hilarity.

Dorcas smacks her friend's arm and snaps, "Don't be nasty, Bridget. I don't see you out there flapping around like a lunatic."

That's all the encouragement Nan needs to take off like a slightly wounded, elderly, bird of prey. She starts slow, but eventually catches her rhythm and starts to hoot like an owl before she begins clucking like a chicken. "Sarah, this is the most fun I've had in ages!"

I hear Emily giggle and mumble, "What the heck?" before she joins in.

Dorcas is totally immobile until Nan runs up behind her and pinches the back of her leg while yelling, "Dorcas, you got a bee up your shirt, gal." That's all that is needed to set her in motion.

"Thank your breasts," I yell. "Tell them how much you love them."

Nan starts to sing out at the top of her lungs, "Do your boobs hang low, do they wiggle to and fro? Can you tie 'em in a knot? Can you tie 'em in a bow? Can you throw them over your shoulder like a continental soldier? Do your boobs hang low?"

I don't know how long we skip around the field with our breasts flapping in the wind, but it was a good long while—we probably could have gone a lot longer—but I hear Nan call out, "Hendrix Greer, is that you, boy? As I live and breathe, come over here and give me some sugar!"

Hendrix Greer? Nan's got to be hallucinating. Rix Greer hasn't set foot in Gelson since his grandfather's funeral six years ago. I turn around to tell Nan to quit playing games when I come face-to-face with an image that filled many of my adolescent fantasies.

I stop dead in my tracks with my mouth hanging open like a hungry baby bird. The Adonis standing in front of us is no mirage, it really is Hendrix Greer, the biggest football star to ever call Gelson home. The biggest star of any kind, actually. He played for Notre Dame before turning pro.

Rix was four years older than me, so we were never in the same school at the same time. But man, his legend reigned supreme over our whole town. It still does. It's just that he's never here to feed local gossip. Don't get me wrong, we still talk about him, but not with firsthand knowledge anymore. Whenever Rix shows up in the tabloids with a new woman on his arm, it's all over the Wash-n-Curl like turkey vultures to a fresh kill.

And here he is, standing right in front of me. I don't say anything and yet I can't seem to close my mouth.

Nan seems amused by the fact I'm tongue-tied, given the

smile on her face, but she helps me out by telling him again, "Son, get over here and let me feel you up."

Rix's laugh is deep and gravelly, and I swear I feel my insides do a back flip.

He picks Nan straight up off her feet and spins her around like she weighs no more than a feather. "Mrs. McTavish, you're a sight for sore eyes. I swear if I knew the good ladies of Gelson had given up wearing their underthings, I would have been home much sooner."

Nan laughs playfully. "Put me down, you big galoot and tell me what you're doing here."

Rix gently drops Nan to her feet and nods to the rest of the class. "Mrs. Abernathy, ladies, it's nice to see you."

Dorcas throws one hand across her chest and the other across the hem of her T-shirt and sort of crumples up in the middle as though she can somehow make herself disappear. Emily's eyes are so wide she looks like she's in jeopardy of her eyeballs popping right out of her head. I still haven't found my voice.

Rix satisfies Nan's nosiness. "The family has decided to go ahead and sell Grandpa's land. I'm here to get the place fixed up."

Then he looks my way. "Didn't you get my letter?"

I think of the certified letter Ethan had signed for and wonder if it was from Rix. It would have been nice to know he was coming so I could have put some pants and a bra on.

Chapter Nine
The Future Tenant of Yurt #1

I finally manage to come to my senses. "I only read as far as the offer to buy the property, and it's not really in my budget right now." I extend my hand and add, "I'm Sarah, by the way."

The smile he gives me is positively blinding. Great big white Chiclet teeth framed by succulently soft lips and a square jaw sharp enough to cut nails on ... gah! This guy must be oozing pheromones at a dangerous level—dangerous for me that is. Yet I'm sure his magnificent self simply grows more as soon as he sets them loose on the world.

Rix Greer takes my hand and gives it a firm squeeze. "I assumed you were Sarah. You look just like you did six years ago at my grandpa's funeral." *Oh-my-god, he remembers me.* He looked at me at his grandfather's funeral.

What in the heck is wrong with me? I'm acting like I'm in eighth grade or something, but darned if I can help it. This perfect specimen of masculinity knows my name, and my body reacts accordingly, which is hard to miss as my flimsy white T-shirt brilliantly showcases my free-range boobs.

Rix notices as well, but manages to shift his gaze away long enough to look me in the eye and ask, "I guess you didn't read the part about me renting out one of your yurts while I oversee construction next door then?"

My knees buckle ever so slightly before I get hold of myself. Rix Greer wants to stay at my farm. Holy ever-loving mercy. This, my friends, is what I mean when I say the universe will provide. Only last night I expressed my angst over a pathetic romantic life, and bam! Not twelve hours later this great big hunk of wonder shows up on my farm looking for a place to stay. Naysayers of the world, take note.

"I can show you to a yurt now if you like." I try to keep the sheer joy out of my tone. A girl doesn't want to appear too eager.

Dorcas nervously asks, "Can we go get dressed now?"

"Don't bother on my account, Mrs. A. If this view is one of the perks of staying in Gelson, I might move back." But it isn't Dorcas he's looking at, it's me. And my-oh-my-oh-my, I'm more than ready to roll out that red carpet.

I manage, "Why don't I meet you out front in about ten minutes?"

He tips his head and answers, "Sounds good, Sarah." I feel his eyes burning a hole straight through my backside as I trot on up to the farmhouse.

"Wait for me!" Emily yells.

When she catches up, she gushes, "Sweet lord, that man is the most gorgeous thing I've ever laid eyes on. And he's going to be staying here? You are so lucky."

Truth be told, I feel pretty lucky. Hendrix Greer staying on my farm is the best thing that's happened to me since my horse Abigail had twins when I was twelve. Twin foals are a pretty tough act to follow.

As I get back to the house, I throw on some cutoffs and a tank top. I even brush my hair and apply a thin layer of lip gloss— you know, to appear hospitable and all. When I walk out the front door, I find Nan and Rix sitting on the porch swing, chatting amiably.

Nan says, "I always knew Cat and Sam would get back together. They just needed a push in the right direction."

"And she was engaged at the time?" Rix asks.

"That's right, but that one's no longer in the picture. Sam asked Cat to marry him last month, and she said yes. Mark my words, it's gonna stick. Now, tell me about you. You got some special lady in your life?"

If the tabloids are to be believed, he's got more than one, so I'm surprised when he answers, "No, ma'am." Then he looks in my direction and adds, "I'm having a hard time finding quality gals like the ones here in Gelson." I'm guessing there's a rather large number of women who are interested in him for his fame and money, but I guarantee one hundred percent of them appreciate his looks, as well.

Nan catches my eye. "We do seem to have more than our fair share, don't we?" With a twinkle in her eye, she adds, "I best go put my girls away. You two carry on without me."

As soon as she walks into the house, Rix says, "That was quite a show out there. Mind if I ask what you all were doing?"

"We were encouraging lymphatic drainage."

His expression suggests that's not something he's used to hearing. Welcome to my world. I do my best to keep people on their toes. He changes topics and asks, "So, which one of these big teepees is my new home?"

Yurts do kind of look like teepees without the sticks poking through the top. "Which one you want? I currently have four that are empty."

"Are they different from each other?"

I shake my head. "Nope. They all have king-size beds, hipbaths, and wood-burning stoves in case it gets cold."

"I'll take the one closest to yours, then." He flirts like a man who's used to having women drop at his feet. Something I could do very easily. He's totally thrown me off balance by arriving like he has.

"I sleep in the house," I inform him primly, hoping not to be too blatant in my adoration.

"I'll take the one closest to the house, then." I feel a rush of pure lust surge through me, but don't take the bait and flirt back. This is the guy I pined for as a teenager, the one who was so far beyond my grasp I knew it could never be. To have him sweet-talking me on my own land has rendered me incapable of coquettish banter. I merely lead the way to Yurt #1 as I've so cleverly named it.

Chapter Ten
I Really Love Your Peaches

I begin the tour in front of my 1930s farmhouse. It looks the same as it always did—two-story with white clapboard siding, dark blue shutters, and a wraparound porch with two swings and multiple rocking chairs. Nervous, I look for something to say. Eyeing a nearby hanging basket, I point to it and tell him, "My mom liked to hang baskets of decorative flowers, but I prefer using medicinal plants."

Rix smiles appreciatively. "I love the look of your family's farmhouse. It's old-fashioned, for sure, but it's comforting—everything you could want in a home."

I love that he said that. It makes me feel like maybe there's still a small-town boy inside that slick "city" exterior. I explain, "The changes I've made are to the land. Instead of being surrounded by corn fields, I had the front two acres closest to the house cleared for my farm stand and the yurts. It has the added benefit of keeping the guest lodgings far enough away from any road noise to promote a calm and healing environment."

I nervously continue, "I never planned to have quite so many yurts, but when friends, and friends of friends, started requesting my help with their health issues, I needed a place for them to stay. Then word got out. Now most of my clients are complete strangers to me."

"Where in the world did they stay before the yurts?" he wonders.

"At first, I put them up in the house, but I found their chaotic auras kind of hard to have around while I was trying to sleep. Plus, the yurts provide the feel of nature that's super helpful for folks looking to heal."

"What about the greenhouses?" The look on his face indicates true interest in his question.

"One of them is used solely for medicinals like lemon balm, hops, mint, chamomile, stinging nettle, and the like, another is for savory herbs for cooking, and the other two are for greens and other vegetables."

Rix whistles appreciatively. "This is quite an operation you've got going. Do you have a lot of help?"

"I have two men who come in and tend the fields and animals, and I hire a bunch of local kids to help during the harvest and to operate the farm stand."

He nudges my arm like we're co-conspirators. "Farm work was the staple of our youth, huh? My first job was walking the beans and de-tasseling corn for my grandpa. Those four a.m. mornings were tough, but the money in my pocket was pretty addictive."

"My dad gave most of our field help to the migrant families who came to town every spring. I used to make pies for the farmers' market on Saturdays for spending money."

Rix confides, "We had your pies every Sunday for dinner— my favorite was the peach. I loved how you added slivered almonds to the crumble topping." He licks his lips for emphasis. My mouth waters in Pavlovian response, as though he's offered to kiss me.

My cheeks flush at his compliment, and like a schoolgirl, I don't know what to say. I'm oddly pleased Rix grew up eating my pies. I'm glad I didn't know that as a kid though, 'cause let me tell you, I might have interpreted it as some kind of old-world promise of marriage. Like every other double X chromosome under the age of twenty-five in town, I had Hendrix Greer on the brain in the worst way.

He winks at me and asks, "Are you going to feed me some of your pie while I'm staying here?"

There's definitely secondary meaning to his words, but I don't let myself go there. "Sure, you can have my pie." My face burns from embarrassment as soon as I say it. *Time to change the subject.*

I hurry my pace and open the wooden door to the yurt for Rix. "How long do you plan on staying?"

"A lot depends on how much work the farm needs. We've been sorely neglectful of both the house and property for the last several years. I need to get over there and assess the damage."

"You haven't been there yet?"

"Nope, I thought I'd check in here first."

"Why wouldn't you stay there?" I ask.

"I might once it's habitable, but without even seeing how badly the place has weathered, I know there's a lot that needs to be done. The kitchen, for one thing. That place was dated in the nineties. It's going to need to be gutted and completely revamped."

"What about your parents' old house in town?"

"We sold it last year when they decided they didn't spend enough time here to be worth the bother of keeping it up."

Rix's parents left town the first year he played for the Chicago Bears. He bought them a big place on the North Shore, and rumor has it he's been taking care of them ever since. The media loved the story and used it to fuel his boy-next-door reputation. Somewhere along the line, the boy next door turned into a playboy.

Rix has dated more celebrities than you'd think possible for one man. Models, actresses, other professional sports figures— he's a regular Alex Rodriguez. The only thing that's kept him from appearing downright slutty is the fact that he's never lived with any of them, yet alone promised matrimony—that's been reported anyway.

I'm not interested in celebritydom, so I don't want to get my hopes up regarding a connection between us. Yet, he did show up at my door just as I was complaining about my lack of romantic life. That must mean something, right?

Chapter Eleven
Locks and Twenty Gs

I show Rix around the 260 square-foot yurt, which doesn't take very long. I explain how the compostable toilet works, show him the shower, and caution him to let the water run for a minute to let it warm up. I even show him how to work the wood stove, although there's little chance he'll need it for warmth now that it's May.

"Do I get a key?" he asks.

"What do you need a key for?"

"I don't know, privacy, security," he suggests.

I'm slightly offended. "I guarantee I'm not going to steal from you."

Rix lets out a sudden laugh. "I didn't think you would. The problem is that when the folks in town find out I'm here, they're liable to come snooping around. Then, there's the press."

"The press? Why would they show up?"

"Ever since I retired from football, they've been up in my business trying to find out what I'm going to do next. One magazine offered a twenty-thousand-dollar bonus to any paparazzi who could get pictures of me in my next venture."

"Really?" I mean, I know the guy's famous, but that seems a bit ridiculous.

He nods his head. "Yup. Anyway, that's the only reason I was interested in a lock."

"I guess I can look into it for you. I'll call Howard Freeman from the locksmith's in town and see what he can do."

"I'd be happy to pay for it."

"I'll let you," I respond. I mean heck, I don't believe in locks on principal, and the thought of adding one to my own personal corner of paradise sure isn't something I'd do on my own.

After Rix puts his suitcases down, I show him the gift shop and cafe.

"Is this where I eat while I'm here?" he asks when we reach my new restaurant.

"If you don't mind, I'd prefer that you eat up at the house. The cafe isn't open yet. If you're still here once *Eat Me!* opens, guests will have their meals here."

"Eat Me!?" His eyes sparkle with laughter.

"My business name is *Eat Me Organic*. It seemed fitting."

"Organic, huh? That must be a lot of messing around."

I bristle at his tone. "The additional work is worth it to grow quality produce that won't poison people."

He shrugs his shoulders. "If you say so, but I highly doubt regular food is killing people. I've always been pretty careful about what I put into my body, and I'm healthy as a horse."

I'm more than a little annoyed by Rix's disregard for the importance of eating high quality food, so I opt to change the subject. "Is there anything else you need before I leave you to go back to your yurt and get settled?"

"No, thanks. I'm going to head next door and start an inventory of what needs to get done."

"Okay, then, I'll see you later."

As I turn to leave, he calls out, "What time should I be up at the house for dinner?"

"Five thirty," I answer.

"Five thirty? I've barely had my lunch by then. Why so early?"

I guess he's forgotten the drill in his years away. "Farm hours. I'm up at five a.m. every morning, so breakfast is at six, lunch is at eleven thirty and supper is at five thirty."

"I'm going to have to make some adjustments to my schedule," he says, looking chagrined.

"Only if you want to eat here. There are still restaurants in town if you'd prefer to have your meals later in the day."

"Maybe so, but they don't serve your pie. I think I'll make the effort to eat according to your timetable."

Seeing his gorgeous face across the table from mine three times a day is a delicious thought. And even though I don't have an extra two minutes for myself, I know I'm going to go out of my way to make homemade pie every morning.

"By the way," I ask, "would you prefer a vegetarian menu or a strictly vegan one? I have a cow and chickens, so I'm happy to provide dairy and eggs."

He looks at me like I'd given him a choice between a nice bowl of crunchy toenails and a booger sandwich. "I'd prefer you'd kill the cow and run it past the grill on the way to the table," he answers.

"I'm not going to kill Shirley! What kind of vegetarian do you think I am?"

"I didn't know you were a vegetarian."

"Rix," I ask, "who told you to stay here while you're in town?"

"My mom," he answers.

"Didn't she tell you anything about the place?"

"What's to tell? You live next door to my grandparents' farm, and I need a place to stay while I get it ready for sale. It seemed like a no-brainer."

I roll my eyes. "You're going to need to dine in town if you want to eat animals."

"No, ma'am," he answers. "If I have to give up meat to get that pie of yours, I'll do it. But I'd be pleased to have eggs and cheese. If you don't mind preparing them, that is."

"I don't mind at all. I'm currently not vegan myself, so I'll make you the same food I make for me and the boys."

"Have you got a boy band staying here with you?" he jokes.

I snort in response. "No, just Cat Masterton's ex-fiancé, Ethan, and my friend Scottie."

"Love triangle?" he teases.

"I've been helping Ethan detox his body for the last few months. And Scottie is Scottie Schweer. He was just a little kid when you left Gelson for the bright lights of Notre Dame."

He nods his head. "Detoxing, huh?" he asks.

"In addition to farming, I run a holistic boot camp. I help people heal from different sicknesses or aid them in rebooting their lives."

Surprise shoots across his handsome face before he abruptly asks, "What's wrong with him, if you don't mind me asking?"

"That's not something I'm at liberty to discuss. I honor my guests' privacy."

He has the grace to look embarrassed. "I guess you're not going to rat me out to the paparazzi then?" he jokes.

I tease back, "I don't know about that. Twenty thousand dollars might be enough to tempt me." I check my pocket and pull out my phone. "I'll have to keep this on me in case you do something photo worthy."

He grins flirtatiously. "What if I'm not alone when I do something photo-worthy?"

That comment causes an explosion of very intimate sensations to race through my extremities making stops at very personal locations. If I'm not mistaken, he's just declared interest in me. I toss him a playful smile and turn to walk out the door. It looks like the universe is stepping up.

Chapter Twelve
Supplements, Laughter, and Love, Oh My!

Emily is on the porch when I arrive back at the house. "Hey, I didn't know what was next on our agenda, so I thought I'd wait for you here."

"Are Nan and Dorcas still here?" I ask.

"They're napping in the living room. I guess running through the dandelions wore them out."

I peek in the window, and sure enough, our two older friends are sawing logs loud enough to put a lumberjack camp to shame. I sit down on the porch swing next to Emily and declare, "Artemisinin is next."

"What's that?" she asks with a little worry in her voice.

"It's a derivative of the wormwood plant. It's been used to treat malaria for decades, but in the last twenty years, Chinese scientists discovered it's a very effective cancer cure."

"If they've known for that long, why isn't the information common knowledge?" clearly upset, she demands.

I sigh mightily. "Cancer is a multi-billion-dollar business. It's not in big pharma's best interest for there to be an inexpensive natural cure."

"Oh, my god, what a horrible thought. Do you really think they know it's a cure and are suppressing the information for profit?"

"That's exactly what I think, but right now that's neither here nor there. The good news is that it's most effective in treating female cancers, including breast and ovarian, as well as head and neck cancers. In one hundred percent of the cases not close to death, and taken with the proper protocol, it stops the growth, shrinks it, or kills it entirely. We're going to start you on it today."

"Wow, great. But why start *me* on it? I got a clean bill of health, is it okay for people who aren't sick to take it?"

"Absolutely. A lot of people use it as a standard detox, while others use it prophylactically. They take it for a week every few months or so to avoid getting sick."

"Amazing," she exclaims. "Do you keep this art, arta, whatever it is, here?"

"Artemisinin. I sure do. Come on in the house and I'll get the other supplements you need to take with it for the best absorption." This part of my job is the bomb. I love sharing holistic remedies that folks have never considered. I'm more pumped when they're as excited about them as I am. Mental outlook is responsible for the majority of healing and when people accept alternative cures with an open mind, they're that much more likely to experience full recovery.

While pulling the various supplements out of my herb cabinet, I say, "A new cancer killer that's just been discovered is a tea made from taking the isolates of fungi off a sloth's fur."

Emily looks at me likes she's about to throw up. "How in the world did scientists' figure that one out?"

"I've got no idea but being that the fur of a three-toed tree sloth is hard to get your hands on—and probably wouldn't be acceptable to vegans—I'm not going to be trying it anytime soon."

At her horrified expression, I add, "Laughter is important, too. Turns out it really is the best medicine. It increases the blood flow to the heart and causes the brain to release dopamine which reduces stress and anxiety."

"I keep a library of funny films on hand. If *Super Bad* and *Napoleon Dynamite* aren't your cup of tea, I've got *Fifty First Dates* and *Bridesmaids*. I'm sure I've got something that'll do the trick for you."

"So, to avoid getting sick, you need to become a vegan for a week out of every month, take natural supplements, and laugh. What else?" she looks skeptical by the ease of the list.

"You could fall in love," I suggest. "Being in love is not only good for mental health, but it also boosts the immune system."

"Cat promised to start hosting barn dances for singles as soon as she's up and running, but other than that, it's kind of hard for a single girl in her thirties to find love in a town the size of Gelson."

"Tell me about it," I commiserate. With thirty-two hundred people, our pool of available bachelors is extremely limited. Especially if you're picky and are looking for an employed man over twenty-five and under forty who doesn't chew tobacco and drink his body weight in beer every night.

"Yeah, but the hottest guy that's ever lived in Gelson showed up at your doorstep and is eyeing you in a way that leaves little to the imagination."

"You think so?" I try not to sound needy, but you know how it is. A lot of times we convince ourselves of something that isn't there because we want it to be true. I could be misreading Rix's signals out of need to fulfill my fantasies. And, oh my, I'm having some fantasies.

"Yeah, Sarah, I definitely think so." Her comment fills me with hope.

I suggest, "Why don't you stay here for a week while you're on your vegan diet? I can teach you some other yoga poses, and even walk you through healing meditations."

Emily sighs. "I'd love to, but I'm a little strapped for cash right now. I've reduced my hours at the hospital to free up time to work on menus with Cat. Until the catering money comes in, it's all I'll be able to do to keep my rent paid."

"You don't have to pay me. I'm offering to help you as a friend."

"Really?" She seems genuinely surprised by my offer.

"Really. It's nice having another friend in town and it's fun having you around."

She smiles brightly and says, "I feel the same way. I'd love to stay. Who knows what kind of fun two single gals can have?"

Chapter Thirteen
Running Through Corn Fields

After feeding the animals, I smudge the house. I normally burn sage once a month to clean out negative energy, but with Emily's emotional arrival last night, I feel the need to combat any undesirable new vibrations.

I finally get to preparing the stuffed peppers; I was going to whip up my cauliflower mac and cheese, but now that Emily will be joining us, meals will need to be vegan. I'll pour Rix and Scottie a big glass of cold milk and hope they don't notice.

I mix cooked quinoa and brown rice with chopped mushrooms, onion, garlic, celery, carrot, dandelion root, and assorted herbs and spices. Then I add some chia seed, flax meal, and water to bind it together. I'm blown away by how gorgeous the rainbow peppers are. I'll stuff the red and yellow ones and chop the orange for the salad.

As soon as I start on the crust for my blueberry pie (I don't have any ripe peaches at the moment or I would have made Rix's favorite), there's a knock on the backdoor. "Come in," I holler.

My friend Cat lets the screen door slam behind her as she staggers in, carrying a load of old newspapers. "The backseat of my car is full of these. What are you going to do with all of them?"

"Hey, lady. Glad you're here," I answer. "I'm going to shred them and add them to the compost for proper decomposition. Drop them in the corner over there." I point toward the laundry room.

After unloading her burden, she plops down at the kitchen table. "I'm beat."

"From carrying newspapers?" I joke.

"From hauling tables and chairs around the barn. I'm trying a bunch of different set-ups to see which ones will look best for the brochures I'm having made."

Cat is a party planner who owned a successful business in New York City before moving home and buying her parents' farm. She was lucky enough to have the Renovations Brothers from HHTV completely renovate it for her new venue. (Scottie's boyfriend Tad was the producer.)

At any rate, the result is stunningly beautiful. Formal events could be hosted in the barn and not look out of place. If a barn could ever be described as elegant, that's what hers is.

"Is Sam helping you?"

"No, he's working the ER all week. I haven't seen much of him, actually." She shifts gears, "Speaking of not seeing people, do you have any idea where Nan has been? I swear she's like a phantom floating through the house."

"She was here until a couple hours ago. She and Dorcas took a nap on the couch, then they took off for the pharmacy to see if they got any new trashy romances in." I explain our morning activities to clarify their need for rest.

"I didn't even know Emily was worried about having cancer until she came by before her appointment. How scary."

"Just because we're young doesn't mean we're immune to bad things happening."

"You know that one better than most, don't you?" She says before checking out the pie. "What kind are you making?"

"Blueberry, with the fresh Spartans I picked up in Chicago. The co-op on the west side got a shipment."

"Would you mind if I joined you for dinner? Sam's working late again, and Nan eats most of her meals with Dorcas and the reverend now. I'm getting kind of lonely out on the farm by myself."

I throw an apron at her. "We'd love to have you. Do me a favor and open a bottle of red wine, then go out back and pick some salad greens."

My friend does as I ask while I toast pine nuts and get started on the naan bread. I turn on some Indian flute music and let the soothingly dulcet tones wash over me while I glide around the kitchen finishing my tasks.

I'm mixing together the ingredients for the pie filling when Cat comes back in with an apron full of greens. She demands, "Why didn't you tell me Hendrix Greer was here? It seems you would have led with that bit of information."

"You saw him, huh? I thought he might have gone next door by now."

"He snuck up on me in the green house to say hello. I nearly peed my pants from shock."

"He's staying here while he gets his grandparents' house ready to sell."

"Man, he looks better in person than he does on the television. You're a lucky girl."

"I'm lucky?" I demand. "You're the one freshly engaged to Doctor Sam Hawking."

Cat beams. "I know, right? It's hard to believe we're back together after all these years. But, Sar, Rix Greer is a celebrity. You've been crushing on him since we were in junior high."

"Some good it did me. Of course, he's here now ..." I let hope and possibility dangle in the air. "He's a carnivore," I add disappointedly.

Cat laughs. "He's an omnivore. If he was a carnivore, he'd eat nothing but meat."

"Still, he wanted me to kill Shirley for dinner."

"You've never judged people for eating meat before. In fact, once upon a time, I believe you were known as the double bacon cheeseburger queen." She lifts an eyebrow to emphasize the gauntlet she's thrown down. Clearly, I don't pick it up because she doesn't know I still am—once a year anyway.

Instead, I say, "He showed up while we were all running around the field thanking our breasts for their service."

"No." My friend belly laughs as she says, "Something like that would only happen to you."

"I'm afraid you're right. We gave him quite a show." Then I start to giggle as I imagine the scene through his eyes. I know how ridiculous this stuff looks to other people, but that's part of the fun. It's liberating to be silly and free and let go of boundaries.

"No wonder he seems so happy to be here," she jokes. "Who knows, maybe he'll decide to stick around for a while."

I've been fantasizing the same thing, but to keep myself from getting too carried away, I remind us both, "He lives in Chicago."

"So what? You're in the city a couple times a week delivering produce. Plus, he's here now, so why not make the most of it?"

"He's used to dating models." My goodness, I'm getting negative all of a sudden.

She scoffs, "Please. You're as pretty as any model he's ever dated. Look at you all tall and willowy with your naturally blonde hair and giant blue eyes. You don't even need makeup to look gorgeous. Just so you know, that kind of perturbs me."

"You're one to talk," I retort.

"How did Rix wind up here? You'd think he'd stay at his grandparents' house," she says, stating the very thoughts I shared with him.

"He says it's a disaster. His mom told him to stay here."

Cat rubs her hands together and says, "I can't wait to see you two together. I'm guessing you're about to have some fun."

Chapter Fourteen
Hiding in Corn Fields

Five thirty comes and goes and there's no sign of Rix. Ethan, Emily, Cat, Scottie, and I sit at the kitchen table—adorned with my happiest patterned batik tablecloth, napkins in bold complementary colors, and even candles—but no gorgeous pro-football player. At five forty-five I put dinner on the table and announce, "I guess he's not coming." No one but me seems to be upset by the news.

Ethan announces, "I found a nice little house to rent in town."

"Which one?" Cat asks. "Cause if it's the little yellow one on Lott Boulevard, they have a gopher problem that will probably drive you crazy."

Having been with Ethan for two years, she knows all of his pet peeves. Although, being that they lived in New York City, I'm not quite sure how she's concluded he's anti-gopher. Maybe he's got a general rodent intolerance that I don't know about.

Ethan taps his right finger on the table two times before doing the same with the corresponding finger on his left hand. Then his feet follow the same pattern before he answers, "It's the one on Bell Street. It's sort of a yellowish green with the window boxes and willow tree out front."

Any house with color is a big step for him. He's made it clear that he's most comfortable with neutrals, so I've made it my mission to bring as much color into his life as possible. No pain, no gain, as they say.

"Oh, that one *is* cute. It's right down the street from me," Emily offers. "And no gophers that I know of." She throws an engaging smile his way.

"Good to know," Ethan says, clearly receptive to feedback.

Cat asks, "What are you going to do about getting your things? Are you going to go back for them or is your mom going to send them?"

He shakes his head. "Neither. My mom's going to put them in storage for the time being. I'm worried my old behaviors might return if I'm surrounded by my past. I'm going to buy new stuff here and start fresh."

"Do you need any help?" Cat asks.

"I don't want this to be your concern, Catriona," he replies kindly. "You have a new life with Sam, and I don't want to interfere in any way."

"I'll shop with you," Emily offers.

Scottie looks between the two of them before shooting me a look that clearly says, "Oh-ho, what's this?" Thankfully he doesn't give voice to it.

"That would be very nice, Emily. Thank you," Ethan enthuses. Tap, tap, tap, tap.

Dinner progresses at a snail's pace. Everyone else seems to be having a nice time, but my eyes are glued to the clock waiting for

Rix to show up. By six thirty, I'm so annoyed I could spit.

At seven, we're sitting on the porch sipping tea and eating pie when we finally see him running through the cornfield that separates my property from his grandparents'. He jogs right up to us and declares, "Sorry I'm late."

"Where's your car?" I demand.

"At my grandparents' house. The paparazzi found me."

"What? How?" And just like that, my irritation fades away.

He shrugs his shoulders. "Not sure. They might have followed me down this morning, but you never know. Sometimes, I think they've wired my car." At my shocked expression, he adds, "Just kidding. But in all seriousness, it's spooky how they can track a person when they want to." I can't imagine anyone wanting a picture of me so badly that they'd stalk me for it. Just another indicator that Rix lives on a different planet than I do.

The last thing I want are a bunch of crazy tabloid photographers around my place and when I say as much, he answers, "That's why I came through the fields. As far as they know I'm still in the house next door."

I do my hostess with the mostess duties and introduce Rix around. He obviously remembers Cat, but he hasn't met Ethan yet. When I get to Scottie, I say, "This is my old friend, Scottie Schweer. I'm not sure if you've ever met."

You'd think Jesus himself had come down from heaven and offered Scottie a foot rub. Awe does not begin to cover his expression. Rix shakes Ethan's hand and then takes Scottie's. "Hey man, nice to meet you."

Scottie replies something along the lines of, "Whaa, maaa, haaa, wooo." Which translates into what, I do not know. Clearly my friend's reaction is quite similar to my own, but he seems to have lost his grip on the language entirely.

My manners kick in. Instantly I offer, "Would you like me dish up some food for you?"

"Please. I'm starving. I've been sitting over there all afternoon trying to stay out of their line of sight, and there's nothing to eat. I take that back. There's a lot of expired canned food." He grimaces, "I didn't want to take any chances."

I go to the kitchen and heat up a plate for Rix while he chats with my friends. I make sure to arrange the peppers and salad as attractively as possible. I even put a bud vase with a daisy on the tray before I bring it out.

"That looks amazing," he compliments. "But I thought you were cooking vegetarian. Stuffed peppers have ground beef in them, don't they?"

"I use mushrooms."

He takes his first bite and offers a groan of pleasure which immediately makes my mind go in another direction. "Delicious!"

Rix finishes everything on his plate and asks if there are seconds before regaling us with the details of his grandparents' house. It's infested with rats the size of cats and bees have built at least two nests in the screened-in porch. "I'm going to hire a cleaning service tomorrow to get everything tidied up so I can see how bad everything really is."

He turns to Ethan. "Do you need any furniture for your new place? Sarah mentioned you were looking to move into town." He says this in such an expectant way you'd think he was offering to drive Ethan right now.

The look on Ethan's face says it all. "No, thank you. I'm

going to buy new." If things aren't impeccably kept or even if they're patterned, he won't be able to tolerate them. Learning that rats have been using the space as home is sure to put him off the idea of the Greers' castoff furniture.

"Up to you, man. I thought I could save you a couple of bucks."

Cat yawns. "I don't know about you all, but I'm done in. I need to call it a night and get home. I've got photographers coming to take pictures of the barn tomorrow."

Emily asks, "Do you need me to help?"

"They aren't going to shoot any pictures of food tomorrow, just the outside of the barn and closeups of the inside. You know, table settings, flowers, burning candles—all the things that set the mood. I'll need you when it's time to photograph the menu."

Rix stands up as she prepares to leave. "Nice to see you, Cat. And congratulations on your new venture."

She smiles up at him. "Thank you. It's nice to see you, too." Then she looks over at me and winks. "Enjoy the rest of your night."

Ethan and Emily quickly follow Cat's lead and say their goodnights as well. Then it's just Rix, Scottie, and me. I lean in to Scottie and say, "You must be exhausted." I'm trying to give him the old wink-wink, nudge-nudge, but he's not picking up on it.

"Why?" he asks.

"Because you got up at four this morning." *Oh please, catch on, Scottie.*

"No, I did ..." I kick him in the foot while Rix is distracted by his ringing phone. Scottie looks annoyed until a flicker of realization seems to light up in his brain. "Oh, that's right, I did," he says somewhat disappointedly. Then stands up and yawns so exaggeratedly it's almost funny. Then he reaches out to shake Rix's hand again and says, "It's been a huge pleasure. I mean, yeah, wow."

Rix looks like he's trying to stifle laughter and manages to keep a straight face long enough to say. "I'll see you at breakfast, huh?"

"I'd love to have breakfast with you. Thanks for asking!" Then he stumbles backwards until he almost falls down the porch steps before turning around and running off toward his yurt.

Rix indicates that he needs to return the call he missed while dealing with Scottie's antics. So, I walk into the kitchen to get him a piece of my super yummy pie, hoping it adds some romance to the evening.

Chapter Fifteen
Blueberry Pie and Black Auras

Rix is still on the phone when I come back out onto the front porch. His side of the conversation goes, "Wow, okay ... That would sure save me a lot of time and energy. Yup ... Uh-huh ... great idea. I'll make the call and set something up. Thanks, Dad. Love you."

My curiosity is positively bubbling over, but I don't want to appear too interested. "Nice chat with your dad?"

He startles as he looks up from his phone.. "Yeah."

"Good news?" I blatantly pry.

He spies the pie. "Is that blueberry? I love your blueberry pie."

Trying to distract me with compliments about my pie? Of course, it mostly works. I'm easily flattered when it comes to my cooking skills. "This isn't the same one I used to make when we were kids. Now, I blind bake the crust and make the filling on the stove." I pause a beat before dropping the bombshell, "I only heat a quarter of the berries then I fold the rest in fresh, so they never cook down. They pop in your mouth like small bursts of happiness." I feel like I've imparted one of the many secrets of the universe on him.

"Cool," he says before taking a bite, obviously not understanding the magnitude of this information. I stare intently as he experiences the pie for himself. Three, two, one, and there it is … His brows knit together slightly, then his eyes widen before he releases a borderline pornographic moan. "Oh. My. God. This is life changing."

That's the response I was waiting for. "What do you think about the lemon zest?"

He smacks his lips. "It knocks it right out of the ballpark! I've had stuff with lemon before, but this is different."

"It's fresh, not baked," I inform him. "I zest it straight on top of the pie after the filling sets, so the volatile oils stay fresh. It's a more intense pop of flavor."

"Volatile oils? Sounds dangerous."

"Ha," I laugh. "Citrus oils are the best. Not only do they boost your mood and immune system, but they kill germs and neutralize free radicals."

Rix takes another bite before saying, "You're an odd duck, Sarah. But as long you make pie like this, we're good."

My mom always used to say that the way to a man's heart is through his stomach. Pretty trite and sexist if you ask me, but true, nonetheless. I'm quite sure the way to anyone's heart is through their stomach. Men aren't the only ones who like to eat.

Rix finishes his pie in relative quiet before asking, "Is there any left for breakfast?"

"There's one piece. I'll put your name on it," I say, as he smiles contentedly.

The sun is low on the horizon as we continue to rock quietly in our rocking chairs. The moment is pure bliss—full stomachs, a gorgeous man, and a beautiful and bountiful landscape. Life is straight-up good.

"I forget how peaceful farm life is at the end of the day," he says.

Farming is hard work, but so rewarding. It truly is a labor of love, for old-school farmers anyway. Industrial farms don't have the same connection to the land.

"I can't imagine living on land that isn't used to grow food," I say. "Do you have a sizable property?" I picture the kind of spread he could afford on a pro-football player's salary and can't wait to hear about it.

He shakes his head. "My parents have about a half-acre, but I spend most of my time at my apartment in the city. No land, but I have a great patio that overlooks Lake Michigan."

"How sad," I blurt out before I can stop myself. I mean, a lake is nice to visit, but it's no farm.

"Not sad, different. I look forward to having a big lawn someday, when I have a family. I want my kids to be able to run and play and feel the earth between their toes."

"Huh," is all I can manage to utter. How a man can grow up like we did and only want grass *someday,* and not even for himself, is beyond me.

"Do you like Chicago?" he asks.

"I don't dislike it," I answer. "I'd never live there, though. The sheer quantity of people would smother my aura. I need room to breathe."

"Great restaurants, though. Good social scene."

"There's plenty of fabulous food right here that I can cook for myself." I don't bother commenting on the non-existent social life. There's no need to make his point for him.

He pats his stomach. "You could be a chef at a fancy restaurant if you wanted to be."

"I'd rather swim naked in shark-infested waters," I answer. He looks shocked, so I add, "Not everyone wants to live in a big city, Rix. Some of us love small-town living."

"Don't you have bigger dreams for yourself, though?"

"Bigger dreams? Like what? Living in a concrete jungle with a bunch of strangers who are constantly on the quest for more money?" Lookout, I've thrown a little shade—totally intentional, of course.

"There's nothing wrong with having money," he defends.

"No, but it doesn't make you special. It doesn't make you better than anyone else."

"I don't think I'm better than anyone else." Whoops, now I know I've offended him.

"I didn't say you did."

"You sure as heck implied it." He stands up abruptly. "I think I'm gonna turn in." I'd normally try to apologize for offending him, but the truth is I meant everything I said. I'm not sorry at all.

His aura is turning black, so I know he's fuming mad. But you know what? I'm mad, too. I yell out, "Your lock hasn't been installed yet, so you might want to shove something heavy against the door."

He storms off without even looking back. Way to throw gasoline on the fire, huh? Hendrix Greer is bringing out the worst in me, and I don't like it one bit. I'm afraid I'm going to have to keep my distance from him for a while.

How do I do that and feed him three times a day?

Chapter Sixteen
Unfulfilling Wild Thing

I sleep restlessly, tossing and turning, flipping and flopping, until I finally give up the ship and get out of bed at four thirty. It's only thirty minutes before I usually get up, but it feels like hours. It's still dark outside when I hit the front porch with my cup of dandelion coffee. I added some chicory root this morning to give it an extra little smoky flavor, which fits my mood perfectly.

Sitting on the porch swing, I stare directly at Yurt #1, wondering how its inhabitant is sleeping. Who am I kidding? Rix is probably sleeping like a baby, not giving our argument a second thought. How inconsiderate can a person be?

I pride myself on being an even-keeled kind of gal. No dramatic emotional highs and lows for me, just nice smooth sailing. Although that seems to be changing. Fewer than twenty-four hours ago, Hendrix Greer blew into town and is in jeopardy of royally upsetting my apple cart. I don't care how gorgeous he is, coping with this kind of drama is not in my wheelhouse.

All the feelings coursed through me yesterday, from an intergalactic high at seeing him for the first time in six years, to fuming mad by the time we called it a night. It was upsetting, to say the least. I cannot let him affect me like that today. The first step is to limit the amount of time we spend in each other's company. At five, I head into the kitchen and leave the following note on the table.

There's cereal in the pantry and both almond and regular milk are in the fridge. Help yourselves.
Sarah

Then I run upstairs and put on a pair of loose shorts and a baggy T-shirt. The light flips on in Rix's yurt as I pass by on my way to the dandelion field for my morning yoga. I quicken my pace so I don't see that man until it's absolutely necessary.

I do ten sun salutations before the actual sun makes its presence known. Ten boring unenthusiastic series of poses that do little to heighten my mood. *Crap.* I try Devotional Warrior pose and Wild Thing pose, but neither is chipping away at my hard shell of unease. I'm good and truly off my center. There's no help for it, I'm going to have to fast today to regain my equilibrium.

Before going back to the house, I lie down in the dandelions and roll around for about five minutes. There's a reason dogs like to do this. Sure, they like to scratch themselves, but they also feel the earth's magnetism charge their bodies. While not exactly hard science, I'm sure there's something to it.

I feel a little better by the time I'm passing Yurt #1 again, until Rix pops out and asks, "Is breakfast ready?"

I don't even turn to look at him when I answer, "Yup." Then I speed up. I go straight to the kitchen and take his piece of pie out the refrigerator, continue on through the backdoor toward the hen house, and dump it over the fence for the chickens.

I don't start to feel more like myself until I'm standing under a hot shower ten minutes later. I'd love to see the look on Rix's face when he can't find his leftovers this morning. I'm not normally such a passive/aggressive sort, but this guy is really getting to me.

After changing into clean shorts, I head out to the barn. I'm going to take my horse Dusty down to the farm stand and start sweeping up to get ready to open up for the weekend. I'll have rhubarb, strawberries, herbs, asparagus, and assorted greens, as well as peas, potatoes, and broccoli. I also sell cut flowers like black-eyed Susans, hydrangeas, and asters. They really dress the place up and draw in the passing cars who aren't necessarily planning to stop.

Luckily, my high school helpers will get out of school the day before we open for business and will be ready to set everything up. The cafe opens the week after, so things are about to really start hopping around here.

Dusty is one of the twins my childhood mare, Lucy, birthed. Her brother, Cornelius, doesn't like to be saddled, so I only ride him bareback. But I can't manage to ride bareback and carry a broom and a bucket full of cleaning supplies.

As Dusty trots down the driveway with me on his back, I notice Rix heading back to his yurt. He doesn't so much as spare me a glance. I can only assume he was less than pleased by this morning's breakfast. The thought gives me a charge of pure pleasure, which catches me off-guard. I'm not one to take pleasure in other people's upset. The Germans call this 'schadenfreude'—a highly questionable emotion at best. I'm twenty-five percent German, so clearly, it's in my DNA.

I'm not at all acting or feeling like myself. Hopefully, after fasting today, my mind will regain balance and I'll start feeling normal again. But, as long as Hendrix Greer is on my property, I have my doubts.

Chapter Seventeen
Cobwebs and Girl Talk

I wave to Arturo and Steve as they drive by in their pick-up trucks for work. These guys have been my right-hand helpers for the last five years. They're indispensable. Both men live in Gelson with their families.

Arturo used to farm his own land but got squeezed out by a big corporation that bought up the properties on either side of him. They offered him an obscene amount of money for his place and he buckled under the pressure. I don't blame him, really. His family were migrant workers when he was a kid. They came to Gelson for six months out of the year from Laredo, Texas and worked for my dad. We became friends and he told me that when he grew up, he was going to have his own farm. That's why I was surprised when he sold it. But I suppose growing up poor makes you appreciate having money in the bank. I once asked him why he didn't buy another property. Turns out he did. He purchased a farm for his parents in Texas. He said that one of these years, he was going to move back with his family and take it over. I'm less than secretly hoping that day never comes.

Steve pulls his truck over and rolls the window down. "So,

Rix Greer is back in town, huh?"

"How do you know that already?" Word travels like locusts in a wind tunnel in small towns, but even so, he's learned the news faster than I would have expected.

"My mom ran into Mrs. Abernathy at the grocery store. Apparently, she had some crazy story about being half-naked when he showed up."

"You going to ask me about that?"

He shakes his head. "No, ma'am. When I heard she was at your place, I was surprised she wasn't covered in mud, too."

Steve has seen some interesting things out here for sure. One of the reasons he's such an important part of my operation is that he doesn't gossip about it. He goes with the flow.

"Yeah, Rix is back. He's getting his grandparents' place fixed up to sell." Then a thought hits me. "He's looking for someone to clean up the house and help him assess the damage. Do you think Ellie might be interested?" Steve's wife cleans for a couple families in town while their three kids are at school. "I'm sure he'd pay well."

He pulls out his phone. "I'll check with her. You got his number?"

"Nope. Have her drive over and see him. Tell her not to be surprised if he's hiding in the house. He's afraid of the paparazzi who found him yesterday and he wants to stay out of their way."

"Will do," he says.

"Oh, and Steve? There are eggs for you and Arturo on the counter in the kitchen. Take as many as you want." One of the perks of working for me is fresh produce, pies, and as many eggs as your family can eat. I don't like a lot of turnover in the folks I employ, especially because I usually end up thinking of them as family.

He tips his hat to me. "Thanks, Sarah." Then he drives on up toward the barn.

I spend the next two hours sweeping out the soil and cobwebs from the farm stand. The structure is very similar to a hay barn, only smaller. Three sides are open to the outdoors with only the back wall being intact. There are three aisles of wooden tables intermixed with wooden barrels for flowers and bins for produce like potatoes, onions, and apples—essentially anything that can roll away.

Once I've swept away the big accumulation of debris, I turn on the hose and spray everything down. I don't bother painting out here because part of the charm of a farm stand is the weathered wood and rusticness of the setting.

I decide to make lunch for my guests after their paltry breakfast. Before I can mount Dusty, Ellie pulls in. Steve's wife is a couple of years younger than he is, making her my age. She's a lovely woman who's not afraid of hard work. Which is good as all four of her kids are under the age of ten.

She jumps out of her minivan and runs over to give me a hug. "Thanks for the cleaning tip. I just came from the Greer farm and Rix hired me on the spot."

"I'm glad," I say. "Is the place as bad as he says it is?"

"Girl, it's a disaster. Rats, squirrels, and birds have moved in. There's a broken window in the back of the house and all the critters took advantage of a sweet opportunity."

"It must be in quite a state."

She nods. "I'm on my way into town to buy cleaning

supplies. There's some funky mildew growing up all the walls." Her body convulses in a shudder. "It'll probably take me a week to get everything cleaned up."

"What do you think of Rix?" I ask, looking for a little girl talk.

"Yummy!" she declares. "Don't tell Steve I said that. But lord, that man is fine looking. You thinking of giving him a reason to stay here in Gelson?"

I snort. "I think he's is a little too citified to consider coming back here."

"You can't blame him, really. He's made it big, and there can't be much for him in a little town like ours."

I couldn't agree less. If I'd made a big name for myself, with a corresponding amount of money, there's nothing I'd like more than to come home. That doesn't seem to be an opinion many people share—especially Rix who doesn't want anything more than to have grass *someday*.

Chapter Eighteen
Gastronomic Gravitas

I gather assorted veggies on the counter and wait for inspiration to strike. After a few minutes of admiring their beauty, it hits me—grilled veggie baguettes! I slice the eggplant, peppers, zucchini, tomatoes, and red onion, then brush them with olive oil before sprinkling them with sea salt and cracked pepper. Then I lay them on the grill plate on the gas stove until they have a nice char.

As I cut open the baguettes, I realize I probably could be a chef if I wanted to. My food is fresh, delicious, always a visual delight, and seriously healthy. Why in the world did I let Rix's comments upset me so much? I decide to take lunch over to his grandparents' place as a peace offering. No sense having a lot of tension while he's staying here, even if he's not the man I'd hoped he'd be. *Clearly the fasting has helped, and my emotions seem to be balancing.*

I lay the cooked veggies on the bread before topping them with a layer of fresh basil. I add slices of thick buffalo mozzarella to everyone's baguette but Emily's. Then I sprinkle a balsamic reduction on top before rolling the sandwiches in parchment paper. I write Emily and Ethan's names on theirs, and then pack Rix's and my lunch in a picnic basket—I've decided it's safe to eat again now that I'm not so angry. I throw in some dark chocolate cherry cookies, so my apology looks more sincere— gastronomic gravitas, if you will.

As soon as I'm in my pickup, I turn on the radio to an oldies station. John Mellencamp's "Small Town" comes on and I feel the emotion of it spread over me like icing on a hot cake. I live this song. I am this song. I need to find a man who understands that and wants the same things I do.

We don't have the innate glamour and excitement of big cities, but that stuff is highly overrated. Who cares that you can't get decent Chinese food after midnight, or ever, really? So what if we don't have museums or rock concerts or theater (other than our local high school production, which is pretty stellar, if I do say so myself). We can visit big cities if we occasionally want that stuff.

What we *have* is everything that matters. We have genuine salt-of-the-earth people who aren't afraid of hard work, plenty of land so we don't feel suffocated by chaos, and we have enough quiet to be still so we can commune with ourselves.

John Mellencamp and I are kindred spirits. I only wish Rix felt the same way. I sit for a moment and thank the universe, *I appreciate your first attempt at fixing my romantic drought, but I need a do-over. The next guy needs to share my values and see the importance of simple living. Please and thank you.* Over and out.

After the song ends, I head down the driveway, appreciating everything I've created here—the yurts, the fields, the dandelions. I'm surrounded by beauty. Between you and me, if

I have to live without a mate for the rest of my life in order to have this, it would be worth it. Although, I'm hoping that won't be the case.

I haven't been to the Greer farm since the week before old Herman died. I used to bring him baked goods and regale him with stories about my then-fledgling dreams of turning my parents' land into my own personal paradise.

"Sounds like you got a hippy commune in mind, girl," Rix's grandfather would say derisively.

"I don't know much about hippies, but if you say so."

"What's wrong with growing corn and soybeans?" he'd want to know.

"Nothing. I just want more. I want to be able to produce at least eighty percent of everything that I need to survive—like the pioneers did."

Then I'd explain the slow food movement to him and the importance of sustainable and locally grown food. "Do you realize that people's bodies are wired to need the food that's local to where they live? There's a reason third-world countries in Africa have the lowest cancer rate and first-world countries like the US have the highest."

The last time I saw Mr. Greer, he said, "Sarah, I don't understand your dream, but it's your dream, so you should run with it. Don't let yourself get old wondering *what if?*"

"Do you wonder that, sir?"

He shook his head. "I do not. I was born on this land and I'm going to die on this land. I've spent my life being true to myself. Everyone should do that."

Amen. I guess I shouldn't judge Rix for being true to himself.

We all have the joys and burdens of our own path, and none of us should make compromises that shake our foundation beyond a healthy limit.

As I step out of the truck, I realize I'd totally forgotten about Rix's warning of the paparazzi being on the prowl.

Chapter Nineteen
Hometown Harems

The door opens before I even knock, but no one appears to be behind it. I hear Rix whisper/yell, "Hurry up and get in here!"

"Hello to you, too," I say as I tentatively step over the threshold.

"Sorry," he apologizes. "They've already got pictures of Ellie coming in. Thank goodness she was carrying cleaning supplies, or you can be sure they'd print them with an article about my hometown harem or some such nonsense."

"Hometown harem sounds like a book Nan would have us read for book club," I giggle.

"What are you doing here?" He looks at me with some concern, like he'd have expected me to have blown poisonous darts at him by now.

"I brought lunch."

He points at the picnic basket. "Is there a piece of blueberry pie in there?"

"Nope," I reply. "The chickens enjoyed the last of the pie this morning."

He shakes his head. "You sure aren't the right woman to make mad, are you?"

"Not if you want my pie," I assure him.

"Listen, I'm sorry if I upset you last night. I was trying to defend my lifestyle choices. I felt a little attacked."

"That's because I *was* attacking, and I'm sorry. If you want to live in a big city and not have the joy and responsibility of land ownership, that's entirely up to you."

"Thank you?" he says, clearly not sure if my apology is sincere. It's a little backhanded, I'll give you that.

I push in toward the kitchen table while looking around. The personal touches were all removed after Herman died. All that's left is some old furniture that no one wanted.

"This is what you were offering Ethan?" I ask as I point to a shabby overstuffed couch covered with a combination of chintz floral and rat droppings.

Rix looks contrite. "Yeah. I guess it's not really good for much more than Goodwill."

"I'm pretty sure Goodwill won't even take it. I think you're going to need to make a trip to the dump." After clearing off the table of odds and ends, I lay out a small tablecloth before unpacking lunch.

I unroll our sandwiches and put them on plastic plates. "Is Ellie coming back? I have plenty for her."

"No, she's going to start tomorrow after she takes the kids to her mom's. She got the lay of the land this morning and made a list of more supplies to buy." He adds, "Thanks for sending her over here."

"Sure thing. Ellie and Steve are a great couple, and their kids are beyond perfect."

We eat our sandwiches quietly, both of us lost in our own

thoughts. I have an inner dialogue going on:

Right Brain: Too bad Rix is sold on living in the city.

Left Brain: It's his life, and he needs to make decisions that are right for him.

Right Brain: But he's missing out on the fresh air, the flowers, the food, the rainbows, the sunshine!

Left Brain: They have those things in the city, too.

Right Brain: Traitor.

Rix probably has a monologue happening:

I can't wait to get back to the city where I belong. Sure, the pie here is good, but the crazy woman I'm staying with gives it to the chickens instead of me. First thing I'm going to do when I get home is call in for Thai food and have three models come over and rub my feet.

I might be a bit off the mark, but I'm positive he's chomping at the bit to get out of here and return to his urban life.

Rix finishes his sandwich and offers, "That was delicious, thank you."

I hand him two cookies and a pint-size jelly jar full of fresh milk to lend credence to my apology. The smile on his face assures me I've made him a happy man. After one bite he critiques, "Wow, these are different from what I'd expect a cookie to taste like. They're not overly sweet, are they? Just kind of— he takes another nibble—perfect!"

"I don't use a lot of sugar in them, so the flavor of the cherries really stands out. Plus, dark chocolate is much less sweet than semi-sweet or milk chocolate."

"What are the crunchy bits?"

"Cocoa nibs." At his confused look, I explain, "They're part of the pod that the cocoa bean grows in."

We sit and chat for a few more minutes, but my chore list is longer than the remaining hours in the day, so I eventually take my leave. "Will you be having dinner with us tonight?" I ask.

He shakes his head. "No. I'm going to meet some friends of my folks in town. They're going to cook me a great big steak," he teases.

I suddenly have an urge for a great big steak myself. "Have a nice time. I'll catch you tomorrow sometime."

I leave with a hollow feeling. How in the world did I ever entertain the idea of a romance with such an unattainable man? I must be more desperate for love than I realized.

Chapter Twenty
Sold Out!

The first day my farm stand opens in the summer is always a bit of a party. Everyone from my friends, to my parents' friends, to my old schoolteachers stops by to say hi. It's a very festive atmosphere, and I spend most of the hours we're open welcoming everyone. Today will be no different.

I put on my nice cutoffs vs. the holey ones that are only still considered clothing because of the few remaining threads that hold them together. Then I make my way down to the cafe to get all the baked goods ready to take down. I stayed up half the night making pies, scones, and cookies to start the season with a bang. It looks like I have enough food to feed the whole town for a week, but it'll all be gone by closing.

I load up the bed of my pickup and spy Rix walking out of his yurt. He stretches, showing off his taut stomach, before looking around to get the lay of the land. When he spots me, he jogs over in my direction.

Let me say that while I'm fully and utterly sure this man and I aren't compatible in any lasting way, I sure do appreciate the view when he's around. My stomach does a little somersault like when I'm barreling down the highway and I hit a dip in the road. When we were kids, Cat and I called those belly tickles. Rix Greer gives me belly tickles every time I look at him.

He eyes the culinary selection I'm packing up and asks, "Anything I can call breakfast?"

I hand him a cheddar and jalapeno scone and say, "You can go up to the house and fry yourself a couple of eggs to eat with that."

"Not cooking for me, huh?"

"I'm the one who made the scone," I scoff. "But that's it. My farm stand opens this morning, and it's all hands on deck."

He walks around the truck and hops into the passenger side. "Mind if I tag along?" He seems pretty confident the paparazzi haven't figured out he's staying here.

"Seeing that you've already decided to do so, I guess I can't stop you," I reply with a hint of sarcasm. The truth is I'm trying to avoid spending too much time in his company. After all, there's no sense panting after a man I have nothing in common with.

There are several cars already lined up when we get to the end of the drive. Rix asks, "Are these customers already? It's only six thirty."

"There're probably a few customers, but they're mostly the kids who'll run the stand over the summer and the band."

"You hire a band to play?"

I shake my head. "No. Wild Pig on the Prairie comes on their own. They play for tips and baked goods. They also pass out their business cards so that folks remember to hire them for summer parties and weddings."

The smile on Rix's face is luminous. "I can't believe those guys are all still around. My dad and granddad used to go and hear them play the first Wednesday of every month at the brew pub in town when I was in high school."

"They still play there," I confirm. "It's a packed house every time."

Wild Pig plays an assortment of old-timey instruments like the steel guitar, bass, and fiddle. They even pull out a washboard and spoons, depending on the song. I should mention that I used to sing along with them all the time but was asked by the brewpub management to stop. Of all the things I have going for me, my singing ability is not one of them. More's the pity because all I want to do is give voice to my inner Taylor Swift when they're around.

Rix jumps out of the truck before I can put it in park and heads in the direction of the grizzled retired farmers who make up the band. He looks as happy as a kid with a ten-spot walking into a penny candy shop.

Hannah and McKenzie Simmons run over and immediately start unloading the baked goods. They're high-school-aged sisters who ran the stand for me last summer. Their brother Jacob occasionally lends a hand as well, but he mostly works for farmers doing their heavy lifting.

The older girl, Hannah, will be a senior in the fall. "Is that Hendrix Greer?" she asks with her mouth so far open it looks like it's an airplane hangar for dragon flies.

"Yup," I answer.

McKenzie, an up-coming junior says, "We heard he was in town, but didn't really believe it. I mean, people here are always having Rix Greer sightings. And you know they mostly invent them to make life seem more exciting."

I look over at the object of their adoration and smile despite myself. He looks thrilled to be chatting it up with the Pigs. "Yes, well, we need to get everything set up in order to open by seven. I promise I'll introduce you to him once we have our first lull of the morning."

We have no lulls. We hit the ground running and it's go, go, go all day. The parking area next to the stand is packed from seven until two when we have to close up shop for the day because we're totally out of merchandise. I like to think the popularity of my stand is the reason we were so busy, but I know that's not the truth. The whole town and probably the three outlying ones showed up to see their hometown hero. But no paparazzi. I'm guessing they still think Rix is holed up in his grandparents' house. And I'm guessing the crowd in front of a farm stand isn't their cup of tea.

Rix worked the crowd like the pro he is. But he didn't only shake hands and kiss babies. He encouraged people to buy. "You've never had tomatoes this good! Try the scones, they're my favorite! You can't leave here without a pretty bunch of flowers for your table!" On and on he went until there was nothing left.

I even went up to the cafe and continued to bake throughout the morning to refill the stock. Scottie was my gopher, running boxes of muffins, cookies, and scones down to the stand to sell, but I had to keep calling him to come back because he was getting distracted, fawning all over Rix.

I'm so worn out by the time the last car pulls out, all I want to do is take a nap. And believe me, there's no time for napping during the summer on a farm. Forget working 9 to 5. It's more like 5 to 9 and you still don't have time to get everything done.

After everyone's gone, Rix says, "Wow, that was wild. Are you always so busy?"

I shake my head. "I think your presence tripled our normal sales." Uncomfortably, I add, "Thank you for that."

"You're welcome." He beams. "That was more fun than I've had in ages." I had a good time too, even though I can barely stand. Rix grabs my truck keys and says, "Go lie down in the back, and I'll drive up to the house slowly so you can catch a couple minutes of shut eye."

Scottie is already in the passenger side waiting for Rix. I'm going to have to remember to tease him about his crush later, but right now I'm so exhausted I jump into the flatbed and roll up a potato sack to put under my head. I'm sound asleep in seconds and have no idea how long I'm out. I don't open my eyes until I hear a deep voice say, "I'm sorry to disturb you, but can you tell me where I might find Sarah Hastings?"

My eyes pop open, and I stare straight into the chocolatiest pool of brown eyes I've ever seen. They're attached to a handsome face sporting a full dark beard and a smile the size of a slice of pizza.

Hello, Universe, has bachelor number two arrived?

Chapter Twenty-One
Bachelor #2

"Hey there, I'm Tony Mendez."

I'm still half asleep, so there are no bells going off in my head.

"The reporter for *Millennial* magazine."

My eyes pop open, and I sit up straight. "Hey, hi. I didn't think you were coming until tomorrow." *Eat Me!*'s opening is being covered by this hipster magazine out of Peoria. They contacted me after their editor experienced one of my aura cleanses. I told her about my new venture, and she promised to give it the cover story of her magazine.

"I decided to come a day early. I hope that's okay."

I jump out of the flatbed. "Sure. Give me a second to check my book and see which yurt to put you in. Larissa wanted you to have the same one she had."

Tony follows me into the gift yurt where I keep the book. "This place is awesome," he gushes. "Cool hookahs." He runs a small wooden rake through the Zen garden I have on display, making zigzags in the sand.

I check my book and say, "Yurt number two will be your home for the next few nights." I'm soft opening this week so that

I can work out any kinks before the grand opening next week. Tony is going to see the farm tomorrow and then trail me and take pictures.

I lead the way to Yurt #2 and run smack into Rix. He raises an eyebrow and asks, "Who's your friend?"

Tony sticks his hand out, "Tony Mendez, *Millennial* magazine." Rix looks at me for clarification.

"Tony's here to cover the opening of *Eat Me!*."

The reporter looks closer at Rix and says, "Hey, you're Rix Greer. Fancy seeing you here."

Rix looks dubious, as I'm sure he's naturally skeptical of reporters. "Yup."

"What are you doing here, man? Getting your chakras aligned or something?"

Rix shakes his head. "Just getting away from the hustle and bustle of the city for a while. I grew up in Gelson. I like to come home every now and again."

Okay. From that I assume I'm not supposed to mention his grandfather's farm. That's okay by me, because as I've stated, Tony is here to report on my cafe, not Rix.

"Cool. Wow. Imagine staying here with an honest to goodness celebrity," Tony says. "You're my dad's favorite football player since Refrigerator Perry."

Rix shoots me a look of annoyance and asks, "Can I talk to you privately for a second?"

I've got no idea what he could have to say that requires privacy, but I answer, "I'll stop by your yurt as soon as I get Tony settled." He nods and walks away.

Tony tours his accommodations and compliments everything

from the decor to the peaceful energy permeating the space. I show him a list of services I provide and suggest he pick a few to experience for himself. His editor wants him to write about more than the cafe. He chooses mud rolling and a chakra cleanse to start.

After setting him up with a cup of ginger tea and an oatmeal cookie, I head over to see Rix.

Once again, he opens the door before I knock. "Hey," I greet. "What's up?"

"Who is that guy?" he demands.

"Tony Mendez from *Millennial* magazine. I believe we both mentioned that to you."

"Yeah, yeah, yeah, I got that, but are you sure he's here to write about your cafe?"

"Yup. Pretty sure. He's had a reservation for a month."

"*He's* had a reservation or someone from *Millennial* has had a reservation?"

"The reservation is under his name, so you can quit being a paranoid celebrity."

He takes offense at my comment. "I'm not paranoid. I'm careful, okay?"

I shrug. "Okay." I head to the door. "If that's all you need, I have to get started on dinner."

He reaches out and touches my shoulder to stop me. "Do you ever do nothing? You haven't stopped moving all day."

"Life will start to slow down in September. This is my busy season, after all." It's always bittersweet, and I always feel a little sad when it's time to let the land rest until a new growing season, so I make the most of the summer months.

"Is there anything I can do to help while I'm here? Ellie pretty much has everything handled at my grandpa's house."

"I can't think of anything. But you could ask Arturo or Steve. They might be able to use your help." It's super sweet of him to offer, but I can't imagine that Rix remembers enough about farm labor to be very useful. I mean, if you forget about five thirty breakfasts, six o'clock mornings in the fields have probably been erased from memory, as well.

"I'll do that," he says. "Be careful with Oscar Issac out there. He looks like he may have interests that lie beyond your cafe."

My eyes brighten. "You think so? I'll make sure to be more welcoming then." Let him stew on that. I mean it, though. I'm not going to poo-poo the second bachelor to show up at my doorstep this week. And according to Tony's fourth finger on his left hand, he's free as the wind. The universe is doing its job and providing. Let's hope this one is a better fit than its first attempt.

Chapter Twenty-Two
Mowing Weeds

"I'm sorry, you did what?" I could not have heard Rix correctly.

He stands in front of me wearing a poop-eating grin while he repeats, "I wanted to do something nice to help you out, so while you were making dinner, I mowed your dandelion field."

"You mowed my dandelion field?!" I put down the meat mallet I use to smash open walnut husks lest I'm overcome by the urge to throw it at him. "Did you just say you mowed down my dandelions?" I demand. "What in God's name were you thinking?"

He starts to look a little less sure of himself, and rightly so. The man is a vandal and a nemesis! "I told you I wanted to help out earlier, and I decided to do that by mowing your dandelions for you."

"Who told you to mow my dandelions?" I demand.

"No one. I noticed that you had a huge field of them, and I thought I'd help you out by mowing them." I don't respond. How can I with a tsunami of rage nearly choking me? Trying not to let my brain succumb to the stroke that threatens, I grab Rix's arm and drag him out of the kitchen.

I haul him down the driveway until I've gotten him to the entrance to the cafe. Then I pull him inside the yurt and hand over a copy of my menu. Seething, I command, "Read it. Out loud, if you please."

He takes the paper I've thrust into his face. "Appetizers, dandelion greens with pea shoots and Chioggia beets in a yuzu vinaigrette, dandelion fritters with cashew sour cream, potato pancakes with dandelion marmalade ..."

He looks sheepish and stops reading, so I say, "There's iced dandelion coffee and dandelion wine as well as dandelion and pistachio ice-cream and dandelion petal confetti sprinkled on EVERYTHING!!!"

"Oh, Sarah, I'm so sorry. Why didn't you show me this before?"

"Because, Rix, never in a million years did I think you'd do something as insanely presumptuous as mow my dandelions!" Then I storm out and lead the way to the gift yurt. He keeps pace, looking uncertain, as if he's not sure whether I'm storming away from him or if I'm leading him somewhere else.

I hand over a brochure of my services which include:

- Dandelion Yoga
- Dandelion Body Steaming
- Dandelion Rolling

"Dandelion rolling?" he asks. "What does that entail?"

"Rolling in the dandelions, you moron. What do you think it entails?"

"Sarah, I swear I only wanted to help. Really, I mean everyone I've ever known hates dandelions and tries to get rid of them. I never knew they were your thing." Then unfortunately for him, he adds, "I mean, they're weeds."

"You're a weed," I spit at him. "Dandelions are from the daisy family. They're beautiful, vitamin-rich flowers, dammit."

I'm so mad I'm positively vibrating. I, Sarah Hastings, queen of calm, high priestess of happiness, empress of enlightenment, want to smack this guy upside the head and keep smacking him until I feel better, which—let's face it—may be a while.

I force myself to breathe slowly and deeply. I close my eyes and count to ten. Then I breathe some more. When I open my eyes, Rix is still there. "YOU!" I point a finger sharply into his chest, "need to get out of here, now." Jab, jab, jab.

"By get out of here, do you mean leave your farm or your sight?"

"GO!!!" I scream. Currently, I'd be happy if he left the planet.

He turns and runs like I'm scarier than any four front linemen he's ever come up against. I force myself to sit down and try to focus on my anger so I can harness it and shrink it. It takes forever. Mr. City Slicker has mowed down the entire crop of my signature ingredient. I have no words.

By the time I walk back up to the house I feel like I've hiked Mt. Kilimanjaro. Anger is toxic, and right now I'm as poisonous as Fukushima.

I run into Ethan in the entryway and say, "Ethan, I need you to make dinner tonight. There's a magazine reporter who's expecting to be fed. Could you please do that for me?"

"Sure," he responds. "Do I say where you are?"

"Tell him I'm performing an anger exorcism. Tell him it's a new service I've started offering."

Ethan taps his fingers against his legs. "Okay. Do you care what I feed him?" Poor Ethan's cooking skills aren't great, and he's only learned to make a few things while he's been here.

"Don't make him anything with dandelions and you'll be fine. Oh, and Emily's vegan this week, so cook accordingly."

Chapter Twenty-Three
Tears and Ideas

I go out to the dandelion field to survey the damage for myself. It's awful. All my beautiful blooms lay there, cut off in their prime. I'm so sad I lie down and cry. I do that for a full ten minutes before an idea comes to me.

I run to the barn and gather as many harvesting baskets as I can carry, then I throw them into the back of the pickup. I'm going to gather as many blooms as I possibly can before the sun goes down. I work for two straight hours before it begins to set.

Once I'm done, I stand back and marvel at the beauty of the scene before me. I get into the truck and drive up to the house as fast as humanly possible. I run in through the kitchen door and find Ethan, Emily, Scottie, and Tony finishing up dinner—Rix is conspicuously missing, smart man. Heaven knows what Ethan served, but their plates are nearly empty, so it must have been decent. They seem to be enjoying a nice chat, so, no harm, no foul.

I yell, "Tony, grab your camera, I have a gorgeous picture you need to take right now."

"Now? Couldn't it wait until tomorrow?"

He can't because tomorrow the dandelions will be limp, wilted, flower corpses. "Sorry, this is a time-sensitive shot."

He gets up and follows me outside. "Let me stop by my yurt and grab my camera."

I drive him the short distance to his lodgings and encourage him once again to make it snappy. We're out in the field moments before the sky erupts in a fiery explosion of color making its peace-out for another day.

Tony stares at the baskets full of dandelions, made even more vibrant by their backdrop, and declares, "Wow!" He hurries and starts snapping photos from a multitude of angles. "It's like Monet set this up to paint or something."

I beam like a proud mother. Talk about making the best out of a horrible situation. When it finally gets dark, Tony asks, "Why did you cut them all down?"

I'm torn. I really want to rat out Rix, but at the same time I don't want to make him look like a fool. I weigh my words very carefully before answering, "Sometimes you have to cut something down if you want it to grow back stronger."

Luckily Rix just mowed them. While the blooms will need to be used pretty quickly, the roots are still intact, so there should be new blooms starting before the week is out. Tony helps me load the truck with baskets and then we drive up to the cafe. We unload them in silence, enjoying the stillness of the summer night.

I get the first bunch of flowers soaking in the wash sink to remove any dust and dirt. I'm only going to keep as many as I can logically hope to use, so it shouldn't take us all night. Maybe only an hour. Tony pats them gently with clean towels before laying them on the counter to dry. "So, Tony," I ask, "are you from Illinois?"

"No, I grew up a couple hours north of Santa Fe. I took a job out here right after college."

"It must be quite a change from New Mexico."

"It is. My dad is a Navajo silversmith. He makes beautiful jewelry that he sells all over the Southwest."

"What about your mom?" I ask.

"She's a potter—half-Navajo and half-Irish. She's started to place a few of her pieces in museums on the West Coast."

"Is your mom Maria Mendez?" I ask in surprise.

"You've heard of her?"

"Yes. I took a really cool pottery class in college, and our professor was a huge fan of her work. He made devotees out of the whole class." I gush, "I love her use of color." Native American pottery can be colorful, but they tend to use shades found in nature. Earth tones from black to a deep clay orange to blues and greens which represent the sky and plant life. Maria Mendez pottery has a bit of a psychedelic flair—hot pinks, purples, bright reds, and yellows. The pottery still looks very true to her heritage, but it's also bold and innovative. I'm highly impressed with it.

Tony and I talk amiably for the next hour while we tend to the dandelions. He asks questions about how I became an organic gardener and holistic healer. I talk openly as if we are old friends. He's clearly an advanced soul and I resonate with him on almost a spiritual level. I wouldn't be surprised if we knew each other in a past life.

It's nine o'clock before we get the dandelions in the

refrigerator and close up shop for the night. Tony says, "This was a lot of fun. I'm glad I decided to come a day early."

I'm glad he did, too. If he'd come tomorrow, he would have missed the photo of the dandelions at sunset. If nothing else, that one picture is going to totally make the article he writes about my place.

I drop Tony off at his yurt and offer, "If you want to do sunrise yoga in the morning, you need to be on the front porch by five twenty."

He smiles. "I wouldn't miss it."

For the first night since I can remember, I don't do my nighttime yoga poses. Instead, I crawl into bed and talk to the universe. I fall asleep practicing the attitude of gratitude.

Thank you for this day. Thank you for the abundance of the earth and the beauty that permeates my world. And thank you for bringing bachelor number two so quickly after I requested him.

Chapter Twenty-Four
My Totem, Shirley

I've literally gone years without a romantic relationship. I've been so busy building my business and taking care of the others that I put that aspect of my life firmly on the back-burner. I didn't know how I could fit it in. I don't exactly have an abundance of free time right now, but suddenly I know Terraz is right, and now's the time to open myself up.

Tony is waiting when I walk outside at 5:15. He's swinging on the porch swing and greets me, "Good morning. Emily was just here. She said she'd meet us in the field." He adds, "She told me a bit about her health scare."

"Yeah, she was pretty freaked out."

"She said you were teaching her how to avoid getting sick. That's pretty cool."

"Thanks." We talk about alternative medicine all the way to the field formally known as dandelion.

We do our yoga poses quietly and in perfect harmony, feeling our bodies and souls unite with the universe at large. When we're done, Tony and I stroll back to the house together. "I slept like a dream," he says. "I connected with my totem animal. It was pretty intense."

I love the relationship Native Americans have with their totem animals. Their totem is their guide. They offer insight and strength as well as teachings. "What's your totem?"

"The eagle. Our culture believes the eagle is the spirit of the divine, the connection to our creator. It signifies courage, illumination of spirit, and risk taking."

I'm beyond intrigued. "What did you dream?"

"I didn't dream. I connected. It's a totally different thing." Then he explains, "I was standing on a cliff's edge and I felt the wind pick up. It was blowing toward me and pushing me away from the edge, so I leaned into it until most of my body was suspended over the precipice. Then I closed my eyes and the eagle flew over me, pulling me into it, becoming one with me. We flew, diving and soaring and experiencing creation as one. It was intense."

I feel myself getting caught up in his vision and can only imagine the euphoria of such an experience. I fly a lot in my sleep, but I always do it as myself, in human form. The thought of taking the shape of a bird is an exhilarating one. "What do you make of your experience?" I ask.

He's silent for a moment before saying, "This kind of thing happens when I need reminding that I'm part of something bigger than whatever I'm caught up in. When I focus too much on the tangible, it reminds me I'm intangible. I'm not just a man in a meat suit. I'm a soul as fluid as the wind. There are no obstacles that can hold me back."

I'm positively captivated by his words. Tony Mendez is an amazingly deep guy.

"I dreamed I was riding on the back of a black bear on a

merry-go-round. He turned around and tried to bite my leg. It scared the crap out me." After a beat, I add, "I don't suppose the black bear is my totem."

"No. Your totem is nothing you would fear. I'm guessing your bear was some kind of message," he says.

"I get those a lot. I normally ask for a meaning, but I totally forgot." Then I tell him, "I don't think I have a totem; I have a spirit guide, though."

He nods. "They can be the same. Do you feel like you have a particular connection to one animal?"

"My cow," I say. "Shirley is like a family member to me. She's solid and present and comforting. She's special in a way I can't even articulate." I think for a moment before adding, "She was born the year I was diagnosed with Hodgkin's. I took that year off school to beat it, and she and I became best friends. She reminds me that life is a cycle; even in the presence of disease, there are new beginnings. She made me realize I was part of creation in a way I'd never felt before."

"Then Shirley is most assuredly your totem," he confirms. "According to Native American belief, the cow represents love of home and community, patience, and fertility."

Fertility, wow. That's something I never think about, regarding myself. Never. As far as I know, I don't even have a biological clock. But as soon as he says the word, images of my future offspring explode out of my subconscious like a lid being taken off a jar full of lightning bugs. I know in that moment, as surely as I know my own name, that I will have children—more than two, even. And they will run on this land and be nurtured by this farm that owns my heart.

I don't say anything for several minutes. My essence jumps right off the timeline and becomes one with my past and future in such a way as I've never experienced. There's no beginning or end to me as I'm consumed by a cosmic reality I've never experienced before, and that's saying something for me.

I know at the deepest level of my being that a new life will come into this world at the same time that Shirley leaves it. I was reborn with her and when she leaves, another life will take her place. Only this time, it will be my child's life. My sweet cow has been more than a pet and companion to me, she's been a placeholder.

Chapter Twenty-Five
On the Other Hand

After yoga, Emily tells me, "Ethan and I are going to hit Market Place and do some shopping for his new apartment."

"Have fun."

Ethan has changed so much in the last few months, it's been a pleasure to watch his growth.

She nods her head and salutes. "Aye-aye, captain." Then she runs into the house to get him. Ethan and Emily have met several times before, but I've never witnessed the kind of energy exchange between them like I have in the last couple of days. How cool would it be if they wound up together? I briefly contemplate a new service, "Fall in Love in the Dandelion Field!"—complimentary with any aura cleanse.

Tony went to his yurt to shower before breakfast, so I'm back on the porch by myself, sitting on a rocking chair and soaking in the beauty of the morning. The air is cool and tinged with enough humidity to indicate that summer is nearly in full swing. Birds sing as they fly from branch to branch between the elm trees, and as the sun climbs higher into the sky, its rays reach farther and farther, as though trying to circle the world before holding hands on the other side.

Against my will, my gaze drifts over to Yurt #1. There are no lights on, so I have no idea if Rix is there or not. His car isn't, but that's not saying anything as he's been leaving it at his grandparents' place and using the path in the corn field to avoid the paparazzi.

Tony and Rix couldn't be more different.

Rix is a small-town guy made good. He's a gorgeous, bigger-than-life celebrity who left home for the bright lights of stardom. It's clear he prefers a lake view to honest-to-goodness toiling on the land. I mean, he hasn't even been home in six years and is selling the family farm.

Tony, on the other hand, is a descendant of native people, steeped in tradition, who experience life through art. All his words and deeds tell me he plans to continue that way of life. I haven't seen his photographs yet, but given his illustrious heritage, I'd be surprised if they weren't staggeringly gorgeous.

Tony's complex. He has a totem, for heaven's sake. What in the world would Rix's totem even be? I'd bet he'd laugh at the thought of such a thing.

Emily and Ethan are going out for breakfast, so I decide to make Tony my cinnamon swirl french toast with maple butter and fresh berries. I haven't made it since Ethan and Emily began their vegan cleanses. Suddenly, I'm ravenous for it.

I run out back to the henhouse to collect the eggs. The girls are already up and clucking about when I get there, so I don't have to physically move anyone from the roosting box. I score a selection of fourteen assorted beauties in varying shades of green, blue, and brown. They look like Easter eggs, they're so pretty.

In the kitchen I pull out a loaf of cinnamon raisin bread that I made four days ago. It's started to go a little stale, which is ideal for french toast. I rinse a handful of raspberries and blueberries and whip up the maple butter in the blender.

Tony arrives the same time as Scottie. My old friend comes over to me, and in the guise of giving me a hug whispers in my ear, "It's raining men. I may never leave."

I look over at Tony. His dark hair is damp, and he's trimmed his beard; he looks delicious. He's wearing a tight white T-shirt that shows off the tattoos on his arms. They look tribal and I wonder if they have something to do with his heritage. I'm not big on too many tattoos, but I quite like Tony's.

"Hello, again," I greet. "Sit down and I'll get you a cup." I don't ask if he wants coffee and I don't warn him that it's dandelion coffee, I just pour it and serve it.

He takes a sip before his eyes widen slightly. "Nice blend. Do I detect a hint of chicory with the dandelion?"

"You know dandelion coffee?"

"My mom started to drink it when she began nursing babies. I guess it really helps the milk come in. She never went back to regular coffee, so I grew up on dandelion coffee. Her blend was a bit stronger." *Tony would never mow my dandelions down.*

Scottie dives into his breakfast like he hasn't eaten in a week, so he's blessedly quiet while I learn more about Tony.

He shares that he lives in a tiny house on three acres of land. Once a week he eats only the food he can forage from his property. He doesn't farm per se, but he has fruit and nut trees, and shrubs, as well as herbs, greens, and wild mushrooms that grow in the woods surrounding his house.

"Are you a vegetarian?" I ask.

"No. I like meat a lot. I grew up hunting with my dad." He notices the look of disappointment on my face. "I'm Native American, Sarah. We don't hunt for sport, just food. We always ask permission of the animal spirit first and then we thank it for its sacrifice."

Scottie takes that moment to start paying attention to the conversation. "Sarah is a bacon-eating vegetarian."

Tony smiles like he's trying to suppress amusement. "I can't blame you there. Bacon is one of the great wonders of the world."

I glare at Scottie and say, "I'm tempted from time to time, but I don't believe in it."

My friend laughs. "What's to believe in? It's not like bacon is a religion."

I roll my eyes and ignore him. "Have you seen Rix this morning, Scottie?" Just as I finish asking, I hear a car door slam.

Chapter Twenty-Six
Not So Happy Corn

Steve, my right hand at *Eat Me Organic*, comes through the backdoor carrying a newspaper and cup of coffee from a local coffee shop. "Morning, Sarah." He eyes the french toast. "Have any extra?"

"Always." I dish him up and introduce, "Steve this is Tony Mendez from *Millennial* magazine. Tony, this is Steve, my wingman at *Eat Me Organic*." He already knows Scottie.

The guys shake hands before Steve opens the paper. "Ellie wanted me to show you this." He hands it over. In big bold letters, the title of the article reads:

Rix Greer Partners with Happy Corn!

I grab the paper, tearing it in my haste, and read the following:

> *Hendrix Greer, retired Chicago Bears football player and ladies' man extraordinaire, partners in a new venture with Happy Corn! The country's largest supplier of popping corn is based in Nebraska, but also has farms in Indiana and Illinois. President Jared Clayton confirms,*

*"We're in negotiations with Mr. Greer to buy his family
farm and for him to be the new face of Happy Corn! It's
an exciting development for the future of popcorn.*

What. In. The. Actual. Hell? I storm out of the kitchen
without a word and head straight to Yurt #1. I bang on the door
like I'm the Big Bad Wolf following a trail of cookie crumbs.
Mixed similes or not, I'm so mad I can't think straight. When
there's no answer, I open it and survey the room. No Rix, but
his stuff is still here, so he hasn't moved out.

I get into my pickup, turn the keys that stay in the ignition,
fire up the engine, and tear down the dirt driveway, leaving a
swirling dust storm in my wake. I'm not even the tiniest bit
calmer by the time I pull into his grandparents' drive. If
anything, I'm even more worked up. Who does this guy think
he is, not caring a wit about our town for years and then selling
a piece of us to the highest bidder?

Banging on the front door, I yell, "Open up, you loser!" I
know I look deranged, but at the moment I feel anything but
composed.

Rix opens the door looking surprised. "Sarah? What's up?"

I stick my pointer finger so close to his nose I could pick it if
I had the urge, which I don't. "You, YOU!!!" I push him into the
house and slam the door behind us.

"Is this about the dandelions? Geez, I said I was sorry. I
promise I'll never do anything like that again. I only wanted to
help."

"Help? HELP!" I scream. "How are you helping by selling
your property to the devil? Does that sound helpful to you?"

He looks confused. "What are you talking about?"

I shake the newspaper in his face like a fistful of maracas. "THIS is what I'm talking about."

He gently takes the paper out of my hand before stepping away from me.

"Well?" I demand.

"Let me read the article, will you?"

I start pacing like I'm trying to create enough friction to start a bonfire. Not that I need the heat—I'm steaming mad already.

Rix quietly reads before asking, "What are you so upset about?"

"Is it true? Are you really selling the farm to those, those ... *people?*" I say people in such a way as to suggest they're more disease-riddled rodents or giant man-eating dragons covered in boils, than actual human beings.

He shrugs. "We're in negotiations. It's not done yet."

"Why?" I demand. "Why would you do such a horrible thing to me?"

"Sarah, you need to breathe." He approaches me cautiously but seems to fear for his safety and stops just out of arm's reach. "Why does this upset you so much? You knew I came here to sell my grandparents' farm. I offered you first crack at it, but you passed. Why do you care who I sell it to?"

"I passed because I don't have the money to buy it." I don't add that I'm trying to free up some of my time for love. That's none of his business.

"Then why do you care who buys it?"

He can't possibly be that clueless, can he? "Rix, Happy Corn! is a corporation. They have no soul, no values. They don't care about anything but making money."

"Slow your roll, Sarah. Start at the beginning and tell me what this is really about."

I inhale and exhale three times before I explain, "It's about genetically modified corn. It's about dangerous pesticides being dumped on the fields when they crop dust. That poison is going to blow over onto my very healthy organic food, and it's going to ruin what I do!"

He shakes his head. "My grandfather crop dusted. How is that different from what Happy Corn! does?"

"Your grandfather crop-dusted *before* I started *Eat Me Organic*, that's how."

His jaw goes rigid, and the tips of his ears turn bright red before he demands, "And that's my problem, how? Do you really expect me to get your permission before I sell *my* land?"

Suddenly and very much against my will, I start to see his point. It's by pure serendipity that I've been able to farm without worrying about pesticides from another farm contaminating my fields. Had Herman still been alive, I probably wouldn't have ever been able to start my business. Instead of answering his question, I ask, "Why did you wait so long to sell your grandparents' farm?"

He shrugs his shoulders. "There was a stipulation in the will that required us to hold onto the property for six years before we could."

"Why?" I ask.

"Don't know. My parents might, though, if you want me to ask them."

"It doesn't really matter now that you're doing it. I guess I have some things to figure out." I'm totally and completely deflated. "How could you consider being the face for this company?"

"I've done endorsements before. They're a big part of my income."

"Rix, Happy Corn! uses GMOs. Do you know that corn earworms die if they bite into genetically modified corn?"

"That's why they modify it right? So that they don't lose their crop to pests."

"If worms die from eating it, what do you think it's doing to the people who eat it?"

His expression indicates that a glimmer of reason finally seems to be entering his thick skull. "Gotcha. But you'd have to eat enough popcorn for a small nation to kill a person."

"Oh, my god, you idiot, the point is that it's not only the corn industry that's doing it. It's wheat, beans, fruit trees, it's all commercially grown food that isn't organic. Then they feed this crap food to the animals and you eat the animals. You're being poisoned by everything."

"You're telling me that by selling my land to the Happy Corn! I'm personally responsible for the demise of civilization?"

"You're contributing to it. Everyone has to take some responsibility."

"Sarah, if we put all the corporate farmers out of business, how would people eat?"

"They'd grow their own food and eat from their own land. And they'd be a heck of a lot healthier for it."

He points out, "Farming is a full-time job. There isn't enough time in the day to work full-time and grow enough food to feed a family."

"They don't have to grow all their food. They can buy organic food from their local farmers' markets or co-ops. They could barter with their neighbors."

He snorts. "You've got some kind of crazy Utopian notions that don't fit into the real world, you know that? What you're suggesting is that people live like they did a hundred years ago. And let me tell you, those weren't easy times. I'd go as far as to say folks back then would have happily traded lives with us if they'd been given the opportunity."

I glare at him like I'm capable of shooting death lasers out of my eyes. "How I ever found you sexy is beyond me."

"You find me sexy? Tell me more," he drawls flirtatiously.

"Found. Past tense." I turn and storm out of his house.

Chapter Twenty-Seven
Bachelor #3, Really?

Rix mostly disappears for the next few days. When we do see him, it's only in passing. Nan told me he's been eating his meals in town, probably devouring all kinds of hideously toxic food. The more I think about his duplicity, the madder I get. Imagine him staying here while simultaneously setting into motion a plan that will ruin my life.

This morning when I walked by his car, I was overcome by the urge to slash his tires. The only thing that saved him was that Tony was with me and I wasn't in possession of a sharp enough object to do the job properly. Although I'm pretty sure I could have gnawed my way through them if I'd been alone.

Tony has been shadowing me and learning everything there is to know about my farm. We've had some amazing conversations about Native American art, the healing properties of cilantro, and the best time of year to experience Machu Picchu. He's interested in a lot of the same things I am, and it's made the time we've spent together fly by. It's also making me more and more convinced of how compatible we are.

So far, he's had a sweat lodge and a mud roll. He's currently enjoying a hot stone meditation. He's on the slate pad that I've heated with boiling water. Before having him lie down on it, I misted the stone with a combination of lavender and tea tree oils, then I placed Moldavite crystals on his chakras to raise the energy in his body.

I believe I've previously mentioned Tony's attractiveness, but let me say, without his shirt on, he looks like a gladiator—all golden and chiseled and buff. I stared at him for a solid ten minutes after he closed his eyes to start his meditation. Tingles shot through me, causing the hair on my arms to stand on end. After returning to the cafe yurt, I may have needed two tall glasses of mint water to cool off afterward.

I'm kneading bread dough and trying to remember every contour of his smokin' hot bod when Emily pops in. "Nan and Dorcas are here. They want to chat." Her aura is bright yellow, which is the color for happy. Emily is positively thriving on her vegan diet.

"They want to chat with you or me?" I have so much to do today I don't really have time to sit and talk.

"They asked me to get you," she answers.

I slam the dough down on the counter a few more times before covering with a cloth while I ask, "Do you have any idea what they want to talk about?"

She smiles. "I do."

"Are you going to tell me?"

"I'm not."

"For heaven's sake, what's up with all the secretiveness?"

"They asked me to get you and not say anything about why they're here."

I have no idea in this world what they could want. When we head out to the porch, I realize they aren't alone. Ethan is sitting on a rocking chair next to a very good-looking man about my age.

The stranger has wavy blond hair and strikingly blue eyes. When he stands, he positively towers over me. He's built like a linebacker. He steps forward and reaches out his hand, "Hi there, I'm John Abernathy."

Abernathy? John, Johnny ... it's all coming together, "Dorcas's grandson?"

"That's me." He beams like he's got halogen headlights illuminating his teeth.

I turn to the minister's wife. "You didn't mention your grandson was visiting."

Dorcas looks moderately contrite. "I told you about him the other day."

That she did. What she didn't mention is that he's one fine looking bacon farmer. I turn to John and ask, "Are you in town for long?"

"About a week," he answers. "I live outside of Springfield. My grandparents need some work done around their house, and I'm their closest relative. I came to help." He smiles at his grandmother like she's the most important person in the world. "I don't want them to have to hire out help."

Nan says, "We were on our way into town and thought we'd stop by to say hello." She looks positively thrilled to be witnessing this meeting. So much so, I don't point out that town is in the opposite direction.

I offer, "Would you all like to come in for some tea and pie?"

Emily announces, "I'm actually going to head back to my place. I want to thank you for all of your wonderful ideas and help."

"I thought you'd be here for a few more days," I say.

"Cat's booked some new parties, and it looks like we're going to be getting busy. It's easier if I'm at home. I'm going to ask if I can plant a garden in the common space at my apartment building."

Ethan says, "If they don't let you, you can plant it at the house I'm renting." Then he looks at me. "Sarah, you've saved my life. I have no words to express what your friendship has meant to me. I'm moving into my new place later today."

Everyone's jumping ship like I've announced I've got the plague or something. I mean, I knew Ethan was going today, yet I can't help but wonder if Emily's interest in being here was directly tied to his presence.

Nan claps her hands together and says, "Your house is emptying out, Sarah." She winks at me. "Kind of makes you want to take off your brassiere and dance around in celebration, doesn't it?" She reaches around her back like she's about to unhook her own bra and declares, "I'll join you!"

John looks alarmed, Ethan shifts nervously in his chair as though this is his cue to leave, but Dorcas saves the day. "Keep your bra on, Bridget. Cat told you if you wanted to learn how to use the new TV, you'd have to do it before two." To the rest of us, she says, "She's busy getting the barn set up for her Highland fling lesson."

Cat is throwing her first singles mixer at the barn and the Mastertons are going to teach everyone how to do the fling.

We've all been looking forward to this for ages.

Nan announces, "Cat got the Netflix and she's going to show me how to use it so Dorcas and I can watch some steamy shows while we knit prayer shawls for church." Dorcas looks decidedly excited by the prospect.

"So, is that a no to tea and pie?" I ask. I'm having a hard time figuring out what everyone is doing here if they're all planning to leave right away.

"About that," Dorcas says. "I'll drive Bridget home." Then she turns to John, "Why don't you join Sarah and I'll pick you up when I'm done."

"Sounds good to me if it's okay with Sarah," John says.

Well, what in the world am I going to say now that I've invited them? "Please, come on in." Then I look at Dorcas, "We'll see you in a few minutes, Mrs. A."

"I might be an hour or so, dear. I'm going to pick up a few things in town first."

Within minutes, everyone is packing up their stuff or have said their goodbyes and I'm alone in the kitchen with a pig farmer who I absolutely refuse to entertain the notion of dating. My vegetarian card would be at stake.

Chapter Twenty-Eight
Dear Universe

John turns out to be a really nice guy. Really nice, like a sexy Mr. Rogers. We spend a full hour discussing farming and life in general. As hard as I try, I can find no apparent flaws. I'm sure he's got them—like maybe he chews with his mouth open or leaves the toilet seat up, but nothing obvious like inappropriate gassiness. More's the pity.

John tells me that Dorcas's son recently retired and handed the business down to him. "It's not my dream job, but it meant a lot to my dad. He really wanted to keep the farm in the family." Gah, so he's clearly a good son. I can't hold that against him.

"Do you have any siblings?" I ask. You know, like a sister who wouldn't mind taking over?

"My brother Charlie lives in Chicago. He's a lawyer." *Darn.* "Tell me about you. Have you been farming for long?"

"Five years, almost six now. My parents moved down to Florida for most of the year for my dad's arthritis. I took over and made the whole place organic."

"That's an incredible undertaking. Really impressive, actually." Then he adds, "I'm raising our pigs organically. You can't be too careful about the food you put into your body."

"Exactly." Some people simply don't understand the benefits of organic. Obviously, I'm thinking of Rix.

"The taste of the meat is superior and brings a premium price, as well. Organic pork is extremely tender and flavorful."

"I'm a vegetarian," I blurt out. I feel like I'm confessing to prostitution in church or something, but John doesn't flinch.

He says, "That's cool. I only eat meat a couple times a week. Mostly to be quality control for our product."

"If you could do something other than a pig farming, what would you do?" Maybe there's hope. Tony's a meat eater, so I can't really discriminate according to that alone. If I did, all three bachelors would be out. Not that I'm still considering Rix. It's one thing to eat meat and another thing entirely to sell your soul for profit.

John doesn't even take a minute to think before answering, "I'd do what you're doing, organic fruits and vegetables all the way. I couldn't imagine being anything other than a farmer. I mean no one works harder than a farmer, but I don't think there's another job on the planet that would be nearly as rewarding."

"I feel the exact same way." Now I *really* like John Abernathy. He's got heart. Anyone who's called to organic farming has to have higher ideals than your average bear—your average Chicago Bear, that is. *That's right, Hendrix Greer, I'm talking to you!*

By the time Dorcas gets back, we're sitting on the front porch drinking our second cup of tea. The time has positively flown by. I'm grateful my book club friend hadn't taken my negative attitude toward her grandson seriously. Although it was probably

Nan who encouraged Dorcas to bring him here. Nan is inherently the pushiest person I know.

Before his grandmother gets out the car, he says, "I don't suppose I could take you out some night while I'm here."

"That would be really nice," I say sincerely. So much for not dating a bacon farmer. The thing is, John is a really a great guy. He loves the land, he might love bacon as much as I do, and he loves farming—two of the three things that mean the world to me.

Dear Universe,

Nice going. I definitely think you're on the right track with John Abernathy. Now, if you can get him to dump his father's dream of his carrying on the family business, I'd have a better idea of knowing if we could have a future together. How 'bout giving me some kind of sign?

Chapter Twenty-Nine
I Did Not See That Coming

After John and Dorcas leave, Tony and I enjoy a candle-lit dinner in the herb garden. A couple of years ago I laid some old square bricks I found at a farm sale to make a small patio in the center. Then I trellised the sides and planted a deep purple clematis. The flowering vines have grown over the top of the table, creating a romantic secret garden kind of setting. I don't usually invite guests to dine with me here; it's my own special spot. But when one has seduction in mind, one must have the proper stage. It's the perfect location to move things along with Tony and see if there's any real chemistry between us.

Over a beet and goat cheese salad with toasted hazelnuts and pickled onions, I confess, "I've really enjoyed your company." Then I smile coyly and bat my eyes a time or two. My flirting skills are a little rusty, but this is one I still remember.

Tony looks up, startled. "It's definitely been one of the cooler assignments I've had lately."

I immediately feel a change in the energy between us. I used the word *company* and he said *assignment.* Has this all been business for him? Has my interest been one-sided?

I think back over the week and realize he's been nothing but professional. Sure, we've had some great conversations, some while he's only been partially dressed, but it's not like we've so much as held hands. I suddenly feel foolish. The rest of the meal is stilted and awkward. Mentally I give myself a good sharp kick.

Finally, over desert, he says, "Listen, Sarah ..." Time stops. The birds halt their singing, the air isn't moving, even the candles cease flickering. I know he's about to say something I don't want to hear and more than anything I want to pretend he misinterpreted my earlier behavior. But, of course, he hasn't.

"I'm seeing someone," he confesses.

I should have taken drama classes in high school because I'm the world's worst actress. In a high squeaky voice that surely isn't mine, I exclaim, "How wonderful! Tell me about her."

He reaches over to touch my hand, but I jump up like a fully wound jack-in-the-box and start to clear the dishes.

"Sarah," he follows behind me. "Please come back and talk to me."

I try to fake a bright tone. "Absolutely I'll be right back, let me clear these plates." Oh. My. God. How did I figure that just because he was good looking and interesting *and* staying on my farm that he was also single? *Darn you, Universe, I thought you were on my side.*

I put the dishes in the sink and run into the powder room to splash some cold water on my face. Looking in the mirror, I practice my, "I'm-delighted-you're-seeing-a-nice-girl" face. It looks a bit more vicious than I'd hoped. I keep trying until I find an expression that doesn't make me look insane or potentially dangerous.

I flash it when I get back out to the table. Tony stands immediately. "I'm so sorry if I've misrepresented my intentions," he said.

Oh, for crap sakes. "Tony, please don't apologize. You're a very nice guy. I've only just realized that I'd like a very nice guy in my life. I took it as kismet that you showed up at the same time I had my epiphany and asked my spirit guide for help."

"If I were single, it would be an entirely different story."

Oh my god, now I feel pathetic.

"Stop." I hold out my hand like one of the Supremes about to break into song. "We're both great people, we've had some great conversations, it's been great." *OMG, Sarah, stop saying great!* "I don't want any weirdness, okay?"

"Okay," he agrees. "Do you still want to hear about my girlfriend?"

Do frogs perform Broadway show tunes in the bayou? "I'd love to," I declare, lying through my teeth. "Tell me *all* about her."

Holy. Crap. Tony spends the next forty (!) minutes telling me all about Xandria Bordaine. She's tall and French and wait for it ... she's a professional ballet dancer. I learn that she's elegant beyond words, loves crossword puzzles, and her dog, Fiona, has canine arthritis. I swear by the end of his monologue I know what kind of shampoo she uses—Yuzu Breeze.

I offhandedly say, "She sounds like the one, Tony."

"Hang on," he says before he runs to his yurt and returns with the turquoise and silver engagement ring he had his dad fashion for her.

Dear Universe,

I have been your most faithful and obedient champion. I tell everyone you always have a plan and that things will inevitably unfold as they should. I tell them to trust you, believe in the unbelievable, and embrace whatever comes. But really, at this moment I'm super pissed at you.

Are you flipping kidding me? When I finally get around to being interested in my own social life, you send me a sneaky, snake in the grass, ex- football player followed by the ideal man who is already taken.

We've been tight, Universe, you and I. But I fear unless you change your ways and get on board with helping me, I might be breaking up with you. Please don't take this as a threat, think of it more as a loving ultimatum. Okay?

Maybe if you could get John to give up bacon farming …

Chapter Thirty
Tortillas and Universal Plans

Today is the day. It is the soft opening for *Eat Me!* and I've been up since four a.m. to prepare. The cafe is a veritable festival of fresh produce. The colors are staggeringly gorgeous—so many shades of red, yellow, orange, purple, and green.

The first thing I do is cull the wilted-looking dandelions out of the refrigerator. Luckily, I'll have enough petals for garnishing the plates. I'll use the wilted flowers in the dandelion fritters.

Arturo stayed late yesterday and harvested the dandelion greens. It turns out that mowing the field didn't hurt anything at all. The only greens that were ready to pick were new growth, ensuring the most tender and delicately flavored salads. Let's not tell Rix that, though.

The customers coming today were all invited as my guests. I chose the people I thought would most likely get the word out about my new place. They'll start arriving at eleven thirty, and the last ones come at one. This will guarantee that no one has to wait for long and I don't get backed up in the kitchen.

After tending the dandelions, I make the bread, biscuits, and cookies, as they're the most time consuming. Then I wash the greens and prep the rest of the ingredients for last minute assembly.

When a car door slams out front, I know it's Arturo's wife, Maria. She makes the best tortillas.

"Hola, Sarah." She comes through the door more bright-eyed than I currently feel. I missed my morning yoga which always knocks me off my game a bit.

"Good morning, my friend. You ready to cook?"

"Always." She ties on an apron before getting her tortilla presses heated. "Which kinds am I making for today?" she asks. Maria is the tortilla queen and has an arsenal full of delectable offerings.

"Let's go with cauliflower, corn, spinach and straight wheat." She does so many more but I'm thinking of the pictures and what will best contrast with the fillings.

"Which ones do you want for the chips?" she asks while turning on the fryer.

"Let's stick to the standard corn today. The yellow will make the guacamole really pop."

Maria gets busy and starts to hum to herself. She's like poetry in motion to watch, like Mother Earth incarnate. She's not thin or heavy; she's not particularly homely or beautiful; she's neither short nor tall. Each one of her physical traits would be considered quite average on their own, but when you put them all together, she's simply stunning. My friend has a beautiful soul.

As she fries the chips, she says, "Tell me about the football player. He's come home, yes?"

"Well, yes and no. I mean he's here now, but he's going to leave as soon as he sells the farm." Then a great idea comes to me, "Why don't you and Arturo buy his land? We could be neighbors!" I'd hate to lose Arturo, but if they bought here, they wouldn't be moving to Texas any time soon.

"I think not, Sarah. Arturo is set on going home, and it's for the best. Our parents aren't getting any younger and they're going to need us to take care of them one of these years."

That's admirable. I mean, I'm all about family. When my folks need me, I'll make sure they're taken care of. But it still makes my heart ping. "I think of your family as my family. You know that, right?"

"Yes, we do. You have been a sister to Arturo since he was a child and I've come to think of you in the same way. But, you know how it is. It's our duty to care for our elders. You will always be welcome in our home." She smiles in such a way that suggests she's harnessed a bit of the sun.

I hate to think of things changing. I know the universe will bring someone to take over Arturo's job here, and I know he and I will always be friends, but sometimes I want to stop the clock so I can soak in the moment. That's why it's so important to live in real time and be centered in the now. Otherwise people can come and go too quickly to appreciate them to their fullest.

"How are your mama and papa? Are they still coming home soon?"

I nod my head absently. "They are. In fact, I'm picking them up at the airport tomorrow."

"So early?" she asks.

My parents' change of plans has been gnawing at me. Not necessarily keeping me up at night, but it's been circling around in my thoughts. My mom and dad wake up at the same time every day. They eat the same breakfast and have the same conversations. They're not boring, just very set in their ways. I can't help but feel something is out of balance for them to be coming home so soon.

I say, "I'm a little concerned about it, actually."

"It's like you always tell me, Sarah. The universe has a plan and as long as we don't fight the ride, it will always be a good one."

"I believe that with my whole heart. If we make the most of the moments and embrace each new person and experience, our lives will be happy."

"Agreed. So, tell me about this football player …"

Chapter Thirty-One
Dead Rodents in Aprons

I didn't invite Rix to the opening. Quite honestly, I don't want him anywhere near my farm today. The article Tony is writing is about *Eat Me Organic*, not some has-been football player bent on my destruction. Yes, I'm dramatic right now, but it's how I feel. The good news is that after our last encounter, I'm pretty sure Rix wants nothing to do with me, either.

"How can we help?" Cat asks as they enter, trailing a blaze of happiness behind them. Cat and Sam are the first ones to show up. My friends are so perfect for each other, it's hard to believe they've only recently reunited.

"You can sit down and look pretty," I tell her.

Sam loops his arm behind Cat's back. "She looks pretty everywhere she goes." Then he leans in and kisses her cheek.

Cat smacks him playfully. "No, you look pretty," she teases before nibbling on his jaw.

"Listen, you two," I say interrupting their love fest, "you both look pretty, now go do it over there at table number one so Tony can capture all your gorgeousness and help sell my business." They giggle and do what they're told.

Cat's parents arrive next. Dougal and Maggie Masterton are quite the pair. Dougal is wearing his kilt, which is his standard attire, and Maggie is sporting a red-checked summer dress that looks like she fashioned it out of an old tablecloth (knowing her, there's a ninety percent chance that's what she did.)

Dougal booms, "Sarah, lass, what a fine day this is." Then he hands me a taxidermied squirrel dressed in a white apron. There's a tiny spatula glued to her paw. "A good luck charm for your new venture."

I awkwardly accept his gift, knowing that he probably worked long and hard to configure this piece of roadkill just for me. "Thank you so much," I manage, trying to hide my distaste. "But you know, *Eat Me!* only serves vegan food, right?"

He looks shocked. "I don't want to serve Midge." *Oh my word, he's named the squirrel Midge.* "I only want her to bring you luck and good fortune." *You know, like only a dead squirrel wearing an apron can.*

Maggie hands over a plate of her shortbread pressed in the shape of smiley emojis. "My lucky cookies. I know today's going to be a great success!"

"Thanks, Mrs. Masterton. Is this, by chance, your special shortbread recipe?"

She beams. "Only the best for you!"

She makes her shortbread with pig fat instead of butter.

"I do, dear. But you don't have to worry, there's no meat in them."

I hand off the shortbread to Maria. Vegetarianism is a foreign concept in these parts. Although, truth be told, I'll probably eat one of her cookies later. They have a slight bacon undertone that can't be beat.

Nan and Dorcas appear next, wearing matching T-shirts that say, *Eat Me, Right Now*. I know it's their way of being supportive, but they have no idea how that slogan will be misinterpreted. I don't enlighten them. I'll simply suggest to Tony that if he takes their picture, he blurs the words a bit.

I introduce my first round of guests to Tony and then head back into the kitchen to start preparing the first course: dandelion fritters on baby greens.

It's too bad I've had to write Tony off as my future mate. That whole *in love with another woman* thing was a real bummer. He would have been perfect for me. But like Maria reminded me, you gotta go with the flow. And while we've had a couple of false starts, it's clear the universe is trying. *Do you hear that, Universe? I'm going to bat for you, don't let me down.*

Hours later, I declare the soft opening of my cafe is a screaming success. Tony chatted with the locals and sampled everything off the menu, before shaking my hands warmly and saying, "Sarah, I love your place! I took some amazing pictures." Then he adds, "I can't wait to compare schedules with Xandria and book a weekend here for us."

"What a great idea," I say, pretending an enthusiasm I do not feel. I say, "great" like typhoid is great. I want to host Tony and Xandria about as much as I want to kill a deer with my bare hands for the sport of it.

After he's packed up and left town, I clean up the cafe and relish the feeling of success. Today was a lot of fun, and while I know I probably won't be that busy once the cafe opens, I'm certain I've made a good impression with my hometown.

Ethan and Emily are both gone, and Scottie went into

Chicago today to stay with Tad for several days, so when I head back to the house, I know it's going to be empty. While I normally love being alone with my thoughts, I'm glad my date with John is tonight.

Chapter Thirty-Two
Dinner for Three

After a quick phone call, John and I decide to have dinner here. Not only will the food be better, but it gives me an opportunity to show off my land—a hard opportunity to resist given that he's as into farming as I am.

Taking care with my appearance, I have put on a less-constricting sarong. It's one of a colorful collection that I ordered to sell in the gift shop. It's essentially a long piece of fabric that I wrap around my body and tie at the neck. Suddenly I feel much better, freer. Not to mention cooler—there's a welcome breeze up my skirt.

While I wait for him to arrive, I pour myself a glass of wine and head out to the back porch. I wonder how I've lived here for so long by myself. Sure, my parents are around a couple months out of the year, but the rest of the time, it's just me.

Arturo and Steve are here during the week, and I see people when I make my deliveries, but it's not the same as sharing my home and life with someone. How have I not felt this deficit before now?

Suddenly, I'm so aware of the stillness around me that I begin to physically ache. My heart actually hurts. My parents have each other, Cat has Sam, Tony has Xandria, Scottie has Tad, Ethan and Emily may be well on the way to something, and Rix has any woman he could ever want. The whole world is paired up, and I have no one.

I stand up and face the late afternoon sun and close my eyes, feeling its warmth fill me. I force my brain to still, and after several calming breaths I say:

Okay, Universe, it's up to you. I know it might seem that I may be jumping the gun on this whole relationship thing. I mean, I haven't so much as kissed a man in ages, but you're the one who had Terraz tell me it's time, so I assume you're not messing around. In that vein, bring it, already.

When I open my eyes and turn around, Rix is sitting in the swing I only recently vacated. "What are you doing here?" I demand.

"I came up early for dinner. I thought I might be able to give you a hand."

"Why are you here for dinner?"

He looks confused. "Because according to your time schedule, it's almost dinner time."

"But Ethan, Emily, and Scottie aren't here."

"And that affects my meal, how?" he asks.

"I guess it doesn't, it's just that you haven't eaten here in a few days, so I figured you wouldn't be coming tonight. And well, I have a date."

He quirks an eyebrow. "A date, really?"

"Yes, a date. Why would that surprise you?" I demand.

He shrugs his shoulders. "I didn't think you were seeing anyone."

"I'm not," I answer. "I mean I wasn't, but maybe I am now." Then I clarify, "It's a first date."

"How exciting," he drawls sarcastically. "In that case, it's a good thing I'll be here to chaperone."

"Rix, it's not the eighteen hundreds. I'll be fine unchaperoned." In fact, I welcome it.

"Maybe, but I am a paying customer, after all, and you've promised me food. I'm here to take you up on that."

He can't be serious. So, I repeat, "You haven't eaten here in days!"

Instead of answering my question, he responds, "I guess you owe me a really good meal then."

"Rix, I have a *date*. You cannot crash my date." That's when I hear the crunching of tires rolling over the gravel out front.

I run around the side yard, totally ignoring the obnoxious football player who has decided to follow me. When I see John get out of his truck, I greet, "You're here. Come on in."

Then Rix shouts, "Yes, welcome, we're so glad you could make it!"

What the hell? I turn and glare at Rix before turning my back on him. "Come on in, John. I was just about to get dinner started."

Rix offers, "Can I get you something to drink while we wait for our food?"

John looks as confused as I am annoyed. He glances from Rix to me and asks, "Did I get the day wrong?"

Rix claps him on the shoulder and answers for me. "Absolutely not. We've been expecting you."

John looks more befuddled than ever and asks, "Who are you?"

Chapter Thirty-Three
Killers and Kisses

Rix sticks out his hand, "Hendrix Greer, at your service."

John looks surprised and delighted at the same time. "Rix Greer? Super nice to meet you, man, I'm a big fan." Then he shakes hands enthusiastically. "Er', do you live here?" he asks.

"I live in the city, but I stay here with Sarah when I'm in town." Then the loser turns to me and winks. Winks!

"He's staying in one of my yurts," I explain.

"The one closest to the house," Rix adds suggestively.

Holy. Hell. What is he doing? He's purposely trying to sabotage my date. So, I say, "Rix is running away from the paparazzi who are trying to confirm a story about one of his love children."

John looks appalled. "Really?"

Before I can answer, the football player approaches me and slides his arm around my waist, then pulls me close to his side. "Don't mind her, she's jealous."

I smack his hand away and step out of his reach. "Follow me, John. You can keep me company while I cook."

John and Rix both follow me into the kitchen. When we get

there, I indicate that my date should sit on a stool at the counter. "Can I get you something to drink, *John*?" I offer, blatantly ignoring Rix.

Before he can answer, Rix says, "You take care of dinner, I'll get our guest a beverage." Then he asks John, "Would you like a beer? A glass of wine? A wheatgrass and kale smoothie?"

Dorcas's grandson appears to be conflicted. He's obviously thrilled to be meeting Rix but seems to be questioning whether or not he and I are on a date, or he and I and *Rix* are on a date. He looks a wee bit nervous that it might be the latter.

"I'll have beer, thanks."

Rix pulls one out of the refrigerator and flips the top before saying, "So, John, tell me what you do."

"I'm a pig farmer. My spread is over near Springfield."

"A pig farmer?" Rix gasps like some Victorian heroine in murder mystery. "Oh my, what does Sarah think about that?" Then he looks at me.

"John has an *organic* pig farm," I explain.

Rix clucks his tongue. "Still and all the same, he's a murderer!"

John looks decidedly uncomfortable with the title. "I'm a farmer, not a murderer."

"Oh, don't get me wrong," Rix declares. "I love meat. It's just that our Sarah here can be very judgmental about people who don't subscribe to her ideals. Can't you, honey?" he says to me.

I slam down the bottle of wine that I've been holding onto for dear life. Both men jump at the noise. "Rix, could I please speak to you for a minute, alone?"

"Alone?" he waggles his eyebrow at me suggestively.

I point to the back door. "On the porch, now!" Then I turn to John and say, "Please excuse me, I'll be right back."

John murmurs something but I don't hear what it is as my head is full of rage, which turns out to be a very loud emotion. As soon as Rix and I are both on the patio, I yell, "WHAT ARE YOU DOING?"

Feigning innocence, he says, "I'm only making conversation with our guest."

"He's not your guest, he's mine. He's *my* date. You should not be horning in on my date."

"Oh, don't worry, John doesn't make me horny at all." He takes a step closer to me.

"I didn't think he did, moron." Then I demand, "Why are you trying to ruin my date by pretending we're some kind of couple?" I let my voice carry, hoping John can overhear our argument.

He takes another step until he within arm's reach. "Because I don't think he's right for you."

"You don't have any say in the matter."

Another step. Then he puts his hands on my elbows and stares into my eyes. His look morphs from combative to something altogether different. He suddenly looks tender and confused, "Don't I?"

Before I can answer, he leans in and gently touches his lips to mine. I'm so shocked I don't move. Rix Greer is kissing me. His lips, all soft, silky, and hungry, feel like heaven on mine. His breath sends chills racing down my arms as well as to more intimate places. I can't help it, I lean into him, prolonging the heat. I feel his very hard muscular chest against my body and let out a sigh that sounds more like a purr.

Rix groans deeply in his throat and gradually parts my lips. I'm fully invested in what we're doing and completely unaware of how long we're occupied. It could be two minutes or twenty, I'm that lost in the erotic sensations flooding my body.

Rix Greer is kissing me like I'm the sunlight and he's just crawled out of a cave for the first time in a year. He's positively devouring me, and it's the most marvelous feeling I've ever experienced.

When he finally pulls back, he says, "I guess you'd better go in and make dinner for your date."

I stumble slightly as he steps out of my grasp. My knees have apparently turned into pudding. "Why did you do that?" Stunned back into reality, I demand in no more than a whisper.

"I heard you talking earlier about not having kissed anyone in ages. It sounded like you were hoping to change that."

Oh, my gosh, he heard me talking to the universe. I wrack my brain wondering what else I said, but I come up blank. "I wasn't talking about you," I finally say.

"I figured as much, but I thought I might be able to persuade you differently."

"Why?" I demand. "Why would you want anything to do with me romantically? We're so different!"

"I'm not the one who's having a hard time accepting you, Sarah. You're the one with the problem."

And he's right. I do have a problem. I have a problem with his blasé attitude regarding organic farming, I have a problem with his selling his land to a corporation who will strip it of all goodness, and apparently, I have a bigger problem than both of those things combined. I have a problem because I loved kissing him. It was by far the best kiss I've ever been a party to, and I want to do it again. But to what end? We obviously aren't compatible on any meaningful level.

Our differences are insurmountable, right?

Chapter Thirty-Four
The Insurmountable Pig

Dinner is a farce. John and I are no more on a date than Tony and I were. He's a nice man and had Rix not just laid one on me, I would go so far as to say there was potential for us. But throughout the meal Rix rubs his foot against my leg or asks me to pass him something and then brushes his hand against mine. My body is at war with my brain the entire meal.

When we finish eating, Rix stands up and clears the table like he's the one hosting this drama. I try desperately to ignore the implied sense of familiarity in my home and ask, "John, can I interest you in some peach pie?"

"Peach pie!" Rix interrupts, "I love your peach pie, it's my favorite."

John replies, "Sure, thanks. Would you mind if I had a cup of coffee with it?"

"Oh, Sarah doesn't believe in coffee," Rix offers.

"Really?" This, from John.

"I have dandelion coffee. Would that be okay?" I ask.

"Um, no, thanks, I'll stick with the pie."

I cut the dessert and serve it with vegan vanilla ice cream. Rix moans and groans through his whole dessert like he's on the receiving end of some intensely personal pleasure. It makes me twitchy in more ways than one. After a swipe of his tongue across his lips, he seductively asks what the secret ingredients are.

I pointedly look at John and tell him, "The ice cream doesn't have dairy in it. I add the coconut milk to make it rich and wickedly delicious." He looks mildly interested. So, I try again, "I always add a pinch of freshly ground nutmeg to it as well, which pops the vanilla flavor like crazy."

John finishes, wipes his mouth with his napkin and politely says, "That was wonderful, Sarah." Then with a look at Rix he adds, "I'm not sure I enjoyed it quite as much as Rix did, but it was really great."

Rix shares, "There's nothing in this world as delectable as Sarah's pie. I've been eating it since I was in high school."

John shifts in his seat uncomfortably and says, "Yes, well, on that note, I should probably get going."

"Already?" I ask. "It's only seven o'clock."

With a pointed look between me and Rix, he says, "I have an early start tomorrow. With all I have to do around my grandparents' place, I should really turn in early."

At seven o'clock? I glare at the interloper. This is all his fault. Then I stand up and say, "I'll walk you out while Rix cleans up." I point at my lodger in such a way that suggests I will send him into the next life if he so much as dares to set foot out of the kitchen.

John and I walk through the living room and out the front door. I move to the swing and ask, "Can you stay for a few more minutes?"

"I guess," he says, not selling his response with any degree of enthusiasm.

He sits next to me, and I gently start the swing in motion with my toes. "I'm sorry about tonight. I didn't invite Rix to join us. He took it upon himself to horn in on our date."

"Don't you two have some kind of history?"

I shake my head. "No. His grandparents owned the neighboring farm, that's it. I promise, I have no idea what tonight was about. I don't think he can stand not being the center of attention."

"Does he always stay here when he's in town?" he asks, clearly not convinced I'm telling the truth.

"He hasn't even been in town in six years and I only opened the yurts a few years ago."

John says, "I think he has designs on you."

"He and I have done nothing but fight since he showed up. I promise he's only acted the way he did tonight to annoy me. And believe me, it worked."

"Really?" he says hopefully. Then he leans back like he's decided to get comfortable.

"Really."

We sit silently for a few more minutes, simply enjoying being in one another's company, then John takes my hand and holds it. He doesn't try for anything else. It's an old-fashioned and respectful gesture, and I receive it happily.

We rock back and forth gently, and John finally says, "In that case, would you like to go out again sometime? Maybe away from your farm and Rix."

"That sounds like a wonderful idea," I say. "What were you thinking?"

"How about that barn dance you all were talking about? That sounds like it might be kind of fun."

"I'll look forward to it," I tell him.

All of a sudden, bacon farming doesn't seem like an insurmountable obstacle.

Dear Universe,

Nice job! I knew if I believed in you, everything would work out. I think in order to give John the chance he deserves, it's time for Rix to hit the bricks. Please look into that.

Chapter Thirty-Five
When the Universe Cuts You Off

I had another bad dream last night. I dreamed I was walking through the county fair, without Cat. I was searching for her everywhere when I heard a menacing growl. Terraz has taught me to ask, "What's the lesson or who has a message for me?" when something unexpected happens. So, instead of being afraid, I look for the answer, which always comes quickly.

Except, last night was unusual. I couldn't remember the question. That's when the fear turned to terror. I stood in a blind panic as a giant black bear came running off the carousel straight at me. I don't remember it getting to me, but the next thing I knew I was lying on the ground covered in blood, next to the corn dog stand.

When I looked up, Terraz stared down at me. My spirit guide rarely comes to me in human form. But there she stood, as radiant and bright as you'd expect an angel to look.

"What happened?" I asked.

"Change is coming, Sarah."

"You mean a life partner, right?"

She ignores my question. "The bear is bringing you courage to face what comes next."

"Um, about that, Terraz"—I point down at my bloody body—"I think you missed the whole part where the bear mauled me."

"The bear didn't do that, Sarah. The change mauled you. The bear showed you how to be strong in the face of change."

Then she disappeared. I woke feeling completely off my center. So much so that I performed twice as many sun salutations to try to shake off the feeling of doom. It didn't work. In fact, I think that darned bear ruined my safe place for me. As strange as it sounds, the memory of the fairgrounds is like a security blanket to me.

I shower and get dressed in something pretty to meet my folks in, but my heart just isn't in it. I spend the whole drive to the airport feeling strangely outside my body and have to force myself to really concentrate on the road.

In baggage claim, I rent a cart to schlep all my parents' suitcases. They usually come home with no fewer than four large suitcases. Standing there, I contemplate how much I love airports. Every time I'm in one I think of the opening scene of *Love Actually* where people from all walks of life are reunited with welcoming embraces. I never notice the harried travelers or the annoyed people. I focus on the joy, the reunions, the love.

My folks were never high strung and controlling. They saw the writing on the wall when I was young that I wasn't going to be like other kids. When my friends took ballet or hip hop in town, my mom drove me to Champaign for belly dancing lessons. When the other girls went to cheer camp, I took a class at the nearest community college in basket weaving. When my classmates started to play the flute and clarinet, I learned how to play the bassoon. Mom and Dad have always embraced my differentness. They gave me the room I needed to be myself.

The passengers start to pour in, and I stand up to look for my folks. I start to worry they missed their flight when I finally see my mom. She's tan and fit as ever, wearing a white suit with low sling-backed heels. She's from the generation that dresses up to fly. She refuses to become lazy, as she calls it, and travel in comfortable clothing.

Mom is walking next to a tall male flight attendant, but I don't see my father anywhere. Then the young family in front of my mother steps aside and there he is. In a wheelchair. My dad has never needed a wheelchair. It's painfully obvious he does now.

He looks every minute of his eighty-three years. In fact, he looks closer to ninety. He's shrunken and gaunt. He's a shadow of the robust man I've known my whole life. He must have lost at least forty pounds since they left. I'm so shocked I don't rush up to them like I normally do. I stand there stupefied.

My mom sees me and waves. "Sarah, dear!" Then she speeds up until she's standing right in front of me. "Close your mouth and don't look so concerned," she says.

"What's going on?" I demand.

She hugs me and whispers in my ear, "I don't want you upsetting your father. Put a smile on your face and we'll talk later."

She doesn't want me upsetting my dad? What about me? Isn't this something she should have mentioned on the telephone and prepared *me* for?

When the unfamiliar version of my father in a wheelchair

arrives, I paste a smile on my face and exclaim, "Hi, Dad." I lean down and kiss his shrunken and slightly stubbly cheek.

He looks at me like he's trying to recall me before offering, "Hi, honey."

I want to cry. I want to demand to know what's going on. But I also don't want to distress him. So, I suggest, "Should I pull the car up to the curb?"

"What a great idea!" my mom says with way too much enthusiasm, like I just suggested piña coladas on the lido deck followed by flamenco dancing lessons with a Latin stud named Carlos. OMG, I'm losing it.

I go to take their luggage with me, but she waves her hand. "We'll load it up at the curb. You get going and we'll meet you outside."

I feel like I'm walking in my sleep, drunk almost. I stagger to the automatic revolving door and try to plan my entry so I don't get hit by the person exiting. It's a close call as I can't seem to focus on the spinning motion.

I nearly step right into traffic and probably would have, had the traffic cop not blown his whistle at me. On the curb, I flash back to my dream and remember what Terraz had said about the bear showing me how to handle fear. I'm suddenly tempted to open my mouth and roar a loud, gut-wrenching, all-consuming scream to warn off anything that dares to upset the balance of my world. My life suddenly doesn't feel like my life.

By the time I get to the car and pull up to the curb, my dad is sound asleep. The man pushing the wheelchair helps load him in the backseat, my mother settles in beside me, and then suggests I park the car.

I find a safe place to pull over, out of airport traffic, and then reluctantly turn to face her. When I finally do, she says, "It all happened so fast, honey. Your dad didn't want me to tell you on the phone when I called last time. He wanted you to have a couple of extra weeks without worrying."

"Worrying about what?" I demand.

"Worrying about saying goodbye." She quietly watches my confused expression before taking my hand. "Your dad's come home to die, dear."

This can't be what the bear was all about. Yet, strangely I know it is.

Chapter Thirty-Six
Truth and Planning

Once the shock passes—and believe me it takes a few minutes—I think about how I have a pretty good attitude toward death. I don't think of it as the end, it is more the soul outgrowing its form. I feel like death is the soul saying, *This body no longer fits me. I need more space.*

Several people, whom I love dearly, have already made their transition—all four grandparents died when I was young, I've lost an uncle, two aunts, and a cousin. My best friend from college passed away five years ago from complications from type 1 diabetes. I've always accepted their moving on easily.

I've done this by allowing myself to feel every emotion as it comes. The shock, the sadness, the loneliness, they all flow through me until I arrive at acceptance. But this is my dad. While I've always known I wouldn't have him into my middle years, I never thought he'd transition while I was just starting my thirties.

Dad sleeps the entire way home, giving my mom a chance to fill me in on everything that's been going on. He has advanced kidney disease and started dialysis a month ago. He goes in three times a week for treatment. Neither of my parents recognized the early symptoms. They figured the excessive fatigue and confusion were normal signs of aging. They didn't go to the doctor until Dad's feet and legs started to swell significantly. By then he was in acute renal failure.

"What about a kidney transplant?" I ask.

"He's not a good candidate. Given his age and overall frailty, they don't put much stock in a new organ taking."

"There has to be something they can do," I declare. In my mind I immediately start to catalogue natural remedies. *Blueberries are loaded with anthocyanidins, vitamin A, and flavonoids that are essential for kidney health. Apples are rich in pectin that can help reduce cholesterol levels which is necessary to treat kidney disorders. Cauliflower is loaded with vitamin C, fiber and folate which will help the body excrete toxins. Red sandalwood tea is a natural diuretic.* I try to remember if I have any of it or if I need to order it.

My mom sees the wheels spinning in my head and says, "You need to talk to your dad before you start going crazy with ideas about how you're going to heal him."

"Of course I'm going to heal him! That's what I do. Why wouldn't he want to be healed?"

"Talk to him, Sarah. You should know that confusion is one of his symptoms and sometimes he has a hard time tracking what people are saying, so be careful with him. I don't want to frustrate him more than he already is."

"That's more reason than ever to start his healing right away," I declare.

My mom reaches over and touches my arm. "Sweetie, your

dad and I are so grateful for you. You came into our lives at a time we'd both thought we were too old to have a child. You kept us going. You kept us young. But, honey, this is your father's life. It's *his*. You talk to him and hear what he has to say, and then you honor his wishes. Do you understand?"

"I understand," I say, because *I know* he's come home for me to help him. Why else would he be here instead of in Florida?

I start to mentally chart how I'm going to go about this. Dad can be resistant to the thought of natural remedies, so I'm going to have to become his personal nurse. I'll ask Arturo and Steve to find another person to help around the farm and to make deliveries. I'll cancel my summer visitors and postpone the official opening of *Eat Me!*. Nothing is more important than helping my dad.

Everything that seemed so urgent this morning doesn't matter in the least right now. My world has undeniably changed, and the only warning I received was a bear charging me at a county fair.

My mom spends the rest of the drive telling me that she's closed up the house in Florida. She talks about her book group and her knitting club. I hear the sound of her voice but I'm not really paying attention to the words.

Instead, I think about Nan's crack about emotional support pigs and decide the first thing I'm going to do is get my dad a dog. It's proven that animals can help heal sick humans and right now I need to pull out all the stops. Plus, how in the world did I not have a dog on the farm yet? I've got six barn cats, fourteen chickens, two horses, and a cow, but no dogs. That's just weird.

When we pull into the driveway, my mom lets out a giant

breath like she's been holding it for a year. Concerned, I ask, "Are you okay?"

She shakes her head. "I'm not sure. All of Dad's talk about coming home to die was only talk until now. Now that we're here"—she pauses to blow her nose—"all of a sudden it's so real."

I reach over and take her hand. "Don't worry, Mom. I'm not going to let him die on my watch. I'll do everything in my power to keep him around another ten years, at least." I've never considered the possibility that my dad wouldn't live long enough to know his grandchildren. Granted, I've only recently begun to think about those grandkids, and I'm the only one who can give them to him … No pressure.

Chapter Thirty-Seven
The Ultimatum

When I park the car, I look at my mom and state the obvious, "I don't have a wheelchair here. The house isn't even wheelchair accessible."

"It's okay," she assures me. "He only needs it when he has to walk for any length of time. All he's going to want to do right now is sit on the porch."

And sure enough, when I wake my dad, he smiles and says, "Let's go sit on the porch." My sweet, wonderful, creature-of-habit dad.

I help him out of the car, and once again I'm shocked by how thin he is. After getting him situated, I run inside to fetch him a glass of ice water—mostly ice as I know he'll have some kind of fluid restriction with kidney disease—and a bowl of blueberries. When I come back out, he pats the seat next to him. "Your mom went inside to freshen up. Come keep your old man company."

While my dad's always been a relatively old man—at least compared to my friends' dads—he's always been vibrant, young at heart. His wrinkles and gray hair have never made him old to me, that was just how he looked.

I sit down next to him and say, "I'm glad you're home."

"Me too, Sar-bear, me too."

"So, you want to tell me what's going on?"

He feigns surprise. "You mean your mother hasn't already done that? I thought for sure she would have filled you in."

"You know very well she gave me the nuts and bolts of the story. I want to hear the rest from you."

"Rest?" he asks, surprised. "What rest? I'm coming to the end of my road."

It's hard to talk with a watermelon size lump forming in my throat. "The doctors say you're dying?"

"That's what they say."

"Have they given you a timeframe?"

"Three to six months if I stay on dialysis. Two to six weeks if I don't."

My heart rate accelerates, and I break out into a cold sweat. *Six months if he stays on it?* That's so bad. I rack my brain for something to say. I finally ask, "Will you let me help you live longer?"

"How?" he asks.

"By altering your diet, giving you supplements, yoga, anything I can come up with." I feel panicky. *Six months isn't enough time to say goodbye.*

He sighs heavily. "Sarah, I'm eighty-three years old. I'm an honest-to-goodness old man. I want to live out my days eating the food I like and not trying to figure out how to touch my toes without falling over."

"You won't even let me try?" I beg.

He smiles at me with such tenderness. "I love you with my

whole heart, honey. You've given me a gift I never thought I'd have again. But I'm ready to go see your sisters."

I've always thought of Naomi and Caroline as my sisters. I used to talk to them when I was little. I named my dolls after them. We have pictures of them hanging on our walls. They are my family as surely as my dad is my family.

I feel like I've been punched in the heart and am having a hard time catching my breath. I've had my dad for thirty-two years. Thirty-two wonderful years. Naomi and Caroline didn't have him for half that time. Tears start to pour down my face, "Daddy," I say as I drop to my knees in front of him. "In order for you to be with them, you have to leave me and I'm not ready to say goodbye to you." I can barely choke out the last words.

He puts his arm around me. "Aw, honey, you knew I wouldn't live forever."

Sure, I've known that. Parents *should* die before their kids. That's the natural order. For my dad to have buried not only his wife, but both of his children, is an unimaginable tragedy. I don't know how he ever carried on. But he did, and now I'm here. And he wants to leave me.

Knowing your parents will die *someday* and being faced with their very imminent death are two different animals entirely. "I'm not ready, Dad."

He nods his head once. "Which is why I'll stay on the dialysis for as long as you want me to." At my confused look, he adds, "If it were up to me, I wouldn't have another treatment."

"But that would only give you two to six more weeks." That can't be what he really wants.

"That's right, honey. But I'll make a deal with you. I'll keep on it until you give me permission to stop, *if* you don't hassle me about my diet or any of that other voodoo you're into."

I stand up and start to pace the length of the porch. "What kind of choice is that? You're telling me if I want to keep you alive, I can't do what I need to do in order to heal you? That's no choice."

"It is a choice, Sar. If I stopped the treatments, I'd go sooner. I hate the treatments. I hate feeling like this, so if I'm going to stay, I have to be able to find joy in my life the way I want to find joy—in the company of my beautiful daughter and my beautiful wife, eating food I love, on the farm I love. Now, is it a deal?"

"What if I said no? What if I said go off dialysis and do everything I tell you until you die, would you do it?" Death is undignified, mourning is undignified. Snot and tears stream down my face and cause me to gasp for breath.

There is an unbearably long silence, broken only by my raspy breathing and hiccups, before his kind baritone voice rumbles, "If you needed to try that badly, I'd do it."

Suddenly, I don't know what to do with myself. The debate between what I need and what my dad wants rages inside me. I feel like I'm about to crawl out of my skin. It's like my emotions are becoming too big for my body and are about to explode out of me. I think I'm having a panic attack. I've never had one before, but as soon as the thought comes into my mind, I realize that's exactly what's happening.

"I can't tell you right now, Dad. I have to think. Is it okay if I think on it?"

"Sure, honey. But you need to tell me by this evening. I have my first dialysis treatment at Carle Clinic tomorrow."

Suddenly, I can no longer stay here. I can't pace fast enough to process this information. I pinch my lips together to keep from wailing and I wipe my eyes before I turn and stumble down the porch steps. Then I run and run and run until I fall over from sheer exhaustion. I am not handling this at all like I thought I would.

Chapter Thirty-Eight
The Chosen People

I hear my feet hit the ground, first one, then the other, increasing in tempo like a drum being beaten in a tribal call to war. Thoughts blow through my head like a tornado has touched down and sent everything scattering to the four corners of the earth. I have no center.

Two weeks ago my biggest concern was the grand opening of *Eat Me!*. Now I'm not even going to open it until, when? My father miraculously gets better? Dies? The mothership lands and demands the best vegan food in town? I don't know. Everything I've worked so hard for my whole adult life has lost its meaning. None of it matters anymore.

My dad is sick, and he doesn't want me to help him live. I help people, it's what I do. I help total strangers that I have no emotional attachment to. But this is no stranger, this is my dad. It's devastating because I know I could help him if he'd let me, but that's not what he wants. How can that not be what he wants?

I run until I'm somewhere in the middle of the cornfield. As a kid I was terrified when I got lost in the corn. With stalks looming high above me, it felt like they were trying to consume me.

I don't stop running until my legs are so worn out I simply fall to the ground in complete despair. The earth is cool to the touch. It smells intoxicatingly rich and fertile. I claw a handful of soil and hold it in my palm. It's black and alive—full of tiny living creatures and micro-organisms. Soil is its own galaxy, full of microscopic stars, planets, and possibility.

My dad always taught me to appreciate the earth. Wherever we'd go, the park, the schoolyard, other people's homes, or on vacation, he'd always pick up a handful of soil and ask, "What do you see?"

If it was dark black, he taught me to see bounty. It was full of organic matter that would feed a wide variety of plant life and in turn, animals. White soil was comprised of high amounts of calcium, magnesium carbonates, and gypsum. Red soil was full of iron minerals. Every kind served their purpose. He appreciated them all.

Dad always loved farming. He relished the thought that he could feed his family and others. That love was passed on to me. I can't accept the fact that a man so of this earth will soon no longer be on it. It's a concept that doesn't make sense to me. And while he'll let me nourish him with the food I've grown for health, he'll also want meat, sugar, and dairy—three things a person with kidney disease should avoid.

He used to quote Thomas Jefferson all the time. *"Cultivators of the earth are the most valuable citizens. They are the most vigorous, the most independent, the most virtuous, and they are tied to their country and wedded to its liberty and interests by the most lasting bonds"* and *"Those who labor in the earth are the chosen people of God, if ever He had a chosen people, whose breasts He has made his peculiar deposit for substantial and genuine virtue. It is the focus in which he keeps alive that sacred fire which otherwise might escape from the face of the earth."*

My dad worked the land he was raised on. He tilled and fed the soil; he planted more than seeds for food, he planted hope and trust that the future would be better for his efforts. He tended his crops and nurtured them with his beliefs. Like Thomas Jefferson, he was the ultimate gentleman farmer.

My mom says it's his life and it's his right to choose how he'll live it. But I'm his daughter. By virtue of that, I'm part of him. Shouldn't I have a say in saving the life that was responsible for creating my own? When his body and mind break down, isn't it my responsibility to offer my knowledge and strength to him?

Parents nurture and tend their children when they're too young to care for themselves. Then they guide them until they're mature enough to make the best decisions. Once they've done all they can, they set their offspring free on the world to hopefully change it for the better. Shouldn't all that hard work be rewarded by care when they're too old or sick to care for themselves? Why wouldn't my dad trust the job he did raising me, by trusting me to help him when he's no longer able to help himself?

I fall asleep in the middle of the field with all these questions racing through my brain. I sleep until the air cools around me. I'm vaguely aware that I'm not as comfortable as I am in my own bed, but it doesn't matter. I need to have my body flush to the ground. I need it to feed me like it does the crops, to offer strength and courage for the decision I have to make.

My slumber is full of travels, messages, and ultimately, answers. The black bear shows up and takes my hand in his giant paw. He leads me to my beloved fairgrounds, onto the roller coaster and shows me how to stand up through the whole ride. Then he teaches me how to roar in the face of fear. When my throat is sore from effort, he jumps off and disappears into the crowd.

I don't wake up until the damp of early morning starts to seep into my clothes and chills me to the point where I need to seek shelter. I wake with the knowledge and weight of my decision.

Chapter Thirty-Nine
The Cosmic Pause

Once I'm showered and in dry clothes, I head to the kitchen to make breakfast. I pull a bag of coffee beans out of the freezer and grind them in my grandparents' hand-churned coffee grinder. This grinder is over a hundred years old and has born witness to generations of Hastings' breakfasts.

Once I get the coffee brewing, I start a pot of steel-cut oatmeal. Then I slice some cinnamon raisin bread for toast to hold everyone over until the oats are ready. At 5:20 like clockwork, my dad shows up in the kitchen and says the same thing he says every morning at 5:20. "My goodness, that coffee smells good."

I smile despite the angst I feel over the conversation we're about to have. I pour him a cup and serve it black, like he likes. Then I sit down at the table with him. "How did you sleep, honey?" he asks.

"I slept in the corn field," I tell him.

"I figured you were out there somewhere. You always slept outside when you had a problem you were trying to work out."

I thought if the answers didn't have to break into the house to find me, I'd get them sooner. I still feel that way.

"What's the verdict, Sar-bear? Am I starting my vegan diet this morning or am I going to enjoy my breakfast?" he asks.

I answer by asking, "How would you like your eggs cooked?"

A smile spreads across his face, "Scrambled with cheddar cheese, ham, and spinach."

There are baggies of chopped ham in the freezer from Christmas, so I pull one out. "Do you want peppers and onions, too?"

"You bet I do! And fresh orange juice, if it's not too much trouble."

I briefly wonder if there's such a thing as too much trouble as far as my dad is concerned. I can't think of anything I wouldn't do for him. I'd probably walk to Florida for the oranges if I had to. Luckily, there's a bowl sitting on the counter from my most recent shopping trip. I don't normally buy citrus this time of year, as there's so much fresh produce being grown on our own land, but my dad loves it, so I wanted to be prepared.

He enjoys his cup of coffee while I prepare foods that he shouldn't be consuming if he was trying to get better. Eggs, spinach, ham, and oranges are all things that should be avoided as they're hard on unhealthy kidneys. I prepare them all.

Renal failure is a tough thing to cure once it's been determined that death is near. It's not impossible, but it would require my dad's full belief and participation. He doesn't want to do what it would take to try, so he's not in the proper mindset to heal himself. For me, this is the real heartbreak.

Ultimately, I decide that I want him to live his life the way he wants, which means he gets to enjoy all his favorite foods while he's here. It's a wonky sort of win/win. No one truly wins because my dad is going to move on, but I get time, and he gets meat, so there you go. We're going to make the best out of a sorry situation.

My mom joins us as the food gets put on the table. She smiles a sad smile, acknowledging to me that my dad is getting his way. "Everything smells delicious, honey."

We eat quietly. Just the sound of forks hitting dishes and the murmur of enjoyment. I wish there was a way to hit a cosmic pause button. In this moment, life seems normal, almost as if the grim reaper wasn't lurking around the corner to take my father from me. I have to remind myself to stay in the moment and not jump ahead. More than ever I have to live my life in real time.

Finally, I break the silence and ask my dad, "How are you feeling this morning?"

"Pretty good. A bit tired, though. I'm almost always tired these days."

My mom quietly adds needed information, "He sleeps about eighteen hours out of the day."

I absorb the impact of her words and my stomach turns over. I don't have six months or even three if he sleeps two-thirds of the day away. I have to make every moment count. "I'd like to go with you to your dialysis appointment today. In fact, I'd like to go to all of them, if you don't mind."

"What about the farm?" my dad asks, alarmed.

"I have Arturo and Steve. They'll take care of everything for us."

"What about the cafe?" my mom wonders.

"The cafe will remain closed for the time being."

Dad says, "I don't want you putting your life on hold to take care of me."

I stare at him with determination in my eyes. "That's too bad, 'cause that's exactly what I'm going to do."

He knows how stubborn I can be, so he also knows when he's licked. He nods his head and doesn't fight me. Instead he says, "I'm a lucky man."

"And I'm the luckiest daughter that ever was," I say back to him. I seem to tap into a deep-rooted strength I didn't know I had and continue, "This is a crappy situation, Dad. But I think we should try to enjoy every moment we have left."

"That's all I've been saying." He smiles brightly.

My mom reaches out to take our hands and we sit relishing our circle of love. "What's next?" she asks.

Chapter Forty

Next

Dad will have dialysis three times a week, Monday, Thursday, and Saturday. Once we get him settled into the hospital, he announces, "Go. Shop. Get lunch or have your toes painted. I'm going to snooze." Each treatment will last for four hours and he prefers to sleep through them so as not to waste precious conscious time.

Mom and I walk out of the hospital with no real destination. Her toes are already painted and I never bother with mine. I don't really see the value in it. I suggest, "Let's go to the co-op. They have these new vegan energy bars that I love. I bet even Dad would enjoy them."

"He might," she says, "but he'll never choose one over a steak." She's right, but I still want to load up the pantry.

We park right next to a pickup truck with a golden retriever in the back. Upon closer inspection, I see seven puppies. And they're adorable. I remember my mission to get Dad a puppy and decide to stay in the parking lot until the owner comes out. Chances are all these cuties have already been claimed, but you never know, the universe might be trying to make up for its recent colossal bomb dropping.

My mom doesn't know what I'm up to. She thinks I'm just petting puppies. She says, "I'll meet you inside, dear; I need to freshen up." She'll never say she has to pee. "Freshening up" is her term for anything that happens within the confines of a bathroom. The bathroom doesn't even get cleaned; it gets "freshened up."

A couple of minutes later a man in his early forties comes over. "Hey," he says.

I look up. Hey, indeed. He's good looking in an earthy sort of way. Sandy brown hair, small crows' feet starting to form in the corners of his sparkling brown eyes. Everything about him says he's approachable and has a good sense of humor. Could this be Bachelor #4? I'm not sure I'm interested in dating anymore, with needing to care for my dad. But if the universe is sending him, who am I to not even look?

"Hey, yourself." I give him a flirty little nudge.

"You checking out my puppies?" he asks.

Unless "puppies" is a weird euphemism for his biceps, then this is the owner of the truck I'm standing next to. I immediately cease all attempts of seduction and declare, "I am. What are the chances you're selling them?"

He reaches his hand into the back and the dogs come running for some love. He roughs up a couple of them playfully and answers, "Five of them are spoken for." Then he grabs the two with lilac collars and pulls them over. "But these two little gals are available."

"Can I buy one from you?" I know this is crazy fast, but it feels right. I ask for a puppy and puppies find me. That's too perfect an opportunity to pass up.

"You can't buy one, but you can buy two. In fact," he adds, "I'll give you two for the price of one. I want to keep these girls together."

"Why?" I ask. I mean, it's sweet, but I don't want two puppies, I want one.

He explains, "They were the smallest in the litter and they formed a strong bond. I think they'll thrive if they're together; the stress of being separated won't be good for them."

How adorable is that? This guy is looking out for the best interest of the dogs, not looking to line his pockets. I know puppies are expensive, so not having to pay for two would certainly go a long way in caring for two. I grab my purse to get the checkbook I rarely use. "How much?"

He shrugs his shoulders. "How about a hundred bucks?"

"A hundred bucks? That's it?"

His smile is slightly lopsided and endearingly sweet. "You look like you need them and I'd hate for something as silly as money to get in the way of you having them." I pull out five twenty-dollar bills and hand them over. "You mean I can have them now?"

He takes the money and says, "You sure can. They're seven weeks old and fully weaned. Would you mind if I got your name and number though?" *Hello, Universe, are you giving me a twofer? Puppies and a date?*

"Not at all! What's your number? I'll call you and then you'll have mine."

He gives it to me before saying, "My wife's a real stickler for making sure all the dogs go to a great home. I'm guessing she might want to follow up with you and give you some instructions."

His wife? Ah, well, at least I got the dogs. "Do you want to ask me any questions so you can assure her I'm a decent person?"

He shakes his head. "No. Something's telling me that my little girls here will thrive in your care. I trust my instincts, my wife might not. She'll feel better if she can talk to you."

"Deal." I shake his hand and load my newest family members into the back of my parents' car. Then I run inside the co-op to find my mom.

When she sees them, Mom is in insta-love with the dogs. "Oh Sarah, they're adorable. Your dad is going to be tickled." I pick up a couple of leashes in the in the co-op along with some other supplies. We walk the puppies around a nearby park so they can do their business. While they sniff around, Mom and I sit down on a bench to give them some water.

"How are you doing with all this, Mom?"

"I have no idea. So far, I've just been reacting to all the changes. But now that we're home and Kenny has agreed to accept treatment, I imagine it's all going to sink in." She takes my hand in hers and gives it a small squeeze. "We'll get through this together, honey. That's what family is all about, right?"

I peek over at her and she looks smaller. For a split second, I see her as a frightened little girl. And it hits me, no matter how many years we acquire in this world, the end of life renders us as vulnerable as the beginning. As I think this, I feel myself ever-so-slightly separate from my body.

My spirit hovers above its normal confines, closer to the divine. I have a feeling it will stay that way for some time—to give me strength to deal with what comes next.

Chapter Forty-One
Puppy Power and Utopia

My dad is completely drained by the time we get him to the car after treatment. Yet one look at our new friends lightens his spirit so much he appears years younger and healthier in a matter of minutes.

"Puppies!" he exclaims. "Where did they come from?" Then he leans back while the girls attack him with wet kisses.

My mom giggles, "Sarah bought them from some man in the parking lot at the co-op."

I catch Dad's eye in the review mirror. His smile is so big I can see his molars. "Thank you, honey." He immediately knows I've done it for him. "Have you named them yet?"

"I was thinking about calling them Naomi and Caroline." I hurry to add, "If you think that's okay."

"I think your sisters would be honored." Cuddling them close to his sides, he adds, "They would have loved to have had dogs like these."

Some people might think it's insensitive to name dogs after my deceased sisters, but I don't. I used to name my favorite dolls after them. I know the dogs will bring my dad nothing but joy.

And let's face it, my sisters are very much on his mind as he gets ready for his reunion with them. So why not?

The ride back to the farm is light and carefree. We don't talk about illness or death or the future at all. We simply enjoy being together.

I see Rix's fancy car as soon as we pull in the drive and pass the yurts. Mom asks, "Who's your guest?"

I haven't thought about Rix since picking my parents up at the airport. I figured we were like that Rudyard Kipling poem, *"Oh, East is East, and West is West, and never the twain shall meet."* You know, a whole out of sight out of mind situation? I should have known that was pie in the sky dreaming with him staying here.

"Hendrix Greer," I answer my mom.

"Really? I haven't seen that boy since Herman's funeral. How is he?" she asks.

I shrug my shoulders. "Fine." Exacerbating, irritating, gorgeous, ruggedly handsome, fabulous kisser—just a few other adjectives that come to mind that I don't give voice to.

My dad laughs. "Fine? Sar-bear, you used to sneak across the corn field and spy on that boy for hours when he was working for his granddad."

The memory of Rix's eighteen-year-old bare chest, glistening with sweat, momentarily disables my ability to speak. My budding hormones experienced a riot of new sensations that year, let me tell you. If I were to be honest, I'd acknowledge that the feelings only intensified over the years. That was before I knew what a sorry excuse for a human being he was.

"He's here to sell his grandparents' farm to Happy Corn!"

"I'm surprised it's taken them so long to put their place on the market. It's given the soil a nice break, though. I bet the next crop grown over there will be the best they've had in decades."

Leave it to my dad to think about the soil. I say, "Yup, it'll be ripe for all the pesticides they're going to spray on it."

Dad and I have gone back and forth over the years about my views of farming versus most every other farmer on the planet. He says, "Honey, if the world's population doesn't decrease, we won't be able to feed everyone. GMOs and pesticides, and all these things you're against, allow us to keep up with demand. Without them, farmers wouldn't be able to afford to keep farming. Most people either can't or won't pay the price for organic food. Without them, people would starve."

"People are already starving and not because there isn't enough food. They're starving out of greed."

"True. But I've been reading up on this global warming thing and you know that in five to ten years scientists predict a large portion of the world's farmland will only be producing half of the food it currently does. The flooding and temperature changes are going to make it impossible to feed everyone."

He adds, "In your lifetime, people in first-world countries could starve to death because they can't afford to feed their families. What's your answer?"

"My answer is for people to start growing their own food. Even if it's only enough for the summer months, it'll cut down on the demand and make it possible for farmers to take over for the rest of the year."

He shakes his head. "Most young people today haven't grown so much as a flower. It's not how the world is."

"But it's how the world should be. People need to get their hands in the ground and get invested in their own survival."

"I agree, until folks take an interest in farming, even on a small scale, there are going to be some tough years. But, honey, most people won't do that until they absolutely have to."

I know he's right. I know my views are Utopian, as Rix called them, but I believe in the potential of people; I don't think they need to go hungry. I think it's possible for them to wake up and thrive. Those are the thoughts I choose to focus on.

As I pull up to the house, Mom exclaims, "Is that Rix on the front porch? My, my, he's grown up nicely."

Chapter Forty-Two
It's Gonna Cost You

It *is* Rix on the front porch, that fiend. I briefly wonder if anyone would notice if I walked around back to let myself into the house, avoiding him and any potential scene that's liable to take place.

No such luck. He sees me helping my dad out of the backseat and runs down the steps to lend a hand. "Mr. and Mrs. Hastings, how nice to see you," he exclaims.

The dogs exit the car in a fit of excitement and Caroline pees on Rix's foot. *That's my girl!* I pick her up and praise, "Who's a good puppy? You are." Rix doesn't look quite as thrilled.

Before the football player can ask about the dogs my dad struggles to his feet and replies, "Good to see you too, son. You in town for long?"

"No longer than it takes to ruin my farm," I mumble.

Rix tells him, "It looks like I may be here for another month or so."

"What? Why?" I demand. "Surely it can't take that long to sell your soul to the devil."

He ignores my comment and answers my dad, "It's taking time to get the house fixed up."

I can't imagine why he's even bothering. I'm sure Happy Corn! will probably tear it down to make more room for their Frankenfood. "Are you planning on staying here that whole time?" I demand.

He turns to me. "Unless you need the yurt for another customer." Then he winks at me and adds, "You've been very hospitable in spite of the fact that you can be a little ornery."

"You've picked that up, have you?" my dad jokes with him.

"She should come with a 'Warning, handle with care!' label," he says.

My cheeks go bright red with heat as I remember the last time he *handled* me. If he stays here another month, he's going to have to promise not to try any more of that funny stuff. I can't say that in front of my parents, though.

Being that I'm going to cancel all my summer guests but Scottie, to care for my dad, the yurts will certainly be available, I'll be losing a lot of income, so I hesitantly answer, "You can stay, but my summer rates are higher than what you've been paying."

"You don't have a long-term discount?" he asks.

"Nope." I don't say anything else. I mean, heck, he has plenty of money and quite honestly, I feel like he owes me for so many reasons—selling his land to a non-organic operation, months of my misspent youth longing after his sorry self, trying to ruin my date, to name but a few.

"Okay." He doesn't fuss about the increase. "But I'm going to want to eat all my meals here again."

Before I can tell him that food is no longer part of the deal, my mom pipes in with, "Of course you'll eat with us." She gives my father a meaningful look before adding, "We'd love to hear about what you've been up to."

Dad seems to perk up at the thought. "You can help me man the grill tonight. I've been looking forward to a big steak."

Rix turns to me and smiles wickedly before answering, "I'd love to, sir. There's nothing like a good piece of meat." I will the muscles on my face not to move, determined not to respond to his innuendo.

Before either of them can start grunting and scratching like Neanderthals, I add, "There will be portobello mushroom burgers as well." They stare at me like I've offered to feed them grass.

My mom comes to my rescue, "That sounds delightful, dear."

The dogs have been running around us, releasing their pent-up energy, and by the time we finally make it to the porch, they're both so worn out they stretch out under the swing and go right to sleep.

I ask my dad, "Would you like me to help you up to your room?"

"I think I'll settle in here on the rocker. I slept during my treatment and I'd like to survey the land for a while." Rix gives me a questioning look. He's clearly wondering what treatment my dad is referring to.

"Well, I'm going to go lie down. I'm pooped," my mom announces.

"I better unload the car," I decide.

Once my dad is in his chair, Rix runs after me, "Need a hand?"

"Sure," I answer. Then I point to the suitcases. "You can carry those." He grabs them with ease and follows me into the house. I point to the stairs and tell him to leave them at the bottom. I'll take them up later.

He sits down at the kitchen table while I put my purchases away, and after a weird few minutes of silence, he asks, "What's going on with your dad?"

"Renal failure. And no, he's not eligible for a kidney transplant. They say he only has a few months left."

Rix gets to his feet and moves toward me. "Oh, Sarah, I'm so sorry." I think he's coming over to hug me or something, and as much as I'd love to fall into somebody's arms right now and lean on their strength, Rix Greer is not the person I can do that with. Especially after that epic lip-lock we shared.

I put up a protective shield around me, one that says *back off or you'll be sorry*. He doesn't read my signals and approaches me with his arms out anyway. When I don't step into them of my own accord, he grabs me by the shoulders and pulls me in.

"Quit trying to be so strong for everyone. You know it's okay to let people help you."

What does he know? I'd happily let people help me if I needed them to. He feels me bristle and instead of releasing me, he holds me tighter. "I'm here for you."

I want to tell him that I don't need him, and I want to push away, but instead I lean into him a little. I tell myself it's only for a moment, but the truth is I let him hold me for much longer than I'd originally intended.

Chapter Forty-Three
Don't Forget to Toast Her Buns!

Nan and Dorcas tear up the driveway like they've knocked over a liquor store and are being pursued by the law.

My mom, who's changed into pedal pushers and a T-shirt, runs down the porch steps to greet them, "Bridget, Dorcas, how nice to see you!

Leave it to Nan to stop by the very afternoon my folks come home. She comes bearing a six pack of my dad's favorite beer and a bouquet of sunflowers for my mom. "Welcome home, honey!" She and her husband were friends with my dad and his first wife, Jeannie. She was the first to make my mom feel welcome as his second wife. A lot of folks felt Dad had no business remarrying and they made sure my parents knew where they stood on the issue. Nan wasn't having any of it and championed their union to anyone who dared speak against it.

My mom kisses both ladies on the cheek and offers, "Come on up and join us for dinner."

Dorcas says, "Don't mind if we do. Let me call the reverend and tell him to heat up some leftovers for himself."

"He's welcome to join us," my mom offers.

"Psh," Dorcas declares, "he'd rather stay home and watch those *Ancient Aliens* shows he's so into these days. I swear he's going to become part of that couch unless he goes and gets himself abducted or something. But if it makes him happy, who am I to complain?"

Nan says, "He's one of the few people who never questioned the crop circles I found in our field during the seventies."

Dorcas says, "*He* believed, dear." Her tone suggests that he was the only one in their marriage who did.

My dad, who is standing beside the grill at the side of the house, waves a spatula in their direction, and shouts, "Hey, gals, you're in time for steak!"

Nan tells him, "Thank the heavens you're home, Kenny. This little gal of yours refuses to let me eat meat on the property and I've had to go and decrease my visitations as a result."

I roll my eyes at her drama. She's done no such thing. As a matter of fact, Nan is over here more than ever since we started our book club, and she brings her own meat every single time.

Rix takes the spatula from my dad. "Why don't you go get yourself a beer and I'll take over the grill?"

Dad has no business drinking beer in his current condition. In fact, he's supposed to limit his liquid intake to only thirty-two ounces for the whole day. He doesn't appear to be adhering to those instructions, either. But, being that he's staying on dialysis, I've promised not to lecture him about what he eats and drinks. It's not going to be easy.

I approach Rix. "Don't forget to put on the mushroom burgers. They'll need a few minutes on each side. And toast the buns," I order.

Nan overhears and calls out, "That's right, Hendrix, don't forget to toast Sarah's buns." Then she cackles in delight.

My mom smiles and winks at Nan. "She does love to have her buns toasted."

"Don't we all," Dorcas chimes in as she giggles.

My dad finally interjects, "Ladies, this is my daughter you're talking about. Please, stop."

"Thank you, Dad."

Nan orders, "Sarah, girl, why don't you go get a pitcher of your famous margaritas? I could sure use a couple."

Nan is so sassy at eighty, I can't imagine what she was like as a young woman. I go into the kitchen to fulfill her request. I'd normally garnish the drink with some dandelion petals, but I don't have any at the moment.

When I get back outside, I hear Nan say, "Shitake mushrooms, Kenny! I'm so sorry to hear of your troubles." She emphasizes the first syllable, so we know what word she really wants to be saying.

"Well, Bridget, you know how it is. Something is going to take us all."

"Boy, ain't that the truth," she responds. "Poor Hugh got bit by the cancer and has been gone for thirteen years now."

"And here I am eighty-three," he replies. "Guess I don't have anything to complain about, do I?" He catches my eye, and I force myself not to offer my two cents.

My mom takes my dad's hand and gives it a squeeze. "We've decided to enjoy whatever time we have left together."

"It's all you can do, dear," Dorcas contributes.

"We're like a Midwestern version of *Steel Magnolias*," I announce.

My dad starts laughing. "Your mother has made me watch that movies so many times, I swear I know it by heart."

My mom smacks his arm playfully. "That's because it's so good. And I don't recall you ever complaining."

"Yeah, but in our version I'm Julia Roberts' character and that just feels weird," he jokes.

"But it makes me Sally Field," my mom says. "There's nothing wrong with that."

Nan yells, "Do me, do me. Who am I?"

She's appalled when we all yell out, "Ouiser!" at the same time.

"Oh, you're just mean. I'm no more that cranky old battle-ax than I am Dolly Parton." She looks over at Dorcas and adds, "We all know who's got that role covered."

Dad saves Dorcas prolonged embarrassment and says, "Rix, tell us everything that's been going on with you. How are your folks? Where are you living these days? And last but not least, do you have yourself a gal? We want to know everything."

And just when I thought I had Rix Greer pegged, I learn something about him I would have never expected.

Chapter Forty-Four
Power Rangers and Cereal

"It's called Greer House," Rix explains. "We get all kinds of professional people, from sports figures to business tycoons to come in and talk to the kids. The only common denominator between them is that they're all self-made."

"Where's your facility?" my mom asks.

"We're currently in the Meat Packing District, where the old stockyards used to be. It's close to public transport, so the kids can hop on a city bus or the L in their neighborhoods."

I'm drawn into the conversation totally against my will. "What ages do you mentor?"

"We start at ten and go through high school. Our goal is to help these kids believe they can do anything they set their minds to. That's why our mentors have to have grown up with limited means. Although we happily take donations from anyone."

Nan wants in on this. "But most of those millionaire types are trust-fund babies raised with silver spoons in their mouths. How many could you possibly have?"

"We've got thirty right now, Nan. They each commit three hours a month. They give our group a motivational talk and answer questions or work with our kids one-on-one, depending on how many are there on a given day."

"But you didn't grow up poor," I point out.

"No, but we were middle class. If I wanted to get a new Power Ranger before my birthday or Christmas, I had to buy it myself. I bought all my own bicycles after the age of ten and still put half of everything I earned into my savings account. Our mentors didn't have to grow up *dirt* poor, just not entitled. They needed to be able to sell that hard work is the way to get ahead."

I wonder, "How many kids are in your program?"

"So far we have eighty. Most of them come for the free food and safe place to hang out."

"What if they're not interested in making big names for themselves?" Dorcas asks.

"We aren't trying to push them into being rich or famous, we just want them to know that anything they set their minds to is possible. They might have to sit through thirty different speakers or maybe even a hundred and thirty before they start to listen to what's being said and absorb any of it."

"What's their motivation for listening at all then?" I ask.

"Every kid who comes for the talk gets a grocery bag with a box of cereal, four energy bars, and canned food that's donated to us every month. Most of them have younger siblings at home. This ensures they can help feed them."

"I'm assuming a lot of your mentors own companies who donate to your program," my dad says.

"Yes, sir. In fact, Jared Clay, the owner of Happy Corn! gave us five hundred thousand dollars last year and supplies all the popcorn our kids eat while they're at Greer House." He sends an unmistakable look my way. It says, "*What do you think of that, Miss Judgy Pants?*"

Crap.

I don't take the bait though. Instead I ask, "How many kids are you hoping to reach?"

"I want to take Greer House national. I'd love to have one in every major city in the country within the next ten years."

I'm impressed beyond belief. I truly thought Rix Greer was some ex-jock playboy who was only interested in money and a good time. He continues, "We have female role models as well. Several of the women I'm reportedly dating are involved."

"Like who?" I demand. Apparently, my curiosity has superseded my need to appear ambivalent about his social life.

"Talia Jackson, for one."

Talia is a supermodel of the highest order. Even I know who she is, and I haven't bought a fashion magazine since junior high school. My fashion sense, farm-girl chic, isn't covered by *Vogue* or *Glamour*. When I read the article about her being Rix's girlfriend, the article mentioned she's only twenty-five years old, and has graced more magazine covers than any other model her age.

He continues, "She grew up in the Bronx. Modeling was her big break, but she graduated from high school with honors. She finished her bachelor's degree in finance last year and is enrolled at Pepperdine to get her master's."

Nan says, "I saw a picture of you two on the red carpet at the Academy Awards. She's cute!" Then she winks. "She your girlfriend?" In addition to being a model, Talia is growing a career in acting, she's quite talented.

"No, ma'am. We're just friends. We met when I approached her about volunteering at Greer House. She calls me when she needs a date for some function or another, and I happily go. She's a great gal."

"You'd think she wouldn't have a hard time getting a real date for herself," I grumble.

He shrugs his shoulders in response. "A lot of guys want to be seen with her because she's a celebrity. They aren't really interested in her, and she doesn't want to waste her time on them."

I change the subject. "Is Mr. Clay planning a trip to visit your property any time soon?"

Rix nods. "He's coming out next week. Why?"

"Why don't you bring him over to *Eat Me* for lunch? I'd love to have a chance to meet my new neighbor."

"You're not planning on souring my deal, are you?" he asks, cautious of my motives.

"Not at all." I don't say anything else because I start plotting how to do just that.

Chapter Forty-Five
A Tornado of Sunshine

I wake up in the morning to the smell of bacon. It's more profound as I'm belly breathing a lot more since finding out about my dad's illness. If there ever was a time I needed plenty of oxygen in my brain to promote calmness and clear thinking, it's now.

Alas, there will be many delicious meat aromas filling the air now that my folks are home. The only way I'm going to be able to stand their siren call is to be out of the house as much as possible.

I quickly brush my teeth, pull my hair back in a ponytail, and throw on some shorts and a T-shirt. I walk through the kitchen to grab an energy bar out of the pantry and find my dad tending his breakfast. He's leaning against the counter like standing is taking its toll on him. He looks old and weak, and it quite simply breaks my heart.

I greet, "Morning, Dad. Why isn't Mom making breakfast?"

"She didn't sleep very well last night, so I told her I'd cook for her this morning." He forces a smile and pushes himself off the counter.

"Hard getting used to the old bed?" I ask.

"I think she's getting hit with a lot of feelings. You know how the bogey man likes to visit and conjure worry when your body wants to rest."

Do I ever. Three a.m. is when he makes his presence known to me. When I have something big on my mind, my brain clicks on and I become plagued by irrational worries. Terraz tells me to ignore them and to focus on the white light, but sometimes the darkness is too powerful.

My dad is now resting one hand on the counter as well as his hip. I take the spatula from him and say, "Go sit down, I've got this." It goes against everything I believe in to cook this for him, but we've made a deal and I'll honor my part no matter how hard it is to do so.

He doesn't put up a fuss. Instead, he slowly makes his way to the table and sits. "I'm tired so much of the time, but I don't want to give up and spend my last days in bed. I want to act normal for as long as possible. Your mom deserves that."

"She loves you so much, Dad," I say unnecessarily. "We both do."

"Your mom came into my life like a tornado of sunshine. My world had been so lonely without Jeannie and your sisters. I was nearly fifty, and to tell you the truth, all I wanted to do was join them. Then one day I'm in the IGA picking up a loaf of bread, and Beth slams her cart right into the back of my legs." He laughs joyfully, "I went down like a bunch of bowling pins."

I love the story of how my parents met and would beg to have it told repeatedly when I was a child. I still want to hear it.

"There she stood, a whirlwind of blonde hair with a smile

that nearly blinded me. She clucked and fussed over me and helped me get my things back in the basket that had scattered when I fell. I assured her I was fine and tried to walk away, but she wasn't having any of it. She told me that I needed to let her cook for me so she could assure herself she wasn't the cause of any long-term damage."

"I told her, 'No, thank you. I'm fine.' Then I got up and walked away. To tell you the truth, a part of my heart opened in that moment, and it scared the bejesus out of me. So, I ran."

"And then what?" I ask as though the outcome hasn't been known to me my whole life.

"And then she hunted me down! That woman found out who I was and where I lived, and she showed up right here at the back door that very night with a pot roast and a pie. I couldn't turn her away without looking sorely ungrateful, but Lord, I did not want to let her in."

"But she came in anyway," I say, prompting him.

"That she did. She came right in and set the table for two like she already lived here. Until that day, this was Jeannie's kitchen. She had everything where she felt it should be. She was queen of this domain. Then Beth came in acting the very same way. It spooked me."

"And ..." I prod.

"And I knew right then and there that even though Jeannie and the girls were no longer in this world, I still was, and I wasn't going to be allowed to die until it was my time. With a snap of the fingers I knew I wanted to start living again."

He continues, "I've been married to Beth for almost thirty-five years. Fifteen years longer than I was married to Jeannie. You and your mom saved me, honey. You gave me something to live for. And I thank you with my whole heart."

I can't help myself and ask, "But not anymore, huh?" I don't mean to be hurtful; I just want to understand.

"No, baby, not anymore. It's my time. I've been given more than most men. I've had two wonderful families, a job I loved, and eighty-three years. No, ma'am, I'm not staying here to be half a person. I'm going to leave this world on my own terms. I'll celebrate every moment I have, but I'm not going to be an invalid. I've too much respect for all of us to step into those shoes."

I want to say a million things to him. I want to tell him it would be my greatest honor to care for him no matter what. I want to beg him not to leave us, guilting him into it if necessary. But, instead, I fry his bacon and thank the universe for the gift we've all been given.

When the bacon is done, I lift it out of the hot fat and put it on top of a stack of paper towels to drain, then I crack a couple of eggs into the frying pan, and squeeze his orange juice. I put breakfast in front of him and sit to keep him company while he eats.

Life is a miracle, giving so much along the way. Yet, it takes from us as well. I believe it was Kahlil Gibran who said something about pain and pleasure being dipped from the self-same well. Those words have never resonated with me more than they do at this moment.

My dad's illness is full of painful feelings, but I'm only now realizing that my pain is in direct correlation to that which has been my blessing, and I have been so very blessed. While I've always known this on an intellectual level, this is the first time I've felt it to the depths of my soul.

Chapter Forty-Six
Stepping Through Time

My parents and I decide to go to Cat's barn dance despite everything. I'm going to meet John, so I can drive my parents in case they aren't up to staying. The barn dance/fling lessons is a gathering meant to bring local singles together. Cat says that's still the plan, but she needs to get the word out and in order to do that she's invited all her family friends to experience the night for themselves so they can create buzz for her.

I rarely wear anything but shorts and tank tops in the summer, but I decide to make an extra effort tonight. I'd like to have some family pictures taken with my parents over the next few months. I figure tonight is a great opportunity for that. I put on a denim skirt and a white peasant blouse that falls over my shoulders. I even apply some lip gloss and mascara.

My parents are all dressed and ready to go when I finally get downstairs. They're holding hands on the porch swing and my mom is resting her head on my dad's shoulder. I stand behind them for a moment and let the image sear itself into my brain. My mom and dad share a love so honest and deep it takes my breath away. I wonder if I'll ever be that lucky.

I clear my throat loudly and announce, "You ready to hit the road?"

Mom sits up and says, "We sure are, honey." She helps my dad to his feet and gently guides him down the steps to the car.

As we're getting in, Rix comes out of his yurt calling, "Wait for me."

What in the world? I realize my parents have both gotten in the backseat and I demand, "What does he mean? Surely he's not coming with us."

I see my mom share a look with my dad in the review mirror. "Your father invited him."

"Why?" I demand.

"Because he's here as our guest and it's the hospitable thing to do," he answers.

"First of all," I announce, "he's a paying guest, which means he's not really a guest at all, more of a customer. Secondly, don't you think you should have asked me first?"

"No. He's the grandson of my good friend Herman. I have every right to ask him. Now shush, he's here." If my dad thinks he's going to turn matchmaker, he's got another think coming. Just because Rix has a social conscience and is giving back to the world, doesn't mean he's right for me.

Rix gets into the car looking like sex on toast. My analogy might need a little work, but the bottom line is he looks *good*, so good my brain stops functioning properly. His jeans are snug and he's wearing cowboy boots and a white cotton T-shirt that leaves nothing to the imagination. He smells fresh like the lemon balm soap I make and put in the yurts. It's all I can do not to lean in and sniff his neck.

I'm unable to manage so much as a hello, so I put the car into gear and take off. Rix says, "Thanks for inviting me along, Mr. Hastings. No one had mentioned tonight's festivities to me." He gives me the side-eye like I intentionally left him uninformed. Which, of course, I did.

I don't bite, though. There's no sense fighting with the man. Instead, I turn on the radio and find a country station that's playing something too loud to talk over. I don't realize what the song is until Rix booms, "I hope Cat's serving tequila tonight!"

Why in the world? "I thought you were a beer drinker," I say.

Then his eyes travel to the radio in time for me to register the Joe Nichols song, "Tequila Makes Her Clothes Fall Off." I snap, "You'd better watch out for Nan, then. That woman loves her margaritas."

"Fair enough," he laughs. Then he says, "I'm surprised Cat moved back to Gelson."

"Why?" I wonder.

"I don't know. Nan said she'd made such a big name for herself in New York City. You'd think it would be hard to walk away from that kind of success."

"Gelson is her home, Rix," I say none too patiently. "Why would it be hard for her to come home to the people who love her?"

"She can do more with her career in a big city, though."

"There's more to life than work and money. Some people know that."

"For some people, their life is their work," he retaliates.

"Too bad for them." Is this man purposely being obtuse? Why can't he see that Gelson is a great place to live? I mean, he grew up here. He knows everything small town life has to offer.

My dad interjects, "Are you enjoying being back home, Rix, or are you chomping at the bit to get back to Chicago?"

He's quiet for a moment before answering. "I feel like I've stepped back in time being here. I love it, but I keep seeing ghosts. Being at my grandparents' house so much, without them," he clears his throat, "it's tough."

My dad releases an understanding grunt. "I know what you mean, son. It was hard on me being in the house alone before Beth came into my life. But if we're not open to change, we only bring more heartache on ourselves."

"I feel like my gran is going to walk around the corner with a plate of cookies. Then, when I look around at the place and it's a disaster, and I'm all alone, it hurts to be there."

My mom offers, "You can always fix it up and fill it with new memories. Then you can tell your kids how you used to play in the barn like they do or how you and your friends used to have cow patty throwing competitions."

"You remember that, huh?" he asks, looking a tad chagrined.

"You bet I do," she declares. "You might recall I took one of those cow patties to the side of the head when I was visiting your grandmother one afternoon."

"Not my finest hour," he declares.

"Oh, I don't know," my mom laughs. "I thought it was funnier than all get out. If I hadn't been on my way to a church potluck, I would have enjoyed the moment more. One thing's for sure, even though you were only eight at the time, it was clear you had a great arm."

Rix says, "I'd happily let you throw a cow pie at me now to get even."

"Oh please, I don't have the strength to do the job properly."
She jokes, "However, Sarah might be willing to act as my proxy."

"What a spectacular idea, Mom." Then I look to Rix, "I can
fit you in tomorrow morning. Meet me in the barn at six a.m."

Chapter Forty-Seven
Slow Dances and Early Nights

It turns out I don't have to worry that Rix is going to repeat his performance from the other night. You know, the one where he tried to make John think that we were a couple? No, sir, as soon as we get to the Mastertons' barn, he's surrounded by a throng of local ladies and remains so the entire evening. I barely catch a glimpse of him as he moves from one to the next. He seems to be enjoying himself immensely, the Lothario.

During our first dance, before the Highland fling lessons start, John leans in and whispers, "I'm having a great time."

Me too, but instead of saying so, I lay my head on his shoulder and let the sweet sound of a Garth Brooks' ballad carry me away.

It's hard to believe how much has changed in my life in such a short period of time. Two weeks ago, I was secure on a path I was sure would continue forever. Summer was starting, which meant long days and hard work, both of which I was very much looking forward to.

But now that my parents are home, suddenly I couldn't care less about work. I'll still spend time in the gardens and bake for the farm stand, but more for my own spiritual centering than anything else.

My dad is spending his last summer on earth, and I'm going to make sure I enjoy all the moments I can with him. I may not make the kind of money I'd expected to, and I might need to skinny in my belt in a couple areas, but nothing is more important than family.

Also, if John and I continue to see each other, I'd like for my dad to get to know him. I want him to know that even though he won't be alive to see it, a new generation will grow up on the land he loves. Even if John isn't the father of that new generation—because let's face it, that would be jumping the gun a bit—my dad needs to know I'm not shirking my duties in searching for his grandchildren's other parent.

The night flies by in a blur of missteps and laughter as the fling lessons begin. Mr. Masterton explains, "Lads, the thing to remember is to jump high enough that your kilt flips up and gives the ladies a hint of your charms." He wiggles his backside suggestively and the crowd laughs in delight.

Mrs. Masterton smacks his butt and smiles, "The lassie's will want to show off their charms, as well." She performs her own leap showing off a good amount of leg. The men in the crowd catcall and whistle in appreciation.

Dougal bellows good naturedly, "Enough of that, boys; this gal belongs to me!" And he grabs his wife as the Scottish band breaks into a Highland reel.

My dad isn't up to participating, but he encourages my mom to join in. Nan takes her in hand and whispers, "Let's give him a show, honey." My dad watches his wife with such love in his eyes you can't help but think he's recalling a time when he could still twirl her around the dance floor himself.

Dorcas has even managed to pull the reverend off the couch long enough to come with her tonight. The barn is full of people of all ages, from toddlers learning to walk to the elderly who can no longer walk unassisted. Everyone is enjoying themselves in the best way they can.

Ethan and Emily sit at a corner table, deep in conversation. Neither of them seems to care that there's a dance going on, they're that lost in whatever topic they're discussing.

I run into Cat in the ladies' room. "I declare tonight a success," I tell her.

She's flushed from her own exertions on the dance floor. "I knew it would be fun, but seriously, this surpasses all my expectations."

"You need to open these lessons up to singles from all over the area. In fact, I bet you'd even get some folks to drive down from Chicago."

"That would be wonderful. It would certainly increase the variety of people we could introduce to each other," she says. "We could even add a speed dating element to the night and make everyone change partners after each song. Then on breaks they could talk to whomever they wanted to."

"Dancing certainly alerts you to any chemistry between you and your partner. And nothing is more important than chemistry."

"Remember that video they made us watch in science class about the birds performing mating dances?" I ask.

"OMG, the manikin looked like a psychotic crack head after

too many Red Bulls." We both start laughing at the memory.

"The fling is no different, really," Cat explains. "If your partner doesn't stir anything in you after one whirl, you pretty much know he's not the one."

I have danced with John the entire night. Being in his arms is like wearing a warm sweater on a chilly autumn morning. It's cozy and comforting, safe and utterly lovely.

Cat says, "You and John sure seem to be hitting it off."

"I know, right? I mean, who would have thought Dorcas would have such potential as a matchmaker."

"And he's a farmer. How perfect is that?" she asks.

I bobble my head back and forth in partial agreement. "A bacon farmer."

"An *organic* bacon farmer," she stresses.

"True enough. One thing's for certain though, he's a great guy and I'm enjoying getting to know him. I think my parents will really like him when they get a chance to talk in a more sedate setting."

After reapplying my lip gloss, I decide to check on my dad. He's enjoying a conversation with his old friend Jim Reardan, but he looks pretty worn out. When Jim goes to get himself another beer, I approach and ask, "How are you doing, Dad?"

He smiles widely trying to act like he's fine, but I know he's not. "Hi, honey. What a fun night, huh?"

"It sure is. I'm glad you and Mom are here for it." He's having a hard time keeping his head up; even though it isn't quite nine o'clock yet, I know he's ready for bed. I don't want to draw attention to his waning strength, so I say, "Listen, I'm beat. I've been up since five and even though I hate for the night to end, I really need to get home and hit the hay."

My dad looks up gratefully. He's knows what I'm doing. "Okay, honey. Help me up and we'll gather your mom. I wonder if the ladies are ready to let Rix leave."

I let Dad find Mom and I go back to John. I explain what's going on and he offers, "I can drive your folks home and then we can come back if you want."

"That's very sweet of you, but I'd like to stay with them."

I've told him about my dad's illness, so he understands. "I'll call you tomorrow and check in, okay?"

"Okay," I agree. Then he leans in and kisses me goodnight. It's a whisper of a kiss, but it promises so much more when the time is right.

I can't seem to find Rix, so I ask Cat if she or Sam could drive him back to the farm at the end of the night. After she agrees, we help my parents to the car where they snuggle up together in the backseat, making me feel like their chauffeur. But the truth is, I think they want to touch each other as much as they can, as long as they can.

While they cuddle and doze, I wonder where the heck Rix went off to and who the heck he went off with. Not that I care.

Chapter Forty-Eight
Animal Care

I get up the next morning and meet my dad in the kitchen, as is fast becoming our habit. I make coffee and ask, "What would you like for breakfast this morning? I could do an omelet or pancakes. You name it!"

"I think maybe I'll wait a bit on breakfast. I'm not feeling too hungry just yet. In fact, I think I might head back to bed," he says slowly.

I try not to show my concern about how quickly he's losing his remaining strength. "Good plan," I say. "You go rest up and I'll go tend the horses. I'll meet you back here later and we'll have a feast, okay?"

I help him up and watch as he drags himself back to bed. The marked change in his energy level scares me. I'm not exactly sure what I thought would happen between now and his death, but I realize this is going to be par for the course. Someday soon he will have a hard time getting out of bed. And then he simply won't be getting out of bed.

I grab a cup of real coffee as it's already made and head out to the barn. I let the puppies out of the cozy space I made for them in a barn stall in lieu of a kennel. They jump and leap, crisscrossing paths in front of my feet, doing their best to trip me up. I've been feeding them in the barn so all the animals can get used to each other.

Once I get Naomi and Caroline's food set up in the corner, I open the horse stalls. Dusty and Cornelius both greet me with a nod of their heads. I put my coffee down and pick up a brush. I work on Cornelius first as Dusty has her nose in her feed bucket and she doesn't like to be groomed while she's eating.

I whisper sweet nothings into Cornelius's ear and kiss his neck while I work. Caring for an animal is such a fulfilling task. They appreciate the attention so much and always reward you in special ways. Cornelius leans his head into mine and taps his right hoof on the ground. I'm so caught up in the peacefulness of the moment that I nearly hit the roof when I realize I'm not alone. Out the corner of my eye, I see Rix standing in the doorway, staring at me.

"You scared the pants off of me," I semi-yell.

He clucks his tongue. "If only …"

I let his comment slide and ask, "What are you doing here? I don't serve breakfast in the barn."

"Apparently you don't serve it in the kitchen, either."

"My dad wasn't hungry, so I told him I'd make it later." I suppose I really should have left something for my paying guest, though.

"Yeah, well, you told me to meet you in the barn at six, so here I am."

"What?" I can't help laughing. "I told you to meet me here so I could throw a cow patty at you to pay you back for what you did to my mom when you were eight."

He shrugs his shoulders. "If that's what you want to do."

"Rix, I'm not going to throw cow manure at you." *As appealing as the thought might be.*

"Then why don't you go for a ride with me?"

"Where?"

"How about out to the dandelion field?"

I roll my eyes. "You mean what used to be the dandelion field?"

He grabs a saddle off the wall. "Which one of these guys gets this one?"

"That's Dusty's. But let's let them eat. Why do you want to go out to the field?"

"I don't particularly, I just wanted to talk to you for a couple of minutes."

I'm not sure why we can't talk here while I'm working, but I figure it can't do any harm to go for a short walk. I put the horse brush back in its cubby and whistle for Naomi and Caroline to join us, it's part of their training. They'd follow me anyway, but I grab a pocketful of kibble to help keep them from wandering off.

We walk quietly for a couple minutes before he says, "You left me last night."

"We didn't *leave* you; we couldn't find you. Where did you go off to?" I ask in an accusatory way.

He shrugs his shoulders. "I went off looking for some quiet."

"Who with?" I ask like a jealous girlfriend.

He gives me a slow smile, obviously thinking the same thing. "Why does it matter?"

"It doesn't. I was too busy to keep looking." Take that.

"I noticed," he says. "John's a pretty nice guy, isn't he?"

"He is." After a quiet moment I add, "And he's a farmer."

Rix scoffs. "A pig farmer."

"An organic pig farmer."

"Listen," he says, "I'm planning on keeping my yurt, but I need to go back to Chicago for a couple of days. I've got some meetings."

I bet he doesn't have any meetings and is just tired of boring country life. I'm sure last night's barn dance made him yearn for a noisy night club with half-naked women draping themselves all over him.

"Go, it's none of my concern." I can tell he's annoyed by my reaction, but what did he expect? I'm hardly going to throw myself at him and beg him to stay.

When we get to the field we stop and I ask, "Is that all?"

He points out into the distance. "The flowers are blooming again." He's right, the field is once again a riot of glorious yellow blossoms. The puppies immediately lie down and roll in the new growth. Rix says, "Isn't that one of your services, dandelion rolling?"

"Yup." I know he's making fun of me. Something as tame as rolling on the ground certainly wouldn't appeal to someone like Rix.

He seems to read my mind and asks, "How much would you charge to roll around the dandelions with me?"

I whistle for the dogs and reach into my pocket for a treat to teach them to heel. Then I turn around and walk away. After about ten yards, I stop and yell, "It would cost more than money.

Suffice it say, you couldn't afford it." Then I continue back to the barn without him.

How dare he make light of what I do? Just because he doesn't understand it doesn't mean it holds no value. I'm glad he's going back to Chicago, and as far as I'm concerned, he can stay there.

Chapter Forty-Nine
The Endgame

I invited John to dinner tonight to spend some time with me and my parents. He's bringing pork chops from his farm and is going to grill them. Meanwhile, I make a lovely caprese salad with some purple, red, and yellow heirloom tomatoes and Thai basil. I reduce balsamic vinegar until it's a thick, sweet syrup to drizzle on top. Then I garnish the whole thing with dandelion confetti. It's positively gorgeous.

I'm pulling the strawberry rhubarb tarts I've made for dessert out of the oven when I hear the doorbell ring. My mom answers it. "John, how nice to see you again. Please come in."

Then my dad enthusiastically offers, "Hello, young man, glad you could make it."

I walk into the living room to find my date standing next to my dad's chair shaking his hand. I untie my apron and approach him for a brief hug, and ask, "How about a beer?"

"Sounds great." He holds up a brown paper bag. "Let me put the pork chops in the kitchen?"

"Sure, follow me." Then to my parents I say, "Why don't we all go out to the back porch? We can keep John company while he grills."

Once we get situated, the night flies by. Over dinner, my dad and John share farming stories.

Dad reminisces, "I remember the time I fell off the manure spreader as a boy and was moments away from becoming part of the fertilizer. I had to roll through that mess like Superman to save myself. I smelled like a barn for a month after."

John cringes. "Those were back in the days when the spreaders had those sharp hooks, right?"

Dad nods. "Oh, yeah. It looked like dragon claws digging it into the earth. Thank goodness we spray the stuff in liquid form now. The worst that can happen is a manure shower."

"Which would not be pleasant, but fortunately not deadly," John concurs.

My mom keeps catching my eye and giving me secret little smiles regarding how nicely John and Dad are getting along. I knew they would.

If Dad weren't sick, we could have many more nights like this. As it is, almost every time we go somewhere, I think, *is this my dad's last* whatever-it-is. Was last night's barn dance his last dance? Will Sunday be the last time he goes to church or has that day already come and gone?

The *last* game is a real gut-wrencher. I think that once the brain starts to process events this way is when the grieving process truly begins. Friday my dad will be eighty-four. It *will* be his last birthday. The certainties are excruciating. I think of his past birthdays and how they were happy events, the promise of the new year coming. Briefly, I let myself feel the epic heart ache that lives in my belly like a parasite. The pain is growing, but it doesn't have to. No. I cannot think this way.

My folks head to bed relatively early. Even though the time difference is only an hour apart from Florida, they both seem to be totally drained of energy. My dad's weariness is due to renal failure. I believe my mom's is the result of a breaking heart.

Once they're upstairs, John and I sit on the porch swing together. He puts his arm around me, and it feels very nice. I let myself snuggle into him and relax.

"I need to go back to Springfield tomorrow and check on the farm. I probably won't be able to get back here for a couple of weeks," he tells me in a reluctant voice.

Springfield is two hours southwest of Gelson. "I'd offer to come visit you for our next date, but I really need to be on hand for my parents." I don't mention that I can't bear to meet a bunch of cute pigs that I secretly want to eat.

"I only wanted you to know that I'm sorry I have to leave."

"As a fellow farmer, I totally understand how busy the summer months are. While I'm sorry to see you go, I get it."

John leans in and gives me the sweetest kiss. It's so light and tender, it leaves me hungering for more. In opposition to what I really want to do, which is jump on his lap and explore his kissability, I find myself pulling away.

Time suddenly seems beyond precious to me, and while I've always had a go-with-the-flow attitude about life, I currently feel that every moment is so special that I don't want to waste any of them.

Which is the reason I uncharacteristically say, "You've taken over your family farm outside of Springfield, and I've taken over my family farm here in Gelson. Before we get in too deep here, maybe we should discuss the practicality of starting a long-distance relationship."

"I hadn't really thought of it like that," John says. "I thought we'd date and see where the future takes us."

"That makes a lot of sense," I reply tentatively. "I normally would have agreed with you, but in light of the fact that we both have huge responsibilities, we're both in our thirties and not getting any younger, I need to know that one of us would be willing to move if we ever get to that point."

He doesn't say anything for a minute but finally asks, "Would you?"

I shake my head. "No. I don't want to live anywhere but right here. That's why I'm asking. Moving is not a concession I'm willing to make for anyone."

John looks a bit crushed. "I don't think I can say either way right now, but I promise I'll think of little else when I go back home."

"I know it's too soon to be talking like this. But with my dad dying, I feel more certain about some things than I ever have before. And I'm certain I will never leave the land he farmed and the house he called home." Talk about a buzz kill.

With his arm still around me, he says, "I respect that." We sit quietly for another several minutes, each of us totally lost in thought, then John unwinds his arm so he can stand up. "I better get going."

He doesn't say anything else. He doesn't try to kiss me goodbye. He just holds my hands and lightly squeezes them. He waves briefly as he drives away.

Dear Universe,

Seriously? Look, I got onboard with the whole opening my life up to a potential mate thing. In fact, I jumped in with both feet, leaving my head somewhere else entirely. And who do you bring for me? 1.) An egotistical football player in love with the big city. 2.) A perfectly lovely artist who's already taken. 3.) A really terrific bacon farmer who isn't sure he'll ever leave his family farm. 4.) A sweet guy who sold me his puppies, who was never a contender, but I'm so mad I'm including him to make my point.

Whose side are you on? And what in the heck is your endgame, to offer romance only to take it away? My ultimatum is no longer loving. Pony up or back off. I've got too much real stuff going on to let you toy with my emotions.

Chapter Fifty
Squirrels with Plans

My spirit guide comes to me in my sleep. I'm lying on the floor of the carousel at the county fair. People have to step over me to get on the ride. For some reason I'm dressed like Maid Marian straight out of *Robin Hood*. My hands are folded under my head and I'm staring up at the hundreds of clear lightbulbs illuminating the ride. Terraz steps up, holding hands with the black bear who comes to teach me how to scare fear away.

They stand over me, staring down in concern, and then the bear lies down next to me. Because this is a vision, or dream if you prefer, I don't find this odd at all. Instead, I say, "I've been roaring at the fear."

"How's that working out for ya?" he asks in a baritone voice with a thick New Jersey accent.

"I don't know. I'm not sure that I feel fear as much as panic. It's like I'm watching the sands of an hourglass run out. I want to stop them, but I can't figure out how to do that."

He nods his big bear head. "I hear ya."

I look up at Terraz and demand, "What's going on with all the men coming and going in my life? I was perfectly content without them, you know. In fact, life was downright peaceful without them."

"Just because you ignore one aspect of your life doesn't mean you're content, Sarah."

"Not everyone needs a relationship, Terraz," I retaliate a bit unkindly.

"Your contract requires you to have one. You signed up with another spirit on the other side to bring children into this world. You must meet him before that can transpire."

I don't doubt her. I fully accept my contract and I believe that I have unfulfilled responsibilities, but the timing of it all seems highly questionable. "Why now?" I ask. "Why can't I spend time with my dad without worrying about a man?"

"It's a gift to your father for him to see that life will continue after he leaves. It's a comfort for him to know that you'll have someone to lean on and to love you," she says.

"But what if John won't consider leaving his farm? Then there's no one, and this whole charade will have been pointless."

"If John's the one, he'll leave it. None of these men have to be *the one* for their presence to assure your father you aren't neglecting that aspect of your life. He just wants you to have someone to share your life with."

"It seems unfair. My heart feels like it's being torn out of my chest. My dad is going to die, and I'm not being allowed to help him, I don't know how to comfort my mom, and none of the men seem to be the right fit."

She shrugs her ethereal shoulders. "That's life, Sarah. What would you tell another to do in this situation?"

"I would say the universe has a plan; live each day the best you can; open yourself up to the unexpected. I would say all kinds of crap that quite honestly sounds empty and pointless in my situation."

Then I turn to the bear and ask, "What would you do?"

He scratches his belly while answering, "I'd pick the one thing I could do something about and form a plan. *Capisce?*"

Okay, so now he's an Italian New Jersey black bear?

"Yeah, I got it. I can't fix my dad or make my mom hurt less. I can't make Rix a different man, and I can't make John want to move someday, so I guess I'll take on the corporation."

Terraz looks concerned. "That's what you're getting from this? Sarah, the thing you should pick is your own perception. That's what Chip was talking about."

The bear's name is Chip? I turn to my furry friend and ask, "Is that what you were talking about?"

"You need to decide that for yourself. I'm only the messenger," he says.

I close my eyes and when I open them again Terraz and Chip have disappeared. In their place are six squirrels sitting around me smoking cigars. One of them speaks up in squeaky voice, "We've got a plan."

And while I've not met these squirrels before, I find I'm very interested in hearing what they have in mind.

Chapter Fifty-One
The Biggest Bump of All

I feel strangely calm when I wake up in the morning. I don't remember too much of what went on in my sleep, but I know something important was decided.

In the kitchen, I find my mom this time, already at the stove. "Morning." I give her a kiss before pouring myself a cup of coffee. Between you and me, I like real coffee better than dandelion coffee but don't drink it because of the caffeine. I fall off the wagon when my parents are home, though, and I quite look forward to it.

"Morning, honey. How did you sleep?"

"Pretty good. Where's Dad?"

"He's going to have breakfast in bed this morning," she says matter of factly.

"Really?" The thought alarms me. Have we already experienced another last without me realizing it?

"He's been pushing himself since we've been home. He hasn't wanted you to see how tired he is all the time."

I'm shocked to hear this. There's no way I would have thought that. In fact, I've been thinking the opposite, that he's let himself sleep more now that he is home.

"Also, he has dialysis today. Leaving the house is getting harder and harder for him."

I feel selfish hearing that. My dad is only going because of me, but I don't feel bad enough to tell him not to go. I do wonder how long I can watch him deteriorate and continue to push him, prolonging his suffering.

I decide to change the subject. "I think I drove John away last night."

My mom puts her spatula down, turns the stove burner off, and joins me at the table. "How did you do that?"

"I told him there was no point in starting anything unless he was willing to leave his farm someday."

"Why in the world would you have said that so soon? You've only been out a couple of times, right?"

"Yeah. But the thing is that I'm never going to leave this farm and what's the point of falling for someone who might feel the same way? It seems like a great big waste of time, not to mention heartache."

"What did he say?" my mom asks.

"He's going back to Springfield today. He's says he'll try to have the answer to that question the next time he sees me."

My mom pats my hands. "I'm sure he will, too. Don't give up on him yet."

But I totally have. In fact, I'm pretty sure I'm giving up on all men right now. I say, "I'm going to head down to the cafe and bake something yummy to tempt Dad. I'll be up in a bit."

"Okay, dear. You do that. In the meantime, I'll try to get him to eat his eggs and bacon and let him rest up for the trip to the clinic this afternoon."

I wind up making my dad chocolate scones, apricot tarts, and Rice Krispie treats, of all things. They're all his favorites and so long as he continues his dialysis, I promised he could have whatever he wants. I feel like we've all too soon reached the point where it's better he gets some food in his body than worry about what kind of food that's going to be.

The car ride to the clinic is very quiet. My dad sleeps, and my mom works a crossword puzzle. I keep peeking back at my dad in the rearview mirror. Every day he looks less like himself—thinner, graying skin. It's like he's already started to leave us.

My mom decides to stay with Dad during his treatment. She wants to hold his hand, even if he sleeps the whole time.

I'm not quite sure what to do with myself. I decide to go to the cafeteria for a cup of tea. Once I'm settled at a table, I call Cat.

Nan picks up her phone. "Girl, where you at?"

"Nan? It's me, Sarah."

"I saw that for myself when your name came up on the screen. What do you need?" she asks.

"I was calling to talk to Cat. Is she there?"

"Yup, but she and Sam are busy building the new chicken coop out back."

"Oh, okay. Well, then I guess I'll talk to her later," I say dejectedly.

"Can I help you with something, honey?" she asks.

"I'm not sure, Nan."

"You upset about your dad?"

"Yeah." I don't say anything else.

"Sarah, girl, listen up. Kenny Hastings is one lucky man. He's had a wonderful life. Sure, it's had its bumps. Some of them big enough to bloody him up a bit. But this here is not a bump."

"How can you say that? This is the biggest bump of all!"

"No, it's not. This is his reward for a life well lived. I'm not sure where exactly we go when we die. I know they tell you one thing in church, and while I believe in the idea of heaven, I can't say for certain what it's gonna look like. But I know this, I know that whatever it is, it's pretty spectacular."

"I tend to think the same thing, Nan. I get that it's my dad's body that's dying, not his spirit. I believe that. I just don't know how to keep going without him here with us."

"You'll do it like you did when he was in Florida. You'll know he's alive somewhere living his life and you'll go on living yours."

"I guess," I say, unconvinced.

"Oh honey, you will. When Hugh died, I thought I'd curl up in a ball and die myself, but I didn't. I trudged through all the feelings and decided to simply be grateful for what I had."

"I'm very grateful, Nan. I really am."

"I know that. You let yourself feel what you're feeling and remember your mama's going to need you. As much as you want to curl up, you can't. You've gotta be strong for her."

Then she changes the subject. "I found us a new book. It's called *Spanked by a Highlander*! I think it might be a little dirtier than our other stories." I hope its subtitle isn't *Fifty Shades of Plaid*. She sounds delighted.

Leave it to Nan to lighten things up. I say goodbye and decide to go buy myself something to eat. I'm not really hungry, but I could use some comfort food. That's when I see him.

Chapter Fifty-Two
Attack of the Hotties

What in the world is Rix doing here? He's sitting at a table checking his phone. Didn't he say he was going to be in Chicago for meetings? I'm torn between hiding behind the sneeze guard of the salad bar to avoid him and confronting him to find out why he isn't where he said he was going to be.

I finally decide to approach him, but someone else gets there first. A man, maybe a little older than Rix, walks up to him and claps him on the shoulder. "Hendrix, my man, thanks for meeting me."

Dear God, Rix's friend is good looking, too. Tall, with black wavy hair and swarthy skin, like he's from the Mediterranean or something. Are there no average looking men left in the world? Everywhere I go these days it's like attack of the hotties or something. Okay, so maybe they're not attacking me, I just mean I've never encountered as many good-looking men in my life as I have in the last few weeks.

I decide to approach Rix. I mean, what's the harm? I walk over to his table and say, "How's Chicago?"

He looks up, clearly surprised to see me, and jumps to his

feet. "Sarah! What are you doing here?"

"My dad is having dialysis. How 'bout you? I thought you went back to the big city."

He gestures to his friend and explains, "I'm meeting Jerry. We're working on a project together."

I give Jerry my brightest smile. One that I hope conveys genuine delight as well as a touch of come-hitherness. "Hi, I'm Rix's neighbor, Sarah. It's nice to meet you."

Jerry gets to his feet while treating me to a dazzling smile of his own. My heavens, he's a stunning creature. He offers his hand and says, "The pleasure is all mine." Then he indicates an empty chair at their table. "Would you like to join us?"

I sit down with every intention of flirting up a storm, not that I'm purposefully trying to make Rix jealous—okay, maybe a little—but seriously if the universe is going to keep throwing hot men in my path, I should really at least try to get to know them, right?

I ask, "So Jerry, what do you do?"

"I'm a farmer," he answers. Who knew there were so many hunky farmers out there? First John and now Jerry. Note to self: Farmers with J names are hot. Explore this theory.

"Really? I'm a farmer, too. I have the property next to Rix's grandparents' place."

Rix nods his head. "That's right, she does. Sarah runs an *organic* farm. She's adamantly opposed to anything but."

Jerry says, "Good for you! It's a hard business to be in, though."

"How so?" I ask.

"People don't like to pay extra for organic produce. It can be a tough sell."

"I don't have a problem. In fact, my farm stand rarely has anything left at the end of the day."

"You must keep your prices pretty reasonable. It's hard to do that when you have to pay a distributor on top of selling wholesale."

I don't want to hear Jerry tell me he's not organic, so I don't ask. Instead I go with, "Do you farm vegetables or animals?"

Rix interrupts, "Be careful, Jer, it's a trap. Sarah's a vegetarian."

I wave off his comment. "John's a bacon farmer, I mean a pig farmer, and I don't have any problem with that." I prefer he didn't farm my greatest dietary weakness, but beggars can't be choosers, right?

"Vegetables," Jerry answers.

To annoy Rix, and not because I mean it, I say, "You should buy Rix's grandparents' place." I don't mean it because he's obviously not organic, but I want to tweak the football player.

Jerry's eyes brighten, "How many acres do you have, Rix?"

"Two hundred twenty. You're not looking to expand, are you?" he asks in a way that makes me think they're sharing some inside joke I'm not privy to.

Jerry shrugs. "I don't know, with neighbors as good looking as yours, it's definitely a thought." Then he turns to me. "I'd love to check out your operation some time."

I smile sincerely. "Rix is staying in one of the yurts on my property. I'm sure he'd be happy to bring you over. Wouldn't you, Rix?"

"Sure," he says. "In fact, we can head that way after our meeting if you want." Jerry agrees readily.

I don't think to ask what their meeting is about because my mind kicks into gear on how best to show off my place. I like to sell the organic produce angle to other farmers, I figure if they see it being done successfully, they might make changes on their own land.

I know Rix isn't going to sell Jerry his grandparents' farm because he already has a deal on the table with that popcorn devil, but maybe I can get Jerry on my side and get his help in shaking some sense into Rix before Happy Corn! moves in and ruins *Eat Me Organic*.

Chapter Fifty-Three
Fresh Love

Once we're home and my dad is settled in his room, I run out to the cafe to bake more. Nothing says, "welcome to my organic farm" like cookies fresh out of the oven. I decide on chocolate chip pecan. I even throw caution to the wind and use both eggs and flax meal. Look out, I'm feeling reckless.

I'm not looking to form a romantic connection with Jerry. I only want to annoy Rix. I know he won't give up his glamorous city life, but I want to give him something to think about. You know, like *life in the country is pretty great and even farmers have a social life.* Although god knows, that's been a totally recent development for me.

I brush my hair and put on some lip gloss. At the rate I'm going with this lip gloss, I'm going to have to buy myself another tube the next time I'm at the pharmacy. Then I go up to the barn and get the puppies. No one can resist the charm of golden retriever puppies, and I'm pulling out all the stops.

When Rix pulls up the driveway, I'm playing fetch with Naomi and Caroline. As the men get out of the car, the girls run over to them looking for some fresh love. Rix picks up Naomi and lets her kiss his face, then he tucks her under his arm for a petting. I'm a tiny bit jealous of my dog.

Jerry plays with Caroline. "You've got the picture-perfect life out here, don't you?"

"I do my best," I assure him. Then I lead them over to *Eat Me*. I explain, "This is my new cafe. I'd planned on having it open by now, but my dad's been sick and I've been taking care of him." I don't go into all the gory details. It's not like Jerry's going to be around that long, so there's no point in sharing all of my personal business.

"Sorry to hear that. Are you going to serve breakfast and lunch here?" Jerry asks.

I nod. "Mostly to my guests who stay in the yurts." At his look of confusion, I explain, "I also run a healing program. I help people detox from the pollutants of our toxic world."

He asks, "You mean like massages and facials and stuff?"

Rix laughs, "The only kind of facial you'll get from this one would be a cow pie in the face."

I take offense. "You should talk. I've never thrown manure at you even though I've been sorely tempted. Flinging crap is your game." I mean that on so many levels.

Jerry looks between us, enjoying the show. "What kind of services do you offer?"

"My guests are usually here for at least a week. I start by removing animal products from their diet and once I find out what their trouble is, I design a schedule of activities for them."

He looks interested enough that I continue, "That could include mud rolling, chakra cleansing, meditation and yoga, and even a eucalyptus beating." There are too many more to even mention.

"Eucalyptus beating?" Jerry looks concerned.

"First you spend an hour in the sweat lodge, then I come in and firmly tap you with eucalyptus branches to encourage increased circulation and to release negative energy. It's great for people who aren't belly breathers."

"What's a belly breather?" Rix asks.

"Belly breathing is breathing deeply and slowly allowing your abdomen to push down and out so you can fully fill your lungs with air. Chest breathers never allow enough oxygen into their bodies. Their breaths are shallower, which can lead to anxiety, unclear thinking, and illness."

"I want to try it," Jerry declares.

"Really?" I ask. I'm so excited by his interest that I offer, "I can do it right now."

"You should do it too, Rix. It'll be fun," Jerry says.

The football player rolls his eyes. "When I get hot, sweaty, and naked, man, you're not the person I see doing it with." He looks at me, the fiend. My body betrays my brain and fills with the most delicious longing. I do my best to ignore it.

"Typically, a sweat lodge is most effective when you've been fasting but seeing as I'm about to give you some homemade chocolate chip cookies, we'll have to improvise. If you like it enough, you can come back and do it right another time."

Jerry stands up. "Let's do this, Rix!"

Rix stands as well. "What's first?"

"I need half an hour to get the sweat lodge hot enough. You have plenty of time to enjoy a couple of cookies and change into the hemp robes in the bathroom of your yurt. Come on out when you're ready. I'll start building the fire to heat the volcanic rock."

"Volcanic rock?" Rix sounds alarmed.

"It the best kind of rock to use. It holds its heat longest and doesn't crumble when I pour water on it."

He groans and looks at his friend. "What part of this is appealing to you, Jer? Getting naked with me or drowning in humidity?"

Jerry laughs. "The experience, man. I've never done anything like this. I love to try new stuff."

Rix turns and leads the way to his yurt, mumbling something about hare-brained, crazy, vegetarian female farmers. Jerry pulls out his wallet and hands me a credit card. "Seeing as he doesn't really want to do this, it'll be my treat." Then he winks at me and hurries after Rix. I look down at his black American Express card curiously. I've never seen one before. I briefly wonder how the heck it's different from the standard green card, when I notice the name printed across the front.

Chapter Fifty-Four
Playing with the Enemy

The tall, dark, and handsome farmer, Jerry, is none other than Jared Clayton, owner of Happy Corn! I never thought of the popcorn king in human enough terms to consider that he has a nickname. How could I have missed that? My heart nearly stops from the shock. I have to force myself to belly breathe a few times in order to get enough oxygen into my brain to think clearly.

Hendrix Greer is going to rue the day he messed with me. How dare he bring the enemy to my farm and not tell me who he is. Fueled by rage—which is an emotion I don't remember experiencing before Rix came barreling into my life—I hurry outside to build a fire to heat the rocks.

I formulate a plan while I work. It's more of a torture plan than a healing one, but I'm going to charge Jared Clayton for every single part of it. I see the men come out of Rix's yurt, and it's all I can do not to rub my hands together like some penny opera villain. These two unsuspecting city slickers have no idea what's in store for them.

Forcing a smile, I walk over to them. "I hope you boys don't have anything else on your agenda for the day. I'm going to give you the full treatment." If they only knew.

Jared, a.k.a. Jerry says, "I'm totally free."

Rix grumbles, "I don't need to be back to the city until tomorrow afternoon."

That's odd, I wonder what happened to him leaving. "Excellent. Then follow me." First, I take them to the open-sided copper meditation pyramids in the sunflower patch. "Pick one and go sit under it quietly. I'll come get you when the sweat lodge is ready."

"You know I'm naked under this robe, right?" Rix asks in alarm.

"What's your point?" I ask.

"I don't want any bugs biting the boys. Shouldn't we have clothes on for this part?"

"Don't worry," I assure him. "I use citronella oil around the perimeter of the pyramids, it keeps the pests away." I don't mention that I may have forgotten to use it this time. Silly, hare-brained, crazy, vegetarian me.

Jerry is all excited and hurries to sit under his pyramid. "What do I do now?"

"Close your eyes and calm your vibration. Try not to think of anything. Let your mind clear so the universe can bring its messages to your heart," I say in a soothing melodious tone meant to help them relax.

Rix grumbles while he tries to decide which of the remaining two pyramids he's going to sit under. He finally gets settled and I instruct, "Don't talk to each other. This is purely an individual journey."

When they're finally still, I very quietly pull out the squeeze bottle of honey I put in my pocket back at the cafe. I drizzle it around their pyramids while saying, "Keep your eyes closed, I'm clearing the negative energies away. Let the breeze blow all the thoughts out of your mind. Let the sun fill you with her warmth." Then because I'm not quite done squirting honey around them, I start an American Indian chant, "Ah-uh-nayah-oh-wa-oh-wa-shon-day-oh-wa." I keep repeating it until I'm a safe distance away.

I use twice as many lava stones in the sweat lodge than is normal for novices. I wait to pull them out of the fire until they're red hot. Then I line the inside perimeter of the tent with them as well as the standard grouping in the center. When everything is set, I go back for the men.

Jerry is still sitting criss-cross applesauce under his pyramid, but Rix is spread eagle, sound asleep. His arms and legs are outside the boundaries, and would you look at that, appear to be crawling with bugs. Excellent.

I announce, "It's time ... Allow yourselves to drift back to the earth plane gently, but don't let any thoughts in. Keep your minds wide open for the next stage of your journey."

Rix opens his eyes and immediately begins smacking the insects off his legs. He glares at me and accuses, "I thought you used citronella oil."

"I do," I assure him. "Those little ants aren't going to hurt you."

Jerry starts smacking insects off his own legs, "I think they threw up on me or something. I've got this sticky stuff all over."

Rix bellows, "Yuck, you're right." Then he shoots an accusatory look my way. "Sarah, what is this?"

"Don't be a baby, Rix. It's probably just remnants of the citronella." I turn and walk away while commanding, "Follow me."

I lead the way to the tent and say, "As soon as I pour the water on the rocks, you're going to want to take your robes off to let the toxins out."

My neighbor looks alarmed. "You want us to sit here stark naked together? Sorry, babe, this is starting to sound a little too kinky for me."

Jerry says, "For Pete's sake, Rix, you're not my type, so put your maidenish sensibilities away. The steam is going to keep you from feeling bad about your manhood. God knows you if you saw mine you definitely would."

Men are such children, aren't they? *Mine is bigger than yours. I have more money that you. My girlfriend is prettier.* They're like a bunch of seventh graders in grown bodies. It's nauseating.

I instruct, "It'll obviously get very hot in here, but make sure you don't stand up during your session. You don't want to step on a lava rock. That's a burn you won't soon forget."

Rix looks a little panicky and asks, "How long are we going to be in here?"

"Thirty minutes or so. Trust me, if skinny little women can do it, you'll have no problem." I'm appealing to his overinflated male ego. I'd be surprised if he lasts ten minutes without begging to be let out.

Once both men get settled, I start pouring jugs of water over the stones. The tent fills up with steam quickly, then I grab their robes and I hurry out to get the next stage of my plan in motion.

Chapter Fifty-Five
Time for Your Beating!

Before even five minutes are up, Rix calls out, "It's really hot in here."

"It's supposed to be," I answer. "It's called a sweat lodge for a reason."

I pull the garden hose out of the green house and point it into the mud pit. Antonio dug me a six-by-six pit with a ledge built around the outer foot. It's deep enough for two grown men to sit in and submerge themselves up to their shoulders.

At twenty minutes, Rix calls out, "How much longer?"

"Ten minutes, you big sissy." I can't help myself. How this man ever played professional football is beyond me.

Twenty minutes later, I finally retrieve them. Jerry is sitting peacefully and calmly, looking like he's really into the experience. Rix is twitching around like he's having a seizure.

"Finally!" the latter declares. But when he tries to stand up, he wobbles to the point where I have to help him sit down again. I try very unsuccessfully not to look down at his impressively naked self.

I instruct, "Don't try to stand. You're going to have crawl out of the tent for the next part of your treatment."

"I'm not crawling out there stark naked!" Rix yells.

Jerry laughs. "I'll go first if it makes you feel any better."

Rix stares up at me. "Where are you going to be while we're crawling?"

"I'll be out there telling you what to do next." Then I taunt, "Scared I'll think you're lacking in some way?"

"No." He immediately picks up the gauntlet I dropped.

I head out before Jerry and Rix emerge from the confines of the sweat lodge. They're both obviously relishing the cool air. You can see the relief on their faces. After several moments, Jerry asks, "What now?"

I point to the mud pit. "Give yourself a minute to adjust, then when you think you can, stand up, walk over to the mud and get in. Sit on the ledge."

Both men seem startled by this part of their treatment, but apparently neither wants to be the one to back out. Jerry is the first to get up and he walks confidently to the pit, happily showing off what the Good Lord gave him. I'd whistle but my mouth has suddenly gone dry.

Rix is next. He puts both hands over his man-stuff and gingerly scurries after his friend.

When they're both situated, Jerry asks, "What's this supposed to do?"

"The sweat lodge has opened your pores. Now the mud will suck out any remaining toxins." I bring them each a bottle of tepid water to drink.

Rix grabs his and pours it down his throat in one go. Once it's all gone, he says, "Yuck, it was warm. Can I get some cold water?"

I shake my head. "Nope. Cold water will decrease your body temperature too quickly and you could experience some shock. Only warm water for the first hour."

Jerry whispers, "I'd sell my soul for some ice." I want to tell him he can't because he's already sold his soul for money. Of course, I can't do that without tipping my hand.

Both men cautiously step into the pit. Rix makes a bunch of grossed-out sounds like soaking in mud isn't exactly his dream come true. Jerry, on the other hand, declares, "This is super cool. I mean totally gross, but still, pretty darn cool. It feels like thick pudding."

Rix shoots his friend a look of disbelief. "Do you roll in pudding for kicks on the weekend or something?"

Jerry shrugs his eyebrows. "Maybe. I'll have you know, my life is probably a lot more interesting than you think it is."

When they finally settle in, Rix asks, "How long do we have to sit here?"

"Ideally, you'd stay in for forty-five minutes, but you can get out now. Make sure not to rub any of the mud off."

"Why the heck not?" he wants to know.

"Because it has to dry on you before it does any good."

"Sarah, you never said anything about this before we got started," he accuses.

"Anyone who knows anything about sweat lodges knows that a mud treatment is part of it." SO not true, but I love tormenting him.

As soon as both men are on dry land, I lead them to a grassy patch and instruct, "Lie down on the ground and let the sun bake the mud on you."

Jerry is the first to obey orders. Once he's settled, he admits, "Call me crazy, but I feel like this is really doing something."

It takes Rix a few more minutes of scoping out the spot he's going to lie on before he follows suit. He does so with his hands covering his privates out of modesty. You'd never know the guy was such a prude by the way he flirts.

"Close your eyes," I say. "I'm going to cover them with a cloth, so the sun isn't too bright for you." I'm so very tempted to pull out my phone and start snapping pictures of them. I could even sell them to that tabloid and do something good with the twenty grand they're offering for pictures of Rix. But as mad as I am, I can't do it. My karma couldn't withstand the ding.

After twenty minutes in the sun, the clay-rich soil has dried on them, making them look like two swamp things that have just crawled out of the grass. Without any warning whatsoever, I turn the hose on them.

So much for not sending them into shock. Well water runs a standard fifty-nine degrees. After a sweat lodge followed by baking in the ninety-two-degree sun, it'll feel icy cold. And it does. Rix screams like a little girl, "What the @$#*? Mother of god! Woman, what are you doing to us?"

Jerry joins in, "Holy balls, that's cold!"

I ignore them and keep spraying. When they're both standing with dirty water dripping off their naked bodies, I push the limits, "Who's ready for a eucalyptus beating?"

Rix is seething mad. "There is no way I'm going to let you hit me with anything, woman! What's wrong with you?"

Feigning innocence, I say, "Nothing. This is all part of cleansing your body from negativity. That's why people come here."

"You're a psychotic dominatrix." He turns to stalk away, but suddenly remembers he's naked. "Where's my robe?"

"In the cafe," I answer.

"Why?"

"Because you don't get it back until you're done with the treatment." Then I offer, "But if you don't think you're man enough to carry on, you're more than welcome to walk up there and get it yourself." I smile as sweetly as I can.

Jerry steps forward. "I'm game. Let's do this thing." The popcorn king is turning out to be quite a sport and darn it, I'm begrudgingly impressed.

I lead both men back into the sweat lodge. It's still hot, but no longer steaming. I pick up a wand comprised of several eucalyptus branches and announce, "Time for your beating."

Chapter Fifty-Six
You Want a Psychotic Dominatrix?

"Ow! OW!! Watch it!!! What are you doing?" Rix yells.

"I'm stimulating your circulation by releasing essential oils, loser. Settle down." I don't normally call my clients losers, but Rix is special.

Jerry grunts every time I strike him with the wand but doesn't offer any complaints. It's almost like he's done this before and knows what to expect.

Twenty minutes in, Rix demands, "Tell me I've earned my robe back."

"I guess so. I'll go up to the cafe and get it for you." I leave them there. I haven't heard a word out of Jerry and think he might have fallen asleep.

"Hurry up," Rix demands.

"On my way," I say. And I am. I'm on my way up to the house to check on my parents. I never had any intention of taking their robes back to them. If they want to return to Rix's yurt, they're going to have to do it in the buff. How dare they deceive me?

When I get up to the house, I run into my mom in the kitchen. "How's Dad?" I ask.

"He's sleeping. Where have you been?"

"Down at the sweat lodge. Rix has a friend here and they're having a couple of treatments."

My mom's eyes perk up. "Tell me about Rix. He's something, huh?"

"If by *something* you mean he's a real piece of work, then yes, he's something all right."

"You still mad about him selling his land to that popcorn company?" she asks.

"Yes, I'm still mad about that. If Happy Corn! moves in next door, I'm going to lose the use of the land that borders our properties." I'll need a buffer area to absorb the chemicals that leach over.

"Honey, Herman didn't run an organic farm, and even though your dad didn't spray, he still used some modified seed. That's how things are done now."

"I don't feel like fighting about this, Mom. I implement organic farming because it's what I believe in. If we can't live our ideals in this life, what's the point?"

"I agree with you, dear. I don't want you to be disappointed is all."

Well, I am disappointed. But before I can say so, there's knock at the backdoor. It's Nan.

"Halloo! Anybody home?"

"Come on in, Nan," I call. "We're in the kitchen."

She comes in through the mudroom all lit up like Christmas morning. "Good heavens, gals, I just saw the most extraordinary sight." She fans herself and sits down at the kitchen table.

"What did you see, Bridget?" my mom asks.

"Men! Naked men as far as the eye can see. Big, strapping lads storming up the drive like a warring clan."

My mom shoots me a questioning look, so I say, "Rix and his friend Jerry."

"Were there only two of them?" Nan asks. "My eyes aren't what they used to be, I'm afraid. I could have sworn there were at least twenty."

"Nope, just the two," I assure her.

"Lordie, what a sight!" Then she stands up and says, "I came in to get you. If we hurry, we might be able to still see them."

My mom shoots me a look. "Why are Rix and his friend coming up the drive naked?"

"I must have forgotten to leave their robes for them," I say innocently.

Nan declares, "Girl, we could charge for this. It could be a real money maker."

"That's not how I run my business, Nan. I'm afraid charging is out of the question."

Nan holds up her phone. "Good thing I took pictures then!"

"Give me your phone," I demand. "You can't take naked pictures of people without their permission."

"Girl, when you're walking around butt nekkid, you're welcoming it."

My mom laughs even though she's trying to look stern. "Bridget, you've got to delete those."

Nan shrugs her shoulders. "Fine, but you want to see them first?"

Before we can answer her question, there's another loud knock on the backdoor. "Sarah, get your butt out here right now!"

It's Rix. I don't answer, but Nan says, "You still nekkid, boy?"

"No, ma'am, I have a robe on."

"Shoot," she says. "Well, you can come in anyway."

Rix opens the door and stalks in. "What's wrong with you?" he demands of me.

"Nothing."

"Why didn't you bring us our robes?"

I shrug. "I must have forgotten. Sorry." I'm no such thing. "Where's Jerry?"

"He's in my yurt showering. Why?"

"I thought my mom might want to meet our new neighbor."

Rix looks more than a little surprised. "What are you talking about?"

"Jared Clayton, owner of Happy Corn!? Isn't he my new neighbor?"

The football player looks like he's hoping the floor will open up and swallow him. Unfortunately for him, he's not that lucky.

Chapter Fifty-Seven
Credit Cards and Confrontations

"How did you know about Jared?" Rix asks.

"He gave me his credit card." I pull it out of my pocket to show him.

Rix groans. "I would have told you."

"Really, when? When he moved in next door?"

He shakes his head. "I don't know. I guess I just wanted you to meet him and get to know him a little without prejudice."

I'm about to storm past him to go outside when I hear a loud crash come from upstairs. We all go running.

"Dad?" I call out. "Are you okay?"

There's no answer. Rix pushes past me and takes the steps two at a time. When I get to my parents' room, he's already at my dad's side.

"Mr. Hastings, are you hurt?" he asks.

My dad rubs his arm. "I banged up my elbow something fierce, I'm afraid."

My mom rushes into the room and hurries over to his side. "Kenny, what happened?"

"I must have gotten up too fast. I got dizzy and down I went."

I don't think that's what happened. I think my dad's dizziness is a result of hypertension. When the body can't excrete all the toxins building up in it, blood pressure rises and can cause unsteadiness. The scary thing is that he had a dialysis treatment this morning. It's a sure sign of the progression of his disease. I paint on the mask I promised I'd wear. I don't know how much my mom understands about what is happening, and though it is breaking my heart to do nothing, the one thing I can do is to keep my promise.

Rix helps my dad to his feet and gets him to the bed. "Why don't you sit down a minute and rest."

"I think I will," my dad says in small voice. He looks at my mom. "I'd better eat my dinner up here tonight, Beth. Would you mind bringing it up?"

"Not at all. I'll bring mine up, too, and we can eat together." She sits next to him and holds his hand.

Sensing they need some privacy, I tell her, "You stay here, Mom. I'll get dinner for both of you."

"I'm grilling your dad a steak, honey. I know you don't like to cook meat."

I wave off her concern. "I've got this." I walk over and give my dad a kiss on the head. "Can I get you something while you wait?"

"How about a cup of coffee?" he asks.

Not only does he not need the extra liquid, but the caffeine will only elevate his blood pressure more. I'm smack in the middle between a rock and a hard place. I say, "Sure thing. You want a cookie to go with that?"

"That would be great, honey. Thank you."

I turn and walk out the door past Rix and Nan to go downstairs. I hear Nan sit down on my dad's recliner and ask, "You want to see some pictures I took on my phone, Kenny?"

Rix follows me down the stairs and into the kitchen. I don't look at him, I'm too busy grinding the coffee beans. I grind until I can't see clearly because my eyes are so full of tears. As I pour the water into the machine, I let out a sob that sounds as anguished as I feel.

Rix comes up behind me and puts his arms around me. "I'm sorry, Sarah. This has to be really hard on you."

I push him away not only out of anger over his subterfuge, but out of frustration over not being able to help my dad. "I don't need your pity, Rix. I need you to get out of here and leave me the hell alone."

He looks hurt, and for a split second I feel bad about what I said, but not bad enough to take it back.

Stepping away from me, he says, "If you need me, I'll be in my yurt."

"Don't worry, I won't need you." And I won't. Hendrix Greer has brought nothing but trouble to my doorstep since he showed up. Life was great before he came back. And right now, I'd do anything to travel back in time and have one more day before that happened. One more day of getting excited for the summer growing season and opening of my new cafe, one more day not knowing my dad was sick and was going to leave us.

Nan comes downstairs while I'm pouring my dad's coffee. She comes over to me and throws her bony arms around me. "I love you, honey. I know this is tough, but life gets that way sometimes. There's nothing you can do but keep going. You hear me?"

"I hear you, Nan." Then a thought hits me. "How did you get here? You're not supposed to be driving."

"Dorcas brought me," she says.

"Where is she?" I ask.

"Don't worry about her. She took an interest in that other nekkid fella. I think she might be trying to make his acquaintance."

And sure enough, after delivering my dad's snack, I walk outside and spot the minister's wife sitting on the porch with Jared Clayton.

Chapter Fifty-Eight
Don't Worry

Dorcas is eyeing Jerry like a Sunday pie. I have never seen her so interested in a member of the opposite sex in my life, and that would include the reverend. It's disconcerting in so many ways. The least of which is the fact that Jerry is half her age.

Dorcas asks, "Do you think you'll be staying for a few days?"

"No, ma'am, I have a meeting in the city tomorrow."

"That's too bad." She looks genuinely disappointed. "Maybe you can come back some time."

I interrupt, "Oh, I think you'll see him again, Mrs. A. Jared here is buying the Greer farm next door."

Rix's friend looks up in shock, "Didn't Rix tell you?"

"Tell me what?" I demand.

"Didn't he tell you that …" he starts to say.

Rix appears freshly dressed from his yurt in time to offer, "Sarah knows everything she needs to know."

"Tell me what?" I repeat only a bit more forcefully.

"Don't worry yourself. I got your message loud and clear in the kitchen. I don't want to burden you with my business."

"Unfortunately, *Hendrix*," I emphasize his full name, "your business affects my business, so if there's something I need to know, you need to tell me."

I turn to Jerry and demand, "Tell me."

He throws his hands up in the air. "Sorry, Sarah, it's not up to me. I think it's best you and Rix work this out for yourselves."

I am so spitting mad that I'm being kept in the dark about whatever is going on next door, I want to punch something, or someone. "Rix, can I see you privately for a moment?" I ask as sweetly as I can muster being that I currently feel as sour as fresh vinegar.

"Why? It's clear you don't want anything to do with me. There's no sense in going somewhere private when I'm not going to tell you anything."

I put my hands on my hips and full-on stamp my foot like a three-year-old who's had her lollipop taken away. My audience appears amused, which makes me even angrier. I turn on my heels and head toward the dandelion field. I think I need to roll for a while.

When I get there, I stop and stare at the beauty in front of me. I love this farm so much. It's part of me. I briefly think about John and feel a sense of rightness that I didn't lead him on. There's no way I'm ever going to leave this land. And anybody I share my life with is going to have to love it as much as I do.

Before I roll, I stand in tree pose for a bit. It helps to center me and brings peace of mind—two things that are sorely lacking in my life right now. Once I feel calmer, I lie on the ground and roll. I roll and roll and roll until I must get two hundred yards from where I started. I inhale the rich aroma of loam and clay in the soil and the woody and pungent scent of crushed dandelions.

I must be outside longer than I realize because when I go back in, I find Nan and Dorcas in the kitchen setting the table for dinner. Nan sees me and declares, "Girl, where've you been? I was getting worried about your daddy not getting his supper, so we got it cooked."

Oh, my gosh, in my pique I totally forgot about dinner. "Thanks, Nan, Mrs. A., I'd better get a tray set up for my parents."

"Don't you fret, honey, I already took care of it. Go wash up and come back," Nan says.

I'm only gone a couple of minutes, but by the time I return, Rix and Jerry are sitting at the table with my friends.

"What are you doing here?" I demand.

Rix serves himself a steak. "Eating my dinner. I believe our deal was for room and board." I look at Jerry and he continues, "I'm sure you don't begrudge my friend a good meal after all the treatments he paid for today."

I cannot sit at this table and pretend I don't want to rip out every last strand of hair from Rix's gorgeous head. I announce, "I'll take my food elsewhere."

I proceed to walk out of the room without my plate and continue through the front door before getting into my truck. I don't know where I'm going, but I know I need to get out of here. Hendrix Greer is making me insane.

I turn on the radio to my favorite station in time to hear Bobby McFerrin sing "Don't Worry, Be Happy." This used to be one of my favorite songs, but at the moment I can't bear to listen to its upbeat, naively positive message. How in the world can I not worry? More importantly, how can I possibly be happy with the state of chaos my life is in?

Chapter Fifty-Nine
Life Will Kick You in the Teeth

I wind up at Rix's grandparents' place like a giant magnet has pulled me in. I sit in my truck for the longest time staring at the old American foursquare farmhouse. It's so solid with its simple lines and stately appeal. It's a lot like my family home, except it doesn't have a large front porch.

I get out of the cab and climb a few steps to the front door when my knees buckle and plain go out from under me. I sit on the steps and let my mind go blank. Then I say out loud, "Mr. Greer, your grandson is a jerk."

I swear I hear his gravelly sounding laughter in my head. Emotionally exhausted, I give in to it. After all, if Terraz can speak to me in my sleep, why the heck can't Mr. Greer talk to me in the light of day? I center myself and focus on the voice I heard. He answers me, "The boy's pretty pig-headed, I'll give you that."

"Are you mad that he's selling your property?" I ask.

"I can't do nothing with it anymore. I had my time and made my choices. It's his turn now."

"But he's going to ruin it. He's going to change it," I say pathetically.

"Sarah, life is about change, you know that. You've never been one to stand in the way of progress."

"How is selling your property progress, sir? It isn't moving things forward, it's moving things backwards."

"How do you figure, girl?" he asks.

"Progress shouldn't hurt the land. It should make it better," I explain.

"That's what you think, huh?"

"That's exactly what I think. What do you think progress is?"

I hear his raspy reply in my ear as surely as if he was sitting next to me. "I don't think progress can be determined on one action alone. I think it's something that's layered up like an onion. Do you know what I'm saying?"

I shake my head. "No, sir, I sure don't."

"Selling this property is only one layer. It's the one that's right in front of your face, so it's the only one you're seeing, but there's more going on than meets the eye."

"I would love to believe that, but I can't see how that's so."

"My grandson is full of pride, Sarah Hastings. He's full of dreams and desires too, but it's the pride that's kicking him around in the dirt right now."

"I don't understand. He's not the one getting kicked. He's the one doing the kicking and I'm the one he keeps practicing on."

"Girl, you smack that boy down every time he tries to get close to you. What do you think that does to him?" he asks.

"I don't care what it does to him. I can't let him get close if he doesn't share my beliefs. What's the point?"

"The point is that sometimes you've got to believe people can change. You've got to believe in your powers of persuasion and encourage that change."

I'm not sure how to respond, but I finally manage, "If I open my heart to Rix, he might crush it. My heart's already breaking, Mr. Greer. My dad is dying. I have to protect whatever part of myself I can because things outside of my control are trying to steal my happiness."

I think of the times that Rix and I have gotten close and I feel a yearning to do what Mr. Greer suggests and trust that he can change. The time Rix kissed me, I thought I'd melt into a puddle. When he learned my father was sick and forced a hug on me that not only held me up but filled me with the belief that I wasn't alone—these are emotions I want to trust.

I would like more than anything to let myself go and believe in Rix, but the nagging thought persists, what if I'm wrong? What if I'm left completely broken and alone? By his own admission, he's only here long enough to sell his land. He can't have any real interest in me if he plans on selling this farm to someone who will in turn pollute my land as well as his own.

"Do you think being alone is the way to keep yourself from hurting?" Mr. Greer asks.

"Maybe," I say.

"I don't think so," he responds. "I think living means taking chances even though things might not work out. Maybe being happy means that sometimes you're unhappy. Life is like country music, girl. It would be nothing without all the highs *and* lows. You can't get your woman back until you lose her. You can't know how wonderful it is to be caught if you won't let yourself fall."

"You're a poet, Mr. Greer." His words are beautiful but I'm not sure they're what I need to hear right now.

"I'm no poet. I'm a man that was lucky enough to live a good, full life. Your daddy and I are a lot alike. That's why we were such good friends. We both know that life kicks you in the teeth sometimes, but even so, you gotta put yourself out there. You gotta be prepared to take a hit or two, if you want the rewards."

"I'm a hard worker, Mr. Greer. I'll work a fifteen-hour day if it needs working. I don't ask anyone to do anything I wouldn't do myself. But I'll tell you the truth, I don't want to live my life on a roller coaster. I want a nice quiet existence that's full of meaningful moments that feed my soul."

"Your soul is starving, girl. You need to get out there and take a chance and really feed it or you're going to wither up."

And then just like that, he's gone, leaving me a whole lot to think about. I can't help but wonder if Mr. Greer was right about my ability to persuade his grandson. I can't help but worry about the vulnerable position I'll be in if I try.

Chapter Sixty
Acceptance

The first thing I plan to do once I get back to my house is check on my parents. Pulling up the drive, I notice that Nan and Dorcas are gone, and Rix and Jerry's cars are parked in front of his yurt. *Good, the house is free of intruders.*

I get out of the car and go inside feeling like the Greek god, Atlas, carrying the weight of the heavens on his shoulders. I'm not sure there's enough yoga in this world to ease my burden.

When I get upstairs, I see that mom is lying in bed next to my dad, reading a book. She notices me and says, "Come on in, honey. Your dad is getting some rest."

He looks even grayer tonight than he did this morning. "He's slept most of the day already. Did he eat?"

"Not much. He ate his whole cookie, though, and declared you the best baker."

He's always done that. Even when I used to pretend to bake him mud pies full of mushrooms and grass. He'd put them up to his mouth and say, "Mmmmmm mmm, my little Sar-bear, you're the best baker in the world!" My heart pings at the memory.

"How's his arm?" I ask.

"Bruised. I'm afraid it took the brunt of his fall. I gave him a couple of painkillers."

My mom scoots toward the middle of the bed to make space for me, so I sit down next to her. "Dad's not going to get better, is he?"

"No, he's not."

"I kept thinking that if he stayed on dialysis, it would give me time to change his mind about letting me help him. I know that's not going to happen."

"Your dad is ready to go, honey. His body is making that possible."

My mom's so elegant lying there with her shoulder-length silver hair. She's always been such a lady. I wonder what in the world she made of me with my constant need to dig in the earth. I was a little heathen and she did nothing but delight in me. She's a wonder.

I finally ask, "Are you ever jealous of them?"

"Who?"

"Dad's first family. Are you ever envious that they got so much of his love?"

She shakes her head. "Not at all. If anything, I'm grateful to them. They taught your dad how wonderful love could be, and they opened his heart to receiving it again. Sometimes ..." she starts to say, but then stops.

"Sometimes, what?" I prompt.

"Sometimes I think Jeannie sent me to your dad."

I've never heard her say this before. "How so?"

"The day I met Kenny I went to the store to get packing tape.

I'd been offered a teaching job in Bloomington, and I thought it might be a good move for me. I mean, there I was in my late thirties and never married. I was like that schoolteacher from *Little House on the Prairie*. And I didn't want to be. I wanted to find someone to share my life with."

Why has she never told me this? Even though I know how the story ends, I'm positively chomping at the bit to hear how she thinks Jeannie was responsible. "And?"

"And I walked by the meat counter and saw a gorgeous pot roast sitting on display and I thought if I'd had a family I could buy that pot roast. It was too big for me alone. But before I could walk away, the butcher said, 'Hey there, Beth, I think this pot roast is calling your name.'"

"He'd never spoken to me before, and I didn't know he knew who I was. Then sure as day, I hear a voice tell me to buy it, so I did. I put it in my cart wondering what in the world I was going to do with such a big chunk of meat. Then I saw a woman I didn't know. She was waving at me from across the store. She waved and waved like she was trying to signal a plane.

"I thought, there's no way she's waving at me, but when I turned around there was no one behind me. I figured, I'd better go over and tell her that she'd mistaken me for someone else. I didn't even see your dad until I rammed my cart into him. Then in a blink, she was standing right there next to me. She smiled as I dropped to my knees to make sure Kenny was okay. She only said one word. 'Stay.'" And I knew in that moment that the pot roast in my cart was for your dad.

"Once I'd made sure I hadn't done any long-term damage to him, I looked for the woman, but I couldn't find her anywhere.

When I checked my groceries out, the clerk said, 'Some lady told me to tell you that his favorite pie is cherry.'"

"Wow." The tiniest touch could have knocked me right over. "Why do you think the woman was Jeannie?"

"When I brought dinner to him that same night, I set the food down in the kitchen, and I swear I knew where everything was. The plates, the silverware, everything. Then when Kenny and I went into the living room after dinner I saw her picture. It was the same gal from the IGA."

I have chills running up my arms. "Why haven't you told me this before?"

"I don't know. I guess maybe because I wanted you to feel secure in your dad's love for me, so I didn't talk to you about Jeannie. But I've always felt that she was my angel, helping me find love and helping your dad rediscover life."

Then my mom takes my hand and squeezes it. "It's time for me to thank her for the wonderful gift she gave me and send her love back to her."

I've never given my dad's first wife much thought. I used to always think about my sisters and I've always felt bonded to them, but in this moment, I feel a flood of love for Jeannie. I believe in angels and goodness, unexpected joy and purpose. I've always felt that I've lived my beliefs, but after bottling up my beliefs so that my father would do dialysis, I've compromised them. And right now, those feelings have been ratcheted up to the moon.

I'm part of a much bigger plan. My family is part of a much bigger plan. And I think I might be ready to accept the fact that I don't need to know what that plan is. I just need to trust it.

Chapter Sixty-One
New Starts

My dad has dialysis this morning, so I make him an extra special breakfast. My mom could use it too, I've noticed her losing weight as well. I figure waffles with fresh fruit and bacon will give them the strength they need. I put everything on a tray and take it up to their room.

Dad is still sleeping when I get there, but Mom is already up and tidying up around him. She's dressed for the day in a pretty pink summer dress. "Morning, Mom, I made waffles."

"Your dad's favorite! Let me give him a little nudge and see if he's ready to eat."

She sits down on the mattress next to him and says, "Honey, you ready for breakfast? Sarah made waffles."

He opens his eyes slowly and a smile comes to his face. "Sounds good, but I'm not hungry quite yet." He looks over at me, "Do you think they'll keep for a bit?"

"I'll reheat them when you're ready. Can I bring you some coffee?"

"Not yet. I need a little more sleep first." And he closes his eyes and drifts off.

I go down to the kitchen and set the table. I expect Rix and Jerry will be up to eat in a few minutes. I leave a note on the counter for them and then take off for the dandelion field for my morning yoga.

It is already warm and muggy, so I know we're in for some hot weather today. I run into Arturo as I walk out the back door. "Hola," I call out.

"Hi, yourself," he says. "Maria made your folks some tortillas. I was going to leave them on the counter for you."

My eyes light up. "The blue ones are my favorite."

"She knows that." Then he asks, "You want the kids picking the strawberries today to bring up any to the cafe for baking?"

"When they sort them for selling, have them bring me the imperfect ones. I'll try to get some freezer jam made." I prefer freezer jam to canning for home use because it doesn't cook out all the nutrients.

"Sounds good," my friend says. "Let me know if we can help with anything. Even if it's not farm related." Then he adds, "It's nice to have your folks home."

"Thank you. It really helps knowing you and Steve are at the helm so I can spend more time with them."

"That's what we're here for, chica."

"There are extra waffles in the oven if you haven't had breakfast yet." He nods his head and walks through the backdoor.

On my way to the dandelion field, I notice that both Rix's and Jerry's cars are gone. They must have left for the city without breakfast. I suddenly feel let down. It's not like I was planning on forgiving Rix totally, but my conversation with his grandfather has been on my mind since yesterday, and I've definitely considered changing my battle plan.

Something is clearly going on between the football player and the owner of the popcorn company, but neither one of them is telling me what it is. Herman's words haunt me. Do I really have what it takes to persuade Rix to keep his land? And if so, how exactly do I go about doing that?

When I get to the field, I'm surprised to find Ethan and Emily already there. "What are you guys doing here?"

Ethan says, "We thought we'd join you this morning, if that's okay?"

"You're always welcome, you know that."

We don't stop to talk because the sun is starting to peek above the horizon and the moment is upon us to welcome a new day. This morning we do ten sun salutations followed by Bird of Paradise pose, which—wait for it—I hold for six minutes! A new record for me. Could this be a sign my fortunes are changing?

After we're done, I invite Ethan and Emily to join me for breakfast. On the way to the house, Ethan says, "We wanted to tell you that we've started dating." Emily is smiling ear to ear.

"Really? When did that happen?" I had a feeling about these two.

"The first morning I joined you for yoga. Emily and I went on a walk later that day and we sort of clicked," Ethan says.

Emily adds, "We've already told Cat. I mean, I know she's moved on with Sam, but being that she and I are working together, we didn't want her to be surprised by our new relationship."

"What did she say?" I ask, even though I know she'll be one hundred percent onboard.

"She's was great," Ethan says. "She said she was happy for us and I know she really is."

I feel a tinge of pride that my farm brought them together. Love really does seem to be in the air. First Cat and Sam, then Ethan and Emily. I have renewed hope that I'll be next. Even though I don't know how it's going to turn out, I decide to open myself up to whatever or whoever comes my way. It's like Herman said, how can I be caught if I won't let myself fall?

Chapter Sixty-Two
When it's Time to Stop

I take my dad's breakfast back up to him, but he's still sleeping. I open the blinds and say, "Hey, sleepy head, it's time to get ready for dialysis."

He stirs slightly and tries to open his eyes but doesn't fully manage it. He whispers, "Honey, I'm not sure I have the energy to go today. Maybe I can miss this one."

The doctors were clear that if he misses even one treatment, it could greatly shorten his life. The balance between the acids and salt in his blood will be disturbed and could lead to heart problems, which could result in sudden death.

I hold my dad's hand and I think back to what my mom said, that he's ready to move on and his body is helping him do so. She's right. My dad has already made his break with this life and all that's holding him back is his last breath. "I think you'll be just fine if you miss a treatment, Dad. Don't you worry about it."

He shifts a bit, and he's immediately back to sleep.

I sit down in the recliner next to the bed and make peace with this moment. Then I eat all the bacon on my dad's breakfast tray.

If ever I've needed comfort, it's now.

My mom is putting bowls of kibble down for the dogs when I walk into the kitchen. She stops to pet them, and they reward her with puppy kisses. She asks me, "Is he ready for me to help him get dressed?"

"He's pretty tired, Mom. He's going to stay in bed and skip his treatment today."

She gasps slightly before nodding her head and smiling. "Good. That's probably for the best. There's nothing like a good rest." She starts to busy herself with the dishes.

I walk up behind her and put my arms around her. "You're an amazing lady, you know that?"

She slumps slightly before straightening her shoulders and joking, "Someone had to teach you, didn't they?"

"Let's plan what we're going to cook for Dad. I want to make sure he gets all his favorites." We make an optimistic list of treats that would fill more days than I fear he has. So, I make sure to prioritize them.

After we're done, my mom says, "I'm going to go sit with him."

My heart feels like it's in a vice that keeps tightening. Even though I'm aware of what's going to happen, part of me still wants to find a way to turn the hourglass over and stop the sands of time.

I don't know what to do with myself. Arturo and Steve are running the farm beautifully, the cafe isn't open, and I have no guests on the property to see to. I start to walk back and forth aimlessly and when the confines of the kitchen get too small, I take my pacing outside.

Before long, I'm running through the corn field. I have no destination in mind, I'm simply running to release the energy bubbling up inside me like a volcano on the precipice of eruption. I can hear my heart pounding in my ears. Faster and faster it goes until it blurs into one long buzzing sound. I don't know how long I run, but I know when enough is enough and I suddenly stop. I turn my face up to the sun and I roar. I roar as loud as I can. Take that, fear! I'm chasing you away.

Every moment of my life, every breath I've ever taken has led me to this moment, on my father's land, raising my fist to fear. "You don't own me!" I scream. "You can't be part of his last days! I renounce you and any hold you have on me!"

Then I fall to the ground and cry. I release every tear and worry in my heart. When I stand up again, I'm a new woman. My old life, the one I've always loved so much, is over. Today is a new day and from this moment on I will face every obstacle with the strength my father gave me.

Dear Universe,

I accept the changes. I accept the passage of time and all that entails. And more than that, I accept that it's my dad's time. Thank you for the gift of his love. Take care of him and love him, honor him, and hold him. I release him to you and your tender care.

Chapter Sixty-Three
New Business

I call the doctor to tell him that Dad is going to stop treatment, and he offers to refer us to hospice.

"What will they do?" I ask.

"They're a wonderful resource. They can provide wheelchairs, hospital beds, they'll bathe him. Anything you need help with."

"Do you really think he has long enough for us to require their services?"

He says, "I think that as long as Kenneth isn't in pain, depending on your support system at home, you probably won't need to avail yourselves of their services for too very long."

"In other words, as long as we can take care of his personal needs, there's really no point."

"Pretty much. But if you need anything, they're definitely worth checking in to."

"Thank you for all you've done." I hang up the phone thinking that my dad's last dialysis treatment was on the day I saw Rix and Jerry at the hospital. Yet another last without my being aware.

The days pass, blurring into one another. My dad rarely gets out of bed.

I haven't seen Rix since the evening of our argument over his farm. He hasn't come back or texted a return date. While I'm curious when that will be, I find that I'm living in altered time. An hour can last a day or a minute. So, I'm not sure what difference it would make if I knew.

My dad barely consumes anything. Both food and water hold little appeal to him. It's already two in the afternoon and he hasn't even woken up yet.

I go and sit out on the front porch to rock away my cares when a truck pulls up the driveway. A man gets out and says, "We have a delivery for your neighbor but they're not home and no one's answering my call."

"Which neighbor?" I ask.

"The Greer farm," he says.

"Do you want me to sign for something?" I ask. I'm not quite sure what he expects me to do.

"No, ma'am, the delivery is too big to leave here. I was hoping you might have some idea where they're at or when they'll be home."

"I sure don't, but I'll be happy to let them know you stopped by."

"Thank you much." Then he tips his hat and leaves.

I spend another hour or six on the porch. I have no idea as the speed of a minute keeps changing.

My mom comes out and says, "Dad's up. He wants to talk to you."

I jump to my feet. "Did he eat?" When she shakes her head,

I want to know, "Did he drink anything?"

"He had about six ounces of water." Even though he's supposed to limit his fluid intake, he still needs water to survive, so I'm happy to hear this.

I run up the stairs and find him propped up on several pillows. "Hey, stranger," I greet. "It's nice to see you awake."

"What time is it?" he asks.

"It's after two," I answer. "Are you hungry? Can I make you something?"

"No, honey. Come sit down by me, okay?" Once I do, he says, "Thank you."

I know he's thanking me for letting him stop dialysis. He's already missed three appointments. "You're welcome."

"Sarah, you need to know how very proud I am of you. Not only are you dedicated to this land, but you've changed it for the better. You've made your dreams a reality and you're making the world a better place as a result. You're an amazing woman, and it humbles me that I got to be your daddy."

I know he's proud of me, but to hear him say it out loud is quite moving. He's not done, though. "I'm leaving the farm to you, honey. Your mom may want to spend more time here than we have in last several years, but I'm turning over the title to you."

"Thank you, Dad. I'll do my best to keep making you proud."

"I know you will. You should know that I've recently made a business deal. I don't want you to be blindsided by it."

"What kind of business deal?" I ask, surprised. My dad hasn't had anything to do with the farm in years.

"I've leased out the back forty, the part of the property you don't use. I figure the money will help you implement some of the other changes you want to make."

"To whom?" Now I'm really alarmed.

"To the new owner of the Greer farm."

"Oh, Dad, what have you done? I was going to have to move some of my current operation out there when Happy Corn! moved in so that I could leave a big enough border to absorb all the chemicals they're going to spray."

I can see my dad is fighting to stay awake, but I'm so shaken up right now I can't let this go. "Why didn't you talk to me first?"

He takes my hand in his and I'm shocked by how cold it is. "Sar-bear, have I ever led you astray?"

I shake my head, so he continues, "Then trust me on this, okay? I promise it's a good business move as well as a good move for the farm. I wouldn't betray you or the land."

"Why can't you tell me about it now?" I demand.

"I'll tell you when I get up from my nap, honey."

"I love you, Dad."

"I love you too, honey." And then he falls back to sleep.

I need to see Rix more than ever and find out what he had to do with this. I can't imagine that my dad would have gone into business with Jared Clayton without Rix's interference. How dare he prey on my sick father? How dare he make things worse than they already are?

Chapter Sixty-Four
Do Something Life Affirming

I never do get to talk to my dad again. He dies peacefully in his sleep sometime after four o'clock. Another last. My mom had gone up to take a nap with him. When I hear her cry out, I know.

I go up to their room and find her curled up next to him with her arms around his very still body. She says, "I love you, Kenny. I love you so, so much. You go on home to Jeannie and the girls. They'll take good care of you." Then she lays her head on his chest and cries.

I walk out of the room. This is their moment, their time to say goodbye. I leave them alone and go back to the kitchen, unsure of what to do. I'm relieved my dad is finally free of his illness. In my mind's eye, I see him young again, laughing and running joyfully in the fields. As sad as I am for Mom and me, I'm happy for him.

I pick up the phone and call Cat. All I say is, "He's gone."

"Oh, Sarah, I'm so sorry. I'm so, so sorry. Do you want me to come over? Can I bring you something?"

"Not yet. It only just happened. Mom doesn't even know I know. We're going to need some time." Then I say quietly, "I needed to tell someone."

"I love you, my friend. I'm going to call you in a couple hours to check in, okay?" she says.

"Okay. Meanwhile, could you start getting the word out. I don't think either Mom or I are going to be quite up to it today. Just let people know. We still need some time alone."

"Will do. I'm here if you need me."

I hang up the phone. I'll make tea, that's what I'll do. Once the tea has been made, I go check on my mom and find her sound asleep next to my dad. I don't wake her.

Instead I go back downstairs and run into Nan. "Nan, what are you doing here?"

"I came as soon as I heard." She throws her bony arms around me and holds on tight. I'm not sure how she got here so quickly unless she was driving past when Cat called her.

"I told Cat not to come yet," I say while hugging her back.

"Good, this is no time to be entertaining." She doesn't seem to see the irony of her being here.

"Then why are you here?"

"Girl, you don't have to entertain me. I'm here to help."

"How so?" I ask.

"Well, for one thing, I brought a pie. Pie always helps at a time like this." I smile despite the emptiness that fills me. "For another thing, I brought Dorcas and you know she's mighty useful with a prayer."

"Where is she?"

"In the kitchen eating pie," Nan says.

"My mom is upstairs with my dad right now. I want to give them their time."

"Absolutely. I kept Hugh home with me for the full legal

twenty-four hours after he passed. We had an old-fashioned wake at home, letting folks come and say their farewells."

"I didn't even think about how long we could keep him home. It's good to know we have some time to work things out."

"Honey, I'm a veteran of this war. I know the ins and outs. That's another way I'm useful."

"Okay, Nan, what do I do first?"

"First, you eat pie. Follow me." And I do.

We find Dorcas at the table, licking her plate. She's horrified to be discovered in such a compromising position and immediately drops her dish. Then she jumps up and hugs me. "Sarah, I'm so sorry for your loss. But you know Kenny was ready to go."

"That's true," Nan says. "We have to put this into perspective. It's not a tragedy like when Julia passed in *Steel Magnolias*. It's a normal thing to have happen at our age."

"Well," Dorcas says, "Kenny had a few years on us. I'm not ready to go quite yet."

"But you could," Nan tells her. "It could happen for either one of us any day now, and it wouldn't be entirely unexpected."

Her friend declares, "But it's not going to …"

Nan rolls her eyes. "Go lick a plate, Dorcas. I need to give Sarah here some pointers on what happens next."

She pushes me down onto a chair and puts nearly a quarter of the pie on the plate in front of me. She says, "When someone dies, it's always good to do something life affirming. You know, something that makes you realize you didn't die, too."

"What are you suggesting, Nan?"

She wipes her mouth primly. "I've always found that sex works the best."

Chapter Sixty-Five
Sex, Really?

"Sex?" I'm totally shocked. "Nan, the last thing on my mind is sex!"

She pats my shoulder. "I know what I'm talking about, honey. Trust me."

I have no idea how to respond, so I try to take her mind off carnal pursuits. "Would you mind making some more pies? It'd be nice to have something to offer folks when they come over to pay their respects."

Nan's eyes brighten. "Sure as shootin', I'm on it." She jumps up and gets busy pulling stuff out of the pantry. Dorcas joins her.

I go back upstairs and check on my mom, but she's still holding my dad. I look at them with borderline longing. My parents have spent thirty-five years of their lives together. They brought a child into this world. They've grown into one being instead of two. I take a mental picture so I can revisit this moment often. Then I quietly close the door so all of Nan's and Dorcas's banging won't wake up my mom.

Instead of joining my older friends in the kitchen, I let myself out the front door. I need to walk. I'm not sure where I'm going, but I'm highly motivated to get there. Putting one foot in front of the other, I start to trek down the driveway. I pass the yurts and feel like I might keep going until I circle the globe and walk through the backdoor.

I haven't cried yet. I've done so much crying since my parents came home, I wonder if I'm hydrated enough to even make tears. I walk right past the farm stand, giving my helpers a small wave, but I don't stop to say anything.

I just move with my eyes on the horizon, like it holds the answers to all the questions swirling in my head. What now? How am I supposed to live as half an orphan? Who will talk to me about the soil? Who will listen to all my crazy dreams and tell me they're not crazy?

I get a couple miles down Highway 47 toward town before I wonder what the heck I'm doing. I don't have my phone or wallet on me. Not that I want to call anyone or buy anything, it just doesn't seem prudent to be wandering down the highway without either of those things.

I stop dead in my tracks and stand there for ages, stupefied, until I see a black sports car barreling down the road at me. I watch it like I'm not even in my skin anymore. I'm hovering somewhere slightly above myself and off to the right a bit. If it hits me, I can be with my dad. There's no downside to dying. My life is three dimensional in a way I've never experienced before.

I focus on my impending doom in the form of German technology and dare it to hit me, but it doesn't. Instead, it slows down until comes to halt maybe ten feet from me. Chicken.

Rix gets out of the driver's side and doesn't even close the door. He stares for a couple of seconds, probably trying to convince himself it's really me before he runs toward me. Nan's words start to play on a loop in my head, "You need to do something life affirming ... life affirming ... life affirming ..."

When he stops in front of me with confusion, concern, and something undefinable in his eyes, I decide to follow her advice and affirm my life by throwing myself into his arms. He welcomes me without hesitation.

Suddenly holding him isn't enough. I want to crawl inside his skin and become one with his warmth and strength. I want to shed my own skin and let him absorb me, so I don't have to feel. I can't do this with just an embrace.

I reach up and pull his face down to my own, attaching my mouth to his like I'm trying to inhale him. His lips are soft and firm and hungry. His breath is as tempting as a cinnamon bun fresh out of the oven and I devour it with the same dedication.

Rix doesn't question my sudden aggressiveness; he gives me what I want. Our kiss is like nothing I've ever experienced before. It transcends mere attraction. It's everything I've ever wanted, everything I've ever missed in my life. It's coming home. Damn. Nan is just as smart as she thinks she is.

We kiss for minutes, hours, days, they all blur together. We consume each other like we've been waiting to do this our whole lives. We don't stop until a truck passes by and the driver lays on his horn in approval. The sound is enough to catapult me back into my body. I try to catch my breath as I distance myself from him slightly.

The look on his face is one of pure confusion. "Sarah," he says like I've just come back from the dead myself, like I'm an apparition he's laying eyes on for the first time in years. "Are you okay?"

Moments after my dad leaves this earth, I've been reborn to it. I shake my head, then nod, before answering, "No ... yes ... I'm not myself."

"I can see that. What are you doing out here?" He looks around. "Did your truck break down?"

"My dad just died."

"Oh, honey," he says pulling me back into his arms. "I'm sorry I wasn't here."

I mumble into his shirt, "You're here now. That's something."

"Yes, ma'am, I'm here now." And he holds me so close I feel like I really might be able to sink into this man and let his strength help hold me up.

Chapter Sixty-Six
Time to go Home

By the time we pull back into the driveway, there are three more cars parked there. I couldn't have been gone more than a half hour or so, but word travels. Especially when it's news of this magnitude.

I jump out of the car, Rix is close on my heels. "Why in the world would people show up so soon?" I demand.

"I'm willing to bet the ones who've come are the ones who love you the most. They're here to support you." That's when I look to see if I recognize the vehicles. Cat's here and so are her parents, and Emily. Okay, that's okay. These are my people. They really do belong here.

Cat is the first to greet us when we walk in. "Oh, Sar, I'm so sorry. I tried to keep my parents from coming, but once Nan said she was already here, there was no holding them back."

"I'm glad you're here. You're my family."

I give her a brief hug, but before I run into anyone else, I need to check on my mom.

When I open the door to her room, I find her giving my dad a sponge bath. She's washing his arms and his hands before moving to his face. She doesn't turn, but she knows I'm there. "Daddy's gone, honey. He's at peace now."

I walk over to her and touch her shoulder. "I love you, Mom."

"I love you, too. So does Dad."

"Can I help?" I ask, unsure of what else to say. Words don't seem powerful enough to convey the emotion filling this room.

My mom hands me a pair of nail clippers. "Kenny's nails have gotten long. Can you trim them up a bit?"

Washing the dead is an ancient custom practiced by many religions. As we care for my dad, I feel like we're doing something sacred, like we're washing away the very things that took him from us. We're preparing him to start the next leg of his journey fresh. Even though the body doesn't travel with him, cleaning it is symbolic and respectful. It's an important part of grieving. We tend to him with all of our love and gratitude.

My mom says, "Your dad is such a handsome man, isn't he? I thought that the first day I met him, and I've thought it every day that we were together. He's the most handsome man I've ever seen. So tall, and strong, so kind and caring. And he was mine. How lucky am I?"

"You were so lucky, Mom. We both were. We both are."

"Jeannie came to me in my sleep last night," she says.

"Really? What did she say?"

"She said, 'Beth, you've done well by our husband and I thank you. The girls and I have come to welcome him home, and we'll be here for you when it's your time. We're all family. We always will be.'"

Those tears I wondered if I could still make, they're pouring down my cheeks like I'm trying to put out a fire. They just fall and fall and fall, like my head is filled with rain clouds.

My mom stands up and turns to me before opening her arms. "Oh, baby," she croons. "This is life. The one thing that's certain when we come into this world is that we're going to leave it someday. And your dad, he led the most beautiful life. Even his death was beautiful."

I let her hold me while I soak her shoulder with my grief. "I'll never hear his voice again," I whimper.

"Of course, you will. You'll hear it all the time. Daddy's going to whisper in your ear until the day you die. Then he'll shout in joy when it's your time and you're reunited in spirit. He's bigger than a mere body."

I know these things. I believe them, but right now at this moment I'm floundering. "What do we do now?"

"We go downstairs, and we grieve with our friends. We let them comfort us and we comfort them. We lean on each other and keep this house of cards from falling down." She reaches out and takes my hand, "We'll do it together, honey."

I take her hand and let her pull me out of the room. "Nan made pie," I say.

My mom nods her head, "Of course, she did." I can't see her face, but I know she's smiling.

Chapter Sixty-Seven
Istanbul, not Constantinople

The days that follow are an odd combination of pea soup fuzziness and bionic clarity. Some moments are just that, tiny blips destined to come and go without leaving so much as a footprint in their wake. While others are so blatantly pristine, they will be etched in my memory for a lifetime.

Scottie comes back, saddened that he missed saying goodbye to my dad. His presence helps fill some of the empty space. In times of illness and death, you really find out who your tribe is, and Scottie jumps right in and fills the position of a brother.

Rix becomes part of our group like he's always been a central figure. He makes coffee and washes dishes, he talks to everyone and listens interestedly while they share memories of my dad, he even shares one of his own.

"My grandfather and Kenny were friends since they were in diapers. They taught me how to shoe a horse and shear a goat. They also taught me how to drink beer while burping the alphabet." Classy, but these were lifelong farm boys, they knew how to have fun without taking things too seriously.

"On my twenty-first birthday, they took me to the brew pub

and told me it was time to learn how to drink like a real man. Grandpa ordered a pitcher of beer and Kenny ordered three shots of whiskey. I thought we were in for a wild night of carousing. But before the waitress could leave, Grandpa asked for a glass of milk and Kenny ordered a diet soda.

"When I asked what heck that was about. Grandpa said, 'I'm nursing a new ulcer, son. Your grandma will kill me dead if I come home smelling like beer.'

"Kenny said, "I've put on a couple pounds lately due to all those pies Sarah's been making. If I don't cut back somewhere, I'm going to bust out of my new jeans.'

"I sat there stunned and said, 'Milk and diet soda? That's how real men drink?'

"Grandpa said, 'Real men with good women taking care of them.'"

My mom's face is luminous. "Kenny never could resist Sarah's pie."

"It's mighty fine pie," Rix adds, his meaning vastly different.

Nan shares that she and Dad went on one date in high school. "Our families were always friends, so when that boy asked me out, I figured why not? But he was seventeen and I was fourteen which is a big separation of years at that age. So, when he leaned in and kissed me, I freaked out and threw potato salad on him. We agreed from that point on that we were destined for friendship alone."

Cat's father Dougal says, "Kenny taught me how to cheat at horseshoes."

"What?" I gasp. "My dad wasn't a cheater! He was just really good at horseshoes."

My mom laughs, "Oh, honey, your dad was a fine gentleman. He believed in truth and honesty, but in the end, he was still a man." Then she adds, "And a horseshoe cheat to boot."

"How in the world do you cheat at horseshoes?" I demand.

"You remember that year you and I made all those magnets to sell for your school fundraiser?" Do I ever! We made over two hundred of them to raise money for my class trip to Washington, DC.

"That's when Kenny discovered magnetic tape. He took off with a roll and started practicing. He found out that if he lined his horseshoes with it, and could get them close enough to the pole, they'd get drawn right in."

"That's why he always brought his own horseshoes?" I ask.

My mom nods. "That's why. He wouldn't let anyone else use them, claiming they wouldn't be lucky for him anymore if he shared."

I don't know what to say. This news makes my dad so much more human and funnier than I already knew him to be. I wish I'd have known, so I could have teased him about it.

My mom begins the business of planning my dad's funeral. She declares, "We'll start out at church and then we're going to have a party, just like Kenny always wanted."

"We'll have it in my barn," Cat offers.

***

That's how we came to have the very best send-off a man could ever hope for. It's a potluck and I swear, nearly everyone in town brings at least one dish they're known for. We have more ambrosia salad than the Union army could have eaten in a month. Yet, miraculously we still go through it all.

Rix drives us from the church to the Masterton farm. When we get there, Wild Pig has already set up and they've brought their full contingent. There are drums, a steel guitar, a bass, an accordion, a fiddle, and some instrument they've jury-rigged together that has four different horns attached to it.

When they see my mom walk in, they start to play "Istanbul, Not Constantinople," which is the very first song my parents ever danced to together. The music is upbeat and sassy and begs your body to move along with it. We give Rix our purses and Mom and I hit the dance floor and celebrate my dad's life.

We dance for hours until we feel drunk on rhythm alone—although a jug or two does get passed that neither Mom nor I shy away from. I dance with Rix, Scottie, Ethan, Sam, and Cat's dad. Then I dance with all the ladies. We cut a rug to "Turkey in the Straw," we sing at the top of our lungs to "Buffalo Gals," and we waltz to "Girl in the Blue Velvet Band." One song leads into the next like a string of beads so beautiful you'd think angels had strung it.

Hours pass and not one tear falls. Dad's getting his last party and it's a humdinger.

Chapter Sixty-Eight
Let's Walk

It isn't until two days after my dad's funeral that I remember I'm mad at Rix. I'm sitting on the front porch when he comes out of his yurt waving like he can't wait to see me.

He's somewhat surprised when I greet his kiss with a, "How DARE you?"

He jumps back and says, "I'm sorry. I thought we were kissing now."

"Not that, you moron. How dare you talk my dad into leasing out our back forty to Happy Corn!? You know they're going to ruin that land, and not only are you okay with that, but now you're going to let them ruin my land, too!"

Rix scoots me over and sits down on the porch swing next to me. "Your dad told you, huh?"

"Of course, he told me. I'm his daughter."

"It seems he didn't tell you everything, though."

"He was going to. He just got tired and wanted to nap first." Rix raises his eyebrow as if to ask why he didn't tell me afterward, so I say, "He died in his sleep."

"Well, then ..." he starts. "It seems that you need to hear the rest of the story before you tear into me."

I scoot over putting more distance between us. "Fine, what's the story?"

"I think I need to take you next door to explain it properly."

"Why can't you tell me right here?" I demand.

He stands up and reaches out to take my hand. After he pulls me up, I try to let it go, but he won't let me. "Let's walk through the corn field."

"Rix, you're delaying and I'm mad, let's drive."

"I don't think so; I think we should walk." He drags me along in his wake. When we get into the field, he asks, "What kind of corn do you grow?"

I begrudgingly answer, "Mostly sweet corn and flint corn."

"The sweet corn for eating fresh and freezing, right?"

"Yes. Why do you care?" I demand.

He ignores me. "And the flint corn?"

"For grinding into meal and feed."

"Okay," he says, "What kind of corn is this?" he asks, while grabbing a leaf as we pass. "Sweet or flint?"

"Sweet. Rix, where are you going with this?" I've rounded the bend on being annoyed and am veering into a whole minefield of mad.

"Good, so the corn bordering my grandpa's property is flint, right?"

"Yessssssss," I hiss.

"Okay." He doesn't say anything else, he just picks up his pace until I'm running after him.

"Why do you care?" I demand.

"Because sweet corn will cross-pollinate with popping corn

and affect the outcome of the product."

Oh, no, he didn't. "I don't care what happens to Happy Corn's! crop. In fact, now that I know that, I'm going to plant sweet corn on the border of our property. What do you think of that?"

He clucks his tongue. "That doesn't sound very nice, Sarah," he admonishes me.

"Why would I want to be nice about this? What do I stand to gain by being nice?"

"I thought you were more socially conscious than to care about your gain alone?"

"Rix, what are you talking about?"

"You'll see," he says mysteriously. "Tell me when we hit the flint corn, okay?"

I don't answer him. I'm liable to pull out a stalk and beat him over the head with it when we hit the flint corn. But I don't. I just walk quietly behind him and say "here" when we pass.

"How can you tell?" he asks.

"I thought you grew up out here, Rix. How is it you don't know?"

"My grandpa only grew sweet corn. He traded with your dad for feed."

"Fine. Sweet corn tends to be a little shorter and the corn silk is slightly lighter in color."

He nods his head and drops a bomb. "I've signed on with Happy Corn! to be their spokesperson."

I knew he was in negotiations, but I thought I still had time to talk him out of it. But then my dad died, and I got sidetracked. Suddenly I feel so deflated I can hardly move. "Rix, why are you doing this?"

"Progress. Also, you should know that I've not only signed on to represent them, I'm going into partnership with them."

I have no words. This man who's been so lovely and wonderful these last few days, the same one I've kissed and cuddled, the one who tells wonderful stories about my dad, is no more than a wolf in sheep's clothing. He's the enemy.

Chapter Sixty-Eight
Just Let me Show You the Bedrooms

I immediately notice how much work has been done on the farmhouse as I stomp out of the field. It's been freshly painted a bright white with rich, glossy black shutters. Rix says, "I'm going to put in window boxes and fill them with flowers to make it feel homier."

"I'm sure Happy Corn! will appreciate all your efforts," I snap.

"I'm not doing it for them, I'm doing it for me."

"You? Why, do you plan on driving down from Chicago to help supervise their operation?"

He shakes his head. "No, ma'am, I plan on living here."

He can't mean it. There is no way I want Hendrix Greer living next door to me now. I could make sure I never had to work the field that bordered our properties, but just knowing he was so close by is sure to mess with my head something fierce. Also, I'm bound to run into him in town. I don't want him living anywhere near Gelson.

"What do you mean, you're living here? You just sold the place to Happy Corn!"

"No, I didn't."

He's going to drive me insane. "You said you signed on as their spokesperson and were going to partner with them."

"That's right, I am. But I decided it would be more beneficial for me to keep my land. So, I'm going to lease it to Happy Corn!"

"I thought you liked the big city with your lake view," I accuse.

"Oh, I'm keeping my place in the city. I'll spend time there in the winter when it's too cold to do any farming." Great, he's just going to ruin my summers, not my whole year.

He climbs up on the porch and says, "Let me show you what I've had done to the inside."

"I don't want to go inside your house," I say petulantly.

"I'm not going to tell you what we plan to do with your property until you do."

I roll my eyes and huff, "Fine, but this is pointless."

As soon as we walk through the front door, I'm positively blown away by the beauty of the room. All of the hardwood flooring has been refinished. The walls have been painted in a neutral shade with an underlying hint of green, almost a pale celery color. It warms the space and makes it feel cozy even though there isn't any furniture.

"Very nice," I say sarcastically. "Now tell me the rest."

"No, no, no, no, the tour has just begun," he declares. "Follow me."

I follow him into the kitchen and am stunned at the simplistic, sleek beauty of it. Everything has been renovated.

There are new countertops, new flooring, a new farmhouse sink that looks big enough to bathe a baby elephant. New cabinets and lighting make it look like it's fresh out of a designer showroom. There's even a huge island with enough stools around it to feed a small army. He opens up a drawer and pulls out an envelope that he puts in his shirt pocket.

"How did you get this all done in such a short time?" I demand.

"Money. It comes in handy, you know."

He moves on to show me the dining room and the family room before heading upstairs. I say, "I'm sure I don't need to see the bedrooms, Rix." Please, as if they're any of my business.

"But I want you to see them," he says a hint too flirtatiously.

"We have five." He opens the first door, "This is the master bedroom." We walk in and it's nothing you'd expect given the expense of the downstairs renovation. There's new carpeting and freshly painted walls, but instead of expensive furnishings making it look like a suite in a fancy hotel, there are four sets of bunk beds with three mattresses each. So essentially, enough room to sleep twelve.

He walks out of the room and I follow, my mind racing with questions. I see three more smaller rooms that each have two sets of double bunk beds, sleeping a total of another twelve. The final room has one king-sized bed in it with a sturdy chest of drawers next to it. "This is my room," he says.

I stare at him like he's grown a second nose. "You're planning on having twenty-four children? Your poor wife!"

Rix laughs. "No, I'm pretty sure three or four is all I can handle."

"I see, so you're planning on letting them have a lot of sleep overs?"

He shrugs his shoulders. "I guess if they want to."

"Rix, are you going to tell me why there are so many beds in this house?"

"Eventually," he says. "Follow me."

This time we go downstairs into the basement where there's a commercial-looking kitchen and a big space that would be perfect for a game room. "Why another kitchen?" I ask.

"Twenty-five people is a lot of people to feed. We might need the extra work room."

"*Twenty-five* people? Are you planning on eating out while your wife feeds everyone?"

"No, ma'am. As I don't have a wife yet, it'll just be me."

"And your twenty-four kids?" I ask incredulously. "How do you plan on getting all those kids without a wife? Are you going to start your own harem?"

He has the nerve to wink at me. "Now, there's a thought. Alas, I've always been the monogamous type, so I can't see it being a very successful harem."

"Rix, what's going here?" I demand. I've had just about enough of his games. He needs to come clean or I'm going home.

"I'm almost ready to tell you. Just follow me." This time I follow him up the stairs and out the back door where he seems to have built himself a playground. There are swings, a slide, even a jungle gym. Next to that there's a small basketball court with two hoops.

"There's no way you've done this all without the whole town buzzing about it. You can't even get a new car in Gelson without it being broadcast in the local paper. How did you manage to keep this quiet?"

"We live out in the country, Sarah. Trucks go by here all the time. Most of my furnishings were delivered from Champaign or Chicago. My workers came from there as well."

"Why wouldn't you use local folks, if you're planning on living here? That doesn't seem very neighborly."

"I agree. But I'm worried folks might not like what I'm doing here, and I want to make sure I explain it to them properly, so they don't get themselves all bunched up about it."

"Well, what are you planning?"

"I'm opening up a camp for the kids at Greer House. I'm going to break them up in groups and have them out here to spend a week to learn the farming business. I figure most of them aren't going to be professional athletes or business tycoons, but this way they get to see another way of life. They could grow up to do something honorable like farming."

My mouth opens and closes, but no words come out. This is a wonderful idea and I'm delighted he's going to do this, but no matter how good of a thing this is for inner city kids, he's still going into partnership with the devil and planning on ruining my land. And that I just can't condone.

Chapter Sixty-Nine
Finally!

"This is a big undertaking, Rix," I say. "Are you sure you're up for it?"

"Not alone. One of the bedrooms will be used to house staff. They'll be responsible for teaching the kids how to cook and clean up after themselves. The basement kitchen will be used to teach them how to can and preserve food."

"How are you going to afford that?"

"Happy Corn! is going to take care of it. Jerry likes to give back, but he also likes a healthy tax deduction."

"How in the world can Jared Clayton be so community minded and still have such archaic farming practices?" I demand.

"First of all, GMOs and pesticides aren't considered archaic, they're considered progress." Before I can interrupt, he adds, "Secondly, I've convinced Jerry to try his hand at an organic line of popcorn. He's been interested in experimenting with it on a small scale but hasn't been successful in finding a property that hasn't used GMOs or non-organic fertilizers in the last three years. Without that he can't get organic certification."

I've had one too many shocks today. My legs go right out from under me until I'm sitting flat on my butt in Rix's playground. "You mean, you're planting organic corn on my back forty?"

"That's what I'm saying."

"And you're not going to spray chemicals and pesticides."

"We are not."

"And you're going to do all that and move back to Gelson during the summer?"

"Yup," he declares.

I very contritely say, "I owe you a huge apology."

"You do."

"Rix, I'm very sorry. I can't thank you enough for what you're doing." Then I ask, "What made you change your mind?"

"I've been having these crazy dreams ever since I've come back to Gelson."

"Really? Like what?"

"My grandfather always comes to me and says the same thing. He says, 'Son, you can have nothing or you can have everything. If you take the easy way, you've got nothing. The hard path is the way to everything.'"

"Wow. That's pretty incredible. What's even more incredible is that you're listening to him."

Rix pulls the envelope out of his pocket, and hands it to me. My name is written on the front in unfamiliar handwriting. I open it and read:

Dear Sarah,

I've always loved our conversations about the land and hearing about your dreams for it. I decided to give you six years to make those dreams come true. Should they decide not to keep the property for themselves, my family has been instructed to give you the first option to buy my farm. Good luck, young lady. Keep believing in progress.

Fondly,

Herman Greer

Rix smiles beautifully and says, "Turns out you're the reason we couldn't sell before now. Grandpa was giving you time and letting the ground rest so it could be certified organic."

"And you decided to stay and not sell after all," I say, full of wonder.

"I knew the day I saw you dancing around your dandelions with Nan and Dorcas that you were someone special. I figured it would be worth sticking around for a while to see how special."

"Thank you," I say again right before I launch myself into his arms. I tackle Rix to the ground and show him just how grateful I am that he came into my life.

Dear Universe,

Finally! It's not that I really doubted you, but it took you long enough. Even though I lost my dad, maybe I should rephrase that ... even though my dad moved on to a new life, I've still met some wonderful men and had some great experiences. Just so you know, I'm still going to need your help guiding me into the next part of my journey. But, oh boy, I'm pretty darned jazzed about it.

Chapter Seventy
Falling Together

Rix meets me in the barn at five thirty a.m., sharp. He's wearing his pajama pants and a pair of flip flops, nothing else. I could stare at the impressive sight of his chiseled glory for hours. "Good morning," he greets before gently taking my face in his hands.

He holds me still while he gazes deeply into my eyes. Returning to his roots has brought Rix a sense of belonging in a way he claims to have never felt elsewhere. Without words, he conveys every feeling in his heart, and I respond with my own silent confession. I've met my other half, and it just so happens it's the boy I've been pining for since my adolescence.

The only way for us to make it as a couple is for Rix to embrace my way of life with his whole heart. The fact that he's cultivating his land organically is a testament to his commitment to a new lifestyle and to me. The fact that he's using his home to help those in need is evidence that he believes in the need to share our bounty. To promote what we do to the next generation will keep our way of life flourishing. The gift Rix is giving me is one that I cherish beyond words. His growth is my growth, my healing.

In return, I offer him loving arms to hold him, willing ears to hear him, and a peaceful and gentle center to help ground him. I will share every gift at my disposal unreservedly and without fear.

Rix's grandfather's words haunt me, "How can you be caught if you won't let yourself fall?" I've chosen to embrace them and have opened myself up so completely that I'm holding nothing back. I'm no longer afraid. I've faced fear and I've chased it away with my strength. I now offer that strength to Rix as we step into the future together.

He tentatively runs his fingers through my hair as I wrap my arms around his neck. I impatiently pull him down to meet my mouth. Chills of anticipation start at my toes and shoot straight to my scalp where his fingers have begun to massage me. I'm addicted to this man like he's bacon. I don't think I'll ever be able to get enough of him.

His lips are soft and firm, and I swear I can taste the future in his kiss, and it's delicious. When we finally pull apart, we're both breathing heavily like we've just climbed a mountain. His muscular arms around me feel like heaven, but it's the promise I feel in them, the security of knowing that this is where I belong, that makes me understand the depth of the gift the universe has given to me.

"Good morning to you," I finally purr in return. "Did you sleep well?"

He tilts his head to the side and bestows a mischievous grin upon me. "I dreamed about you all night. I almost broke into your house to get you."

"That wouldn't have required a great deal of breaking. As you know, I don't lock the doors."

He smacks his forehead. "I plumb forgot! But now that I've been reminded ..." he lets the rest of his thought hang in the air like a tantalizing threat.

"When are you moving over to your grandparents' house?" I ask.

"Are you trying to get rid of me, woman?"

I shake my head slowly. "No, sir. In fact, I was going to give you Yurt Number One as a gift. I like having you in the yurt closest to the house," I flirtatiously remind him of why he chose those particular lodgings.

"I'd rather be *in* the house," he drawls wickedly.

"About that, my mom is still here, so I don't think the fruition of that particular dream is in your near future." Then I bestow a bawdy wink. "You ready to go?"

He takes my hand in his, and it's all I can do not to jump back into his arms. Rix and I fit in a way I would have never thought possible. On the outside we're so different. Up until this point, his life was full of bright lights and glamour. Mine was full with quiet moments and dirt under my fingernails. Yet here we are. The boy I had longed to have notice me in my youth is walking next to me in peaceful camaraderie, like he's finally where he belongs—at my side.

When you grow up on a farm, there's no denying that history, and our shared history is rich. I can feel his grandfather and my father's happiness surrounding us. It's part of us as surely as if it's woven into our DNA.

Rix's farm boy childhood is coming back to him more and more every day. He follows me around learning the ways of organic farming in preparation for the part he'll play in Happy Corn!'s new venture.

I teach him how to mix fertilizers out of bone meal and kelp. I teach him which plants respond best to which animal manures, and I show him how to bury coffee grounds next to the blueberry bushes to increase the acidity in the soil. I share all of my knowledge in the hopes it will bind him to the earth even more.

Once we hit the dandelion field, we reluctantly let go of each other and face the dawn. We begin our series of sun salutations. Just us, the earth, the sun, the dandelions, all doing what we were meant to be doing in perfect harmony. When we finish ten series of poses, I ask, "What do you want to do now? You want to go in for breakfast?"

Rix shakes his head slowly. Then he sits down on the ground. "No, ma'am. I'm not hungry for food." He reaches his hand out to me. "Come here."

I sit down next to him and he shakes his head again. "Not over there. Come sit on my lap."

Oh my, this day is starting out promising. I straddle Rix's lap and feel the certainty that I never want to be anywhere else. I lower my mouth to his and show him how he makes me feel. I inhale his breath into my body, and I feel whole.

After several minutes of a truly blissful connection, he pulls back. "Miss Sarah, I'm about to do something very naughty if we don't stop this right now."

"How naughty?" I tease.

"Naughty enough that you'd be beet red for a week if either Arturo or Steve came upon us unexpectedly."

"Promises, promises," I reply. Then I move to stand up, but he stops me.

Rix lays flat on his back, pulling me with him and says, "Roll with me."

"Really?" I ask delightedly.

"Really. It's time I learn why you love doing this so much."

"Okay," I say, certain that I'm going to convince him to become a devoted dandelion roller. "First thing you do is put your hands up over your head like this." I cross my wrists before clasping my hands together. "Then you cross your ankles and you just roll." I take off to illustrate the motion.

I hear him grunt as he launches himself right before making a spitting sound. "I think I just ate a bug!" he yells.

"Then keep your mouth closed," I respond. But I wind up saying it through laughter as the sheer joy of rolling in the dandelions with Rix Greer nearly overpowers me. The feeling of the earth beneath me, the smell of the dandelions around me, and the knowledge that I'm doing this with the boy next door is the most divine combination in the whole world.

Epilogue
Opening Day

Today is the official opening of *Eat Me!* I'm a couple months behind schedule, but it's the first of August, and I figure I'll stay open through the end of September. There should still be enough harvest to sustain a smaller menu.

I've rebooked the yurt reservations that I canceled. Mom is going to stay with me at least through Christmas while she adjusts to her new life without Dad. So far, she's been stronger than I could have ever imagined. Her acceptance and composure have been humbling.

The puppies rarely leave her side. It's like they've adopted her as their cause. As strange as it sounds, I feel like Dad is reaching out to her through them.

Maria is in the cafe when I get there. "When did you arrive?"

"About an hour ago, chica. I want to make sure we have enough different kinds of tortillas, so everyone gets what they want."

I put on my apron. "I better get started on the muffins." I jump right in and totally lose track of time. An hour goes by when Rix opens the door and announces, "I need some coffee, woman! What do you have?"

I give him a long, lingering kiss before answering, "I've got dandelion and I've got dandelion with chicory. Which do you want?"

"You know actual coffee comes from beans, right? Totally vegan."

"Yeah, but I can't grow them, so you're out of luck. Why don't you go up to the house? I'm sure Mom has a pot of real coffee you can drink."

He kisses me one more time and says, "I'll be back!"

Nan and Dorcas arrive next. Dorcas hands me a beautiful vase of sunflowers and Nan brings bacon. I make her take it outside.

By ten thirty, the yurt is full. It's a good thing I put umbrella tables outside for the overflow. I stop by Cat and Sam's table and sit down. "Thank you for coming to support the cause."

Sam says, "Are you kidding? This is going to be our go-to breakfast place. Who knew vegan pancakes were so delicious!" He pulls a piece of bacon out of a baggie on his lap. I raise an eyebrow, and he explains, "Nan's handing them out at the end of the driveway."

I look around at other tables and sure enough, several of them seem to have a stash of bacon. For Pete's sake. That's going to offend my true vegan clientele, which I apparently don't have. Also, it's not like Nan is going to show up every day and hand out bacon. *I hope not anyway.* There's no way I could keep resisting it.

I stop and say hi to Ethan and Emily. They appear to be quite the solid couple. They're eating bacon, too.

My mom is sitting with some ladies from her church group. They're laughing a lot which, as you know, is one of the best things to promote good health. Naomi and Caroline are lying asleep at Mom's feet.

Scottie and his boyfriend Tad are at another table enjoying some rare time together.

Rix comes out of the yurt to find me. He gives me a great big bacon-flavored kiss and says, "Jerry's on his way. He said to tell you he'll be here by noon."

I stand here, arm and arm with my honest-to-goodness boyfriend, Hendrix Greer, and look out at my farm and feel real pride. Life has brought so many changes in the last few months, but we've ridden the wave and come out on top. In this moment, I don't think I've ever felt happier.

I'm not sure what comes next, but I vow to live every day in present time and appreciate all the moments for what they are, gifts from the universe.

***

Dear Universe,

Wow. Clearly you have a plan that we're not always privy to. Thank you for pushing me into the bigger picture, even though I sometimes fought you on it. Thank you for the people you've brought to share my journey and thank you for not taking my threats to abandon you seriously. I'm ready to welcome whatever comes next with open arms and I promise to not fight you on it.

Dear Friends,

I hope you love Sarah as much as I do! She's unique and offbeat and a really bad vegetarian, but she has a great heart. Her story is very special to me, and she demanded it be told at a time when I hadn't planned on writing it. You see, my dad had just died, and I felt that I needed to take a break from authoring to let myself grieve. It turns out that by sharing Sarah's journey with you, I was able to work through some of my own sadness.

Life is a great big fat wonderful roller coaster of emotion. I'm so grateful to have fans like you who will ride those waves with me!

I thank you for the time you've spent with me in Gelson, Illinois and welcome you to join me in Creek Water, Missouri to meet the Frothingham family. Keep reading for a sneak peek of book one in the Creek Water Series, "The Event."

Book one in the *Creek Water Series,* "The Event."

Chapter One

In my esteemed opinion Creek Water, Missouri, population 14,012, is the armpit of the world. Scratch that, it's a ripe pustulent boil on the butt of the Northern Hemisphere. If it wasn't my hometown, and I wasn't desperate for employment, I'd never consider moving back. Ever.

I just got off the phone with my Uncle Jed—the Beverly Hillbilly reference is not lost on me—and he's offered to make me manager of a new commercial venture he and my other uncle, Jessie (yes, like Full House) are starting up in the old warehouse district. The revitalization of Creek Water continues as my peers have discovered it's cheaper to live at home and not go out into the real world like I did. Problem is, I got myself into a tiny bit of trouble in the real world.

I was driven in my formative years to prove that I could make something of myself without any backing from the illustrious Frothingham family, of which I am one. I was sick to death of people thinking everything was handed to me on a silver platter just because of my last name. So, I worked hard to get excellent grades in school, and I earned myself a scholarship to college.

After graduation, I moved to New York City determined to leave my small-town small-minded roots behind. Things were going great too, until *The Event.*

I worked as head buyer for Silver Spoons Enterprises in Manhattan, an exclusive gourmet/kitchenware boutique chain on the eastern seaboard. I was stationed at our flagship location on East Seventy-Third St.

The Event was the corporate dinner dance at the Metropolitan Museum of Art, where all the big wigs gathered to pat each other on the back and recognize top performing employees. I thought I was a shoo-in for the Demitasse Award, honoring the most creative contribution to the company during that fiscal year. I was personally responsible for the whole "Linens for Dinner" campaign, which promoted the ideal that urban and suburban millennials alike, only use cloth napkins to dine, not only cutting back our carbon footprint by lessening paper waste but adding a touch of elegance to our lives. We sold more linens that year than in the previous ten years combined. It was *that* successful.

So there I'd sat in my way too expensive dress—I splurged because I knew how important it was to make a good impression on the executives *and* because it was the perfect little number to accept my honor in—when Jameson Diamante announced the nominees for the Demitasse.

There were only three of us; me with my linen campaign, Juliet Smithers from the Southampton store for her "Drink More Wine!" crusade, and Allison Conrad from Atlanta for her "Pretty Please, Ya'all" call to reinstate formal invitations on engraved card stock.

Why don't we just kill the planet, Allison, with all the trees we're going to murder for your cause?

I was poised on the edge of my seat ready to throw my hands across my heart and gasp something along the lines of, "What? Me? My word, I'm so surprised!" I'd imagined how I'd get up and showoff my six-hundred-dollar understated elegance to the whole room.

Jameson announced, "This year's decision was not an easy one to make, with all three ladies greatly contributing to our brand, but in the end, we chose the contender who was responsible for the most innovative campaign."

Here's where the chain of events gets a wee bit cloudy. I swear he'd called my name, so I stood up as planned, but my friend and tablemate Alexis says that isn't what happened at all. Apparently, old Jameson had called out Allison's name, and she and I both went up to accept the award. How deforesting the planet is innovative, I do not know. I did hear through the corporate grapevine that Allison had gone to Jameson's hotel room with him after the ceremony like a Kardashian auditioning her new sugar daddy. But I digress. Back to *The Event*.

I grabbed the silver spoon out my fellow nominees' hand and proceeded to give my speech. All of it. Which for some reason I was allowed to do. It was a beautiful speech. I thanked my mother for her graciousness and manners, and I thanked my grandmother for teaching me how to fold dinner napkins into swans. I was about to thank Silver Spoons for having the wisdom to hire me, when Allison grabbed the Demitasse out of my hand. I may have chosen that moment to snatch it back and hit her over the head with it—obviously not very hard as she never pressed assault charges, thank God.

It's all conjecture really. All I can say for certain is that I hastily fled the ceremony, trotting down all eight hundred thousand stairs of the Met in four-inch heels, in a cloud of disgrace and disappointment. I took a cab to a nearby bar, where I proceeded to drink my body weight in tequila before waking up in an unknown apartment in Brooklyn.

Tequila and I have a sordid past. One incident of overconsumption resulted in my belting out my karaoke version of "I Will Always Love You"—the Dolly Parton version, not Whitney Houston's, so poorly I'm sure ears bled; another, found me french kissing a giant stuffed frog before throwing up on it, and the last time, before the Brooklyn incident, was when I urinated in my sorority sister's shoe because I was so drunk I couldn't find the bathroom. Now I can add 'indiscriminate behavior' to the list.

Let me just say, I'm not loose by anyone's estimation. I believe in using linens at every meal, for Pete's sake! But the truth is, I spent the night with a stranger and if he wasn't Armie Hammer from that movie *Hotel Mumbai*, because that's who I thought he looked like, then I have no idea who he was. To make matters worse, we apparently didn't use any protection. I soon discovered that I, Emmaline Anne Frothingham, of Creek Water, Missouri, was going to become a mother at the tender age of twenty-eight.

Chapter Two

The reason I'm so bitter about my roots is because when I was eight-years-old my daddy, Reed Frothingham, died and the whole town of Creek Water—with the exception of our family—acted like Mama and I were leaching off my uncles for our survival. Which is simply not the truth. We were left a decent sized inheritance, not huge as most of the family money was spent during my grandparents' generation—we have the sterling silver snail tongs to prove it—and my uncles didn't start making good investments until after I'd become a half-orphan. It is by surname alone that we aren't considered nouveau riche.

Mama and I had enough money to keep our house and pay our bills, but she had to go back to work so we could have the extras. She kept the books for the uncles and in that way managed to stay part of the family business, which as I mentioned earlier has become revitalizing Creek Water. Mama didn't invest any of our money because she worried that risking it might send us to the poor house. My uncles didn't have a good track record at the time.

I *needed* that scholarship to Duke as there simply was not enough money to pay for that caliber of education any other way.

Yet, no one acknowledged my hard work and instead treated me as though I was using money I wasn't entitled to. Every time Mama and I did something extra, like go shopping in St. Louis, some busybody would inevitably say, "Your uncles are so good to you!" completely negating our ability to take care of ourselves. The uncles tried to set them straight, to no avail.

This is why I was determined to get out and make something big out of my life. I was going to prove once and for all that I was more than a charity case.

Of course, that was before I'd accepted the gift of a stranger's swimmers and decided to bring new life into this world. I continued working at Silver Spoons through most of my pregnancy. I worried that after *The Event* they might try to find a way to let me go. But if I was pregnant, they couldn't do so without fear of a lawsuit. I told my boss about my situation as soon as I found out. I realize that was a little manipulative on my part, but Gloria Gaynor and I, we're survivors.

When I told Alexis, her response was, "Emmie, why in the world are you going to have this baby? You can't raise a child alone in New York City!"

My response was simple. "I made my bed, now I'll have to lie in it." But to tell you the truth, I was nowhere near the martyr I made myself out to be. When I laid with my feet in the stirrups at the doctor's office and heard a heartbeat coming from inside my body, one that wasn't my own, it was *insta-love*. I don't judge what other women do or do not do with their reproductive systems, but mine was making a person, and I wanted to know everything about who she would become. (I just knew she was a girl.)

"You need to go back to that apartment and let that man know he's going to be a father. He'll have to pay you child support," Alexis said very practically.

I probably should have, and maybe even would have, had I taken note of his address. The truth is, I was still drunk when I woke up and all I could think to do was hightail it out of there before I had a witness to my walk of shame. I had absolutely no idea how to find the father, so I decided to forget he existed.

After going to my doctor to make sure I was disease-free—I'll never put myself in *that* situation again—I settled down and tried to enjoy my pregnancy. In my ninth month, Silver Spoons decided to cut my position, claiming they couldn't afford a senior buyer and two junior buyers, so they offered me six months' severance to go away. I probably could have sued them for wrongful termination, but I was fat and tired and all I wanted to do was lay on my couch and watch classic romantic comedies until my baby was born. So, that's exactly what I did.

Available now!

About the Author

Whitney Dineen is an award-winning author of romantic comedies, non-fiction humor, thrillers, and middle reader fiction. She lives in the beautiful Pacific Northwest with her husband and two daughters. When not weaving stories, Whitney can be found gardening, wrangling free-range chickens, or eating french fries. Not always in that order. She loves to hear from her fans and can be reached through her website at https://whitneydineen.com/.

Join me!

Mailing List Sign Up
whitneydineen.com/newsletter/

BookBub
www.bookbub.com/authors/whitney-dineen

Facebook
www.facebook.com/Whitney-Dineen-11687019412/

Twitter
twitter.com/WhitneyDineen

Email
WhitneyDineenAuthor@gmail.com

Goodreads
www.goodreads.com/author/show/8145525.Whitney_Dineen

Blog
whitneydineen.com/blog/

Please write a review on Amazon, Goodreads, or BookBub. Reviews are the best way you can support a story you love!

Other books by Whitney Dineen — All are available on Kindle Unlimited!

Romantic Comedies
Relatively Normal
Relativey Sane
She Sins at Midnight
The Reinvention of Mimi Finnegan
Mimi Plus Two
Kindred Spirits
Going Up?

Thrillers
See No More

Non-Fiction Humor
Motherhood, Martyrdom & Costco Runs

Middle Reader
Wilhelmina and the Willamette Wig Factory
Who the Heck is Harvey Stingle?

Children's Books
The Friendship Bench

CPSIA information can be obtained
at www.ICGtesting.com
Printed in the USA
FSHW021956210421
80713FS